SWEET MISS SEETON

THE HERON CARVIC MISS SEETON MYSTERIES

By Heron Carvic

PICTURE MISS SEETON
MISS SEETON DRAWS THE LINE
WITCH MISS SEETON
MISS SEETON SINGS
ODDS ON MISS SEETON

By Hampton Charles

MISS SEETON, BY APPOINTMENT
ADVANTAGE MISS SEETON
MISS SEETON AT THE HELM

By Hamilton Crane

MISS SEETON CRACKS THE CASE
MISS SEETON PAINTS THE TOWN
HANDS UP, MISS SEETON
MISS SEETON BY MOONLIGHT
MISS SEETON ROCKS THE CRADLE
MISS SEETON GOES TO BAT
MISS SEETON PLANTS SUSPICION
STARRING MISS SEETON
MISS SEETON UNDERCOVER
MISS SEETON RULES
SOLD TO MISS SEETON
SWEET MISS SEETON

HERON CARVIC'S MISS SEETON

SWEET MISS SEETON

HAMILTON CRANE

BERKLEY PRIME CRIME, NEW YORK

SWEET MISS SEETON

A Berkley Prime Crime Book
Published by The Berkley Publishing Group
200 Madison Avenue, New York, NY 10016

The Putnam Berkley World Wide Web side address is
http://www.berkley.com/berkley

First Edition: December 1996

Library of Congress Cataloging-in-Publication Data

Crane, Hamilton.
    Sweet Miss Seeton / Hamilton Crane.—1st ed.
        p.   cm.—(Heron Carvic's Miss Seeton)
    ISBN 0-425-15471-8
    1. Seeton, Miss (Fictitious character)—Fiction. 2. Women
detectives—England—Fiction. 3. England—Fiction. I. Title.
II. Series.
PR6063.A7648S94   1996
823'.914—dc20   96-880
                                                                   CIP

Printed in the United States of America

10 9 8 7 6 5 4 3 2 1

SWEET MISS SEETON

CHAPTER 1

A stray moonbeam tipped the corner of an uncurtained window and slowly spread a clear, calm, pitiless light around the little room.

The ashes were long cold in the grate beside which, in happier times, brass fire-dogs had barked companionably at the toasting fork on its nearby hook, and the leather bellows had huffed warmth and life into coal from the copper scuttle. The hearthrug had borne mute witness that such life had its inconvenient side . . .

No longer. No coal; no fire; no sparks. No rug. No set of fire-dogs, no bellows, no copper coal-scuttle . . .

No hope.

The little figure silhouetted in moonlight sat quietly by the window until a deep, mournful sigh filled the room with the ghosts of past comfort and the spectre of present loss. A loss which, day by day, must grow ever more acute until it became impossible to bear . . .

As it had now become.

The blurred eyes of the little figure turned from the silent reproach of the empty hearth to tearful contemplation of the black-and-white outdoor bleakness of paths and flower beds and asphalt drive, stark beneath the moon.

Moonlight made the world not sparkling silver but cheap, weary pewter, grey and dull and heavy. There would be no bright memories of frost-filigreed branches or cobwebs spangled with diamond dew going gentle into that good night; there would be nothing but the dark emptiness of despair.

Darkness and hunger and cold, of spirit and body alike; no light, no warmth, no comfort.

And no thirst. The little figure on the window-seat lowered her gaze to her hands. In one hand was a glass of water, almost full. In the other—thin fingers tightened their feeble grip on the brown plastic phial—was . . . oblivion.

Her hands, as she thought this, shook. A few drops of water spilled over the edge of the glass; she clicked her tongue at the carelessness that had stained her best silk dress, then smiled for her vanity. It hardly mattered now.

She lifted the hand holding the brown plastic phial, and shook it. There was a reassuring rattle. She set the glass down on the bare board of the window seat and brushed those final foolish drops from her skirt, then felt with fingers that were suddenly numb for the lid of the plastic phial, and began to twist it open.

She tipped the contents, saved over many pain-wracked days, into the palm of her hand and picked up the glass to drink one final toast to her lost world before the world lost her. It would lose her—but it would not miss her.

Who in the world would miss one small, unimportant, elderly spinster?

At her kitchen sink, a small, elderly spinster rinsed the last of the breakfast dishes, humming a tuneless tune as she set her plate, cup, and cutlery to drain in the plastic rack. She washed out the mop one final time, squeezed it, and hung it on its hook beside the tea-towel. Still happily humming, she took the kettle to the cold tap to fill it for her mid-morning cup of coffee. The lapse of more than thirty years could not weaken the Blitz-learned habit of taking advantage of the water supply while it was there.

Thoughts of elevenses made Miss Seeton glance up at the kitchen clock. A slight pucker appeared between her brows; then she looked out of the window at the frost-powdered garden and smiled. "The weather, of course," she said. "Dear Nigel has more than once observed how very low temperatures can make it difficult to start a motor—something to do with the battery, I believe—and, of course, a milk float runs entirely on electricity. Unlike the post, which can sometimes be so smelly." She wrinkled her nose and sighed. "The van, that is. Diesel—or is it petrol? But even worse than turpentine."

More than seven years earlier, Miss Seeton had chosen to take early retirement, settling in the country after a lifetime in London. One of the many benefits of her choice had been that, as a former teacher of art, she no longer had to work with oils and clean her brushes with turps. Crayon, charcoal, pastels, and watercolour were her preferred mediums now that she drew almost entirely for pleasure.

Almost entirely. There are occasions when the artistic talents of Miss Emily Dorothea Seeton are harnessed by the most unlikely persons . . .

Miss Seeton was checking her list before heading for the shops when, from the front door, she heard at last the welcome rattle and thump of the letter-box. She smiled as she trotted down the hall and saw the folded *Times* on the mat and heard the fading jingle of the milk float as it rumbled off along the village's only street: The Street, as this thoroughfare is proudly known to those who live in Plummergen. Miss Seeton, who lives there by inheritance, is quite as proud as any.

It was a little early, perhaps, but when one normally read

one's paper while digesting one's breakfast, perhaps it would not be too ridiculous to read it now while drinking a cup of coffee. It wasn't, after all, as if there were any particular urgency about her little shopping trip. The post office opened at eight, stayed open for lunch, and shut at six: it was just a matter of stamps, and writing paper, and a few groceries . . .

Miss Seeton settled herself and her conscience with *The Times* and a steaming cup at the dining room table and began to read. *Small Earthquake In Chile.* Not too many people, she hoped, had been hurt. *Revolution In Stentoria: Foreign Office Advice For Travellers.* To stay away, she supposed. *Chancellor Promises A Prosperous New Year.* The trouble with politicians, she felt, was that they were always promising and always making excuses when those promises weren't kept. Or didn't seem, to the lay mind, to have been kept, even if the politicians somehow made it sound as if they had been all the time.

Shaking her head, Miss Seeton turned to the arts page. *Stuttaford Announces New Prize.* This was more interesting. Miss Seeton read on.

"The Stuttaford Foundation, one of the oldest and most generous art charities in Britain, today reveals plans for an annual award of £25,000 to be given for an original work, in any form, paying tribute to its Victorian founder. The competition is open to professional and amateur artists alike and will be judged at the end of the year by a panel to include Mr. Paget Stuttaford, a direct descendant of Sir Andrew Stuttaford, the eminent financier and philanthropist. Sir Andrew's vast fortune, it will be recalled, was established by successful dealings in the tobacco and confectionery trades. His tea-clipper *Isabella*, named in honour of his wife, the former Lady Isabella Paget, on one occasion came close to beating the more celebrated *Cutty Sark* in the homeward race from China until she was dismasted within sight of land by a Channel storm. Sir Andrew, who was already noted for his generous nature and his love of the visual arts, set up The Stuttaford Foundation in memory of those who died in this endeavour.''

Miss Seeton stopped reading to study the accompanying photograph. Paget Stuttaford, a serious young man, clenched a pipe between his teeth as in one hand he held a jar of the celebrated ''Isabella'' Blended Coffee, and in the other a tin of Stuttaford's Best Quality Drinking Chocolate. Something about his expression suggested to Miss Seeton that he was, in fact, a nonsmoker. She knew little about such matters, but assumed that he had been persuaded to adopt this pose in the interests of publicity. Twenty-five thousand pounds, after all, was a great deal of money, even if—Miss Seeton resumed her reading—the sum was to be divided between three persons.

''The winner will receive a cheque for £15,000, while the second prize will be £7,000.'' The writer of the article saw no reason to advise a *Times* readership that the third prize would be £3,000. ''Entrants have until the end of December to create a suitable memorial to the spirit of the late Sir Andrew Stuttaford.'' Across Miss Seeton's imagination floated a plump, smiling man with a waistcoat and Dundreary whiskers, wreathed in a swirl of grey mist that upon closer inspection proved to be the steam from a mug of cocoa. ''They should,'' went on *The Times*, ''perhaps bear in mind that the philanthropist's acute tone deafness, a family trait, might render difficult a judicious consideration of any musical work of art.''

Poor Paget, it seemed, couldn't hold a tune. Well, Miss Seeton knew that she couldn't, either—or at least not very well: but well enough for her purposes. And she could enjoy listening to opera on the wireless or on television; she could enjoy a trip to the theatre in person whenever she wanted. She was, she knew, most fortunate. She had, of course, no thought of entering the competition—the attendant publicity should she win (Miss Seeton blushed for the immodesty of the very idea) would be most unwelcome—but even if she had such a thought, she had no real need of the money. Throughout her working life she had done her best to save. There had been no need to dip into her savings to buy the cottage bequeathed to her by dear Cousin Flora. With no mortgage, her pension, and her—Miss Seeton blushed again—other income . . .

Yes, she was most fortunate indeed to have no serious worries over money. Unlike so many others . . .

Superintendents of police are as entitled as anyone to the odd free day, even if they are often so busy chasing criminals, or catching up on essential paperwork, that they will waive their entitlement in the interests of justice.

Superintendent Brinton of the Ashford force was no exception to this rule. While the whole nation had gone on holiday over the Christmas and New Year period, citizens of the crooked persuasion had resumed work rather more promptly than their law-abiding counterparts. Brinton's "in" tray was currently piled high with assorted files on bank robbery, assault, break-and-enter jobs, and one Domestic, in which the killer had telephoned the police himself and made full confession before the body of his wife had been stretchered out of the door.

Despite his workload, Brinton had decided that half a day must be devoted by him to affairs other than constabulary. He could trust the rest of his team—even young Foxon, whose taste in clothes belied his brains—to cope with the investigative routine for a few hours . . . couldn't he?

"If I can't," he informed his reflection in the mirror, "then I'll bust the lot of 'em back to uniformed constable. And take early retirement . . . or maybe I won't." There was the small matter of his pension to consider. Small indeed, if he retired before time; it'd be bread and water for the rest of his natural life and his wife grumbling when they had to save electricity by switching off the central heating and just boiled the odd kettle for a hot-water bottle or a cup of tea. Weak tea.

"Ugh." Brinton, who liked his cuppa as strong as he liked his peppermints, shuddered. He wrenched at the knot of his tie. Maybe not with this shirt; this suit. He needed to look . . . dependable. Respectable. Trustworthy. And *not* like a copper, even if the chap he was going to see knew damn well that he was—which didn't make it easy, because coppering was about the most respectable job he knew.

But it could be dangerous. And he didn't want to remind people of the risks if he could possibly avoid it . . .

From the wardrobe he produced a quiet grey tie with a faint blue stripe, echoed in the deeper blue of his shirt. He gave himself a final glance in the mirror. Not bad. If he didn't know who he was, as a copper he'd guess he might be . . . a bank manager, perhaps.

Not bad at all. He smiled.

Plain Mr. Brinton squared his shoulders, picked up his cardboard file of bills, called a cheery goodbye to his wife, and marched out of the house to his car. His appointment was for half past ten. It wouldn't do to be late.

"Mr. Brinton, good morning! You're very prompt. Do come through, won't you?" Percival Jestin, youngest manager in the City and Suburban banking chain, shook hands with his visitor and led the way to his office. No standing on his dignity for young Jestin when most of the people he had to deal with were locals who'd known him since before he was a twinkle in his father's eye. He'd gone to school with their children: pulled their daughters' hair, kicked a football around with their sons. He knew he'd be "that young Perce who did so well for himself" to the end of his days and was sensible enough not to brood over it.

Brinton, being childless, was able to meet him on rather more professional terms. Percy took great pains to settle the burly policeman in a comfortable chair, then went slowly—reluctantly?—round to the official side of his desk. It struck Brinton that the bank manager was strangely pleased at the prospect of talking with someone who (he might guess, given the early-January, post-Christmas date of this interview) wanted to borrow money from him.

No, not pleased: relieved. And that was certainly strange . . .

"How can I help you, Mr. Brinton?" Mr. Jestin had caught his visitor's quick frown and hurried to placate him. "No problem with your account, is there? If you have any complaints about our service—"

"No! No complaints at all, Mr. Jestin." Brinton did his best to sound completely satisfied, but there was embarrassment in his voice as he went on. "As for problems, now . . . well, most likely there will be. In a few weeks. That's why I've come to see you now." He fiddled with the elastic loop fastening the cardboard folder on his lap. "I'm afraid it was Christmas. The wife . . . presents and so on . . . a bit more entertaining than we'd planned . . . it all sort of . . . sneaked up on us. And when I sat down to catch up with the sums, and realised the bills would start coming in before much longer . . ."

"Thank goodness it's only once a year," returned Percy in sympathetic accents. "Oh, I know just what you mean, Mr. Brinton. You're by no means the only one to be caught out. You'd think that after almost two thousand years we'd *expect* Christmas to come round each December, but it always seems to catch us on the hop." His smile was friendly; there was no hint of reproach. "So I suppose you'd like to arrange an overdraft? I don't see any great difficulty. Our terms are very reasonable, I think you'll find. Especially for someone who's banked with the City and Suburban for as long as you have.''

Brinton, who'd come prepared for a spot of grovelling, blinked. The folder he'd been about to open stayed closed. If he was being offered a low-interest loan without having to confess just how badly he'd managed his finances during the past month or so, he wasn't going to risk a spanner in the works by producing evidence that might be used—he had to grin—against him.

Percy Jestin grinned back. ''Very reasonable terms,'' he repeated cheerfully. ''Let's see, now. You're earning how much per annum?''

The conversation thereafter became technical. Percy did sums in pencil on a piece of paper (which reassured the client) and checked them on his desktop calculator (which reassured him). The generation gap was never so noticeable as when it involved technology. He called for copies of Brinton's statements over the past three years and approved the negligible amount of red ink appearing therein. He discoursed with eloquence upon current and deposit accounts, debated the various benefits of standing orders and direct debits, and congratulated the superintendent for having paid off most of his mortgage, and for having a job with such . . . undoubted security.

Brinton appreciated the younger man's tact. ''Well, I doubt I'll ever be made redundant, Mr. Jestin. Not unless every villain in Kent decides to reform. And you know as well as I do how likely that is.''

Percy Jestin, who owed his position as branch manager to certain villainous activities on the part of his immediate predecessor, nodded and sighed. That sigh struck Brinton as being somehow excessive for a young man who was doing so well in his chosen career.

The young man caught the older man's curious glance

and moved restlessly on his chair. "Er—yes," said Mr. Jestin. "A secure job and the regular income that goes with it: I'd call you a pretty safe bet, Mr. Brinton. How much would you like to borrow? And for how long would you like the repayment period to last?"

Brinton was speechless. This just couldn't be happening. He'd thought, at first, that Percy must have been making some routine joke about reasonable terms for long-term customers to put him at his ease before the serious negotiations began. But now he had to face the fact that it had been no joke at all. Mr. Jestin was behaving in a way few bank managers treated their clients unless they were thriving local businesses, multinational corporations . . . or crooks.

He had to smother an instinctive groan. Not Jestin! Not so soon after the last one! A branch manager's power over the activities of his staff was supreme. Head office couldn't keep an eye on everyone all the time. Pull enough wool over enough eyes and you could salt away a tidy little sum in a numbered Swiss account, under a false name, before the auditors caught up with you. And how often did they pop you in prison right away? Not often. Usually it was bail, while the prosecutor prepared the case. And the number of folk who'd skipped the country while on bail . . .

This time he couldn't prevent a groan escaping him, and the shudder that shook his burly frame made the pencils dance on Percy's desk. "Mr. Brinton, are you all right? Do you feel ill?" Mr. Jestin eyed his visitor with some alarm. "Shall I slip out for a glass of water?"

Slip? Skip! This awful echo of his previous thought had Brinton biting his lips with the effort of not allowing another groan to warn the manager that suspicion had been aroused in the official breast. At least let the chap sign the overdraft papers before he heard the chink of handcuffs!

"I'm fine, thanks, Mr. Jestin." Brinton gulped. "Well,

a bit on edge, I suppose. Wondering what they're up to back at the shop while I'm not there keeping an eye on them . . .''

He looked at his watch, checking it against the clock on Mr. Jestin's wall. Percy followed his gaze and nodded.

''We can have the details sorted out for you by this afternoon, Mr. Brinton. If you'd like to come back around three . . .'' He hesitated. He cleared his throat. ''If that would be convenient. But . . .''

CHAPTER 2

Percival Jestin, novice bank manager, had addressed the experienced superintendent of police in tones of . . . eager uncertainty, thought Brinton with a sinking heart. Was the lad about to confess before he had a chance to be caught?

"But, Mr. Jestin?" he prompted.

Now it was Percy's turn to gulp. "Well, Mr. Brinton . . . I'm rather glad you called in this morning. Because . . . if you can spare the time, there's a—a confidential matter I'd like to discuss with you . . ."

Brinton spared him a few moments for further gulping, then prompted again: "Confidential, Mr. Jestin?"

Percy tried to sound decisive. He was not altogether successful. "Something's worrying me . . . and I don't know whether I'm right to worry or whether it's just"—he shrugged—"looking for problems where they don't exist. And perhaps they don't—but after last time . . ."

"I understand, Mr. Jestin." Well, he didn't really, but a few sympathetic noises wouldn't do any harm.

Percy squared his shoulders and breathed hard once or twice. "It's . . . the old folk, Mr. Brinton."

Brinton reeled. Was Jestin already starting a collection

for the next round of Christmas hampers? He watched the
young man watching him. Jestin was definitely worried.
No, it was more serious than asking for a donation.

"Five or six customers from this bank alone," announced Mr. Jestin. "And I'm sure they can't be the only
ones, but I haven't been in my present position long enough
to . . ."

Brinton grinned. "To be accepted as a new shoot on the
managers' grapevine? It'll come, lad—uh, Mr. Jestin—but
we'll do without the others for now. Tell me about these
five or six you say you yourself know about."

Percy's eyes dropped to his hands, folded uncomfortably
on his blotter. "It's their accounts, you see. They've been
pretty well emptied over the past few months—and not for
the obvious reason, I think. Most of them are so old they've
outlived what close family they have—and that age-group
doesn't throw money around on presents for distant relatives or friends, do they?"

"Two world wars and a depression make people learn
to watch the pennies, all right."

"That's what I thought." Reassured by Brinton's tone,
Percy sat upright as he went on speaking. "But they've
gone down almost to the last penny, some of them beyond
into the red, and one old lady even killed herself the other
day. The others write rubber cheques for everyday expenses
and just apologise nicely when I have to warn them about
unauthorised overdrafts—or they put the tuppence-ha-
penny that's left in a deposit account and complain that the
interest isn't enough to live on—and I've tried writing and
talking to them to find out why their finances are in such
a mess, but nobody will tell me!"

He was wringing his hands now, and Brinton could understand why. This was the lad's first responsible job; the
last thing he wanted was a reputation for hounding impoverished old-age pensioners into bankruptcy or beyond, to

the modern equivalent of the workhouse. Shades of Charles
Dickens. ''Uh—respectable old folk?'' came the logical enquiry as Brinton applied himself to the problem.

''Salt of the earth,'' said Jestin promptly. ''I can guess
why you ask, Superintendent, but I honestly don't see any
of them as blackmail victims. For one thing, isn't blackmail
usually a—a regular payment over a long period, not a
lump sum? And even if they *were* being blackmailed—
because I'm not so daft I don't know the most surprising
people have secrets—why so many of them? More or less
at the same time? Men *and* women? All well past retirement age?''

Brinton nodded. ''I see what you mean.'' He applied
himself a little more. ''The old lady who died. What can
you tell me about her?''

Percy sighed. ''I suppose bank confidentiality doesn't
matter anymore when you're dead—and intestate.''

''No heirs? No relatives?''

''Nobody, Mr. Brinton.'' Percy's smile was sad. ''Only
a cat. Miss Byng—Philippa Byng—was a dear old lady
who should have been living out her last days in peace with
a pension and a moggy and a nice bit of garden—and she
didn't. She committed suicide because she was flat broke
and too proud—or too afraid—to ask for help.''

''That generation prides itself on staying independent,
lad—uh, Mr. Jestin.''

Mr. Jestin shuddered. ''I know. To them I'm still wet
behind the ears, but it's my job to look after them—and
they won't let me! And I'm afraid some of the others might
be going the same way as Miss Byng, and I don't know
why—and I don't know what to do about it! I just don't
know!''

''I don't know. It sounds a downright waste of good food
to me, Miss Emily.''

Surviving even one world war left vivid memories of past privations. Martha Bloomer, Miss Seeton's devoted domestic paragon, had been a girl in 1939. Like Miss Seeton, she had lived in London for the duration. Cockney Martha and her family would not forget the Blitz or the doodle-bugs or the rockets; with the rest of the country they remembered having to queue in near-hopeless hope outside shops with no glass in their windows and no goods on display. Miss Seeton's tale of how her dear mother had stood for two hours outside the fishmonger's in pursuit of rumoured kippers, and how the winner of what must have been the last fish in Hampstead had allowed her neighbour next in line to buy half of it, had been capped by Martha's memories of running out each night to feed the back-garden rabbits and hens with a tin bath on her head against what sometimes seemed like a permanent rain of shrapnel.

It was now not Martha, but Martha's husband Stan who was officer-in-charge of chickens: and they were not Bloomer birds. They belonged to Sweetbriars. Miss Seeton had been bequeathed by Cousin Flora not just her cottage, but with it the dear friends who had helped the increasingly frail Mrs. Bannet to remain happily at home until her death at the age of ninety-eight. As the old lady's garden had become too much for her, farm worker Stan from over the road, where The Street narrowed to cross the canal bridge, had volunteered his horticultural services in exchange for a share of any saleable surplus in the flower, fruit, or vegetable line. While Martha took care of the house, Stan looked after the fowl house. It was an arrangement so convenient for all concerned that there had been no question of Miss Seeton's wish to continue in the same way when she came into her inheritance seven years before. Were not Martha and Stan, after all, as close to her as family could ever be?

"Well, Martha dear," said Miss Seeton now, doubtfully. "Well . . . I agree that it does sound a somewhat . . . unusual means of—of expressing oneself. But modern art . . .''

Honesty here prevailed and Miss Seeton fell silent. One must, of course, try to keep an open mind, but . . .

''Modern, fiddlesticks.'' With an unnecessary bang, Mrs. Bloomer thrust her broom into an already dust-free corner. ''Art? I've seen it in the papers and on the telly, and it's rubbish. Bits of scrap metal I'd pay a man to take to the tip—great lumps of concrete full of holes—a couple of pink blobs with a triangle someone calls a masterpiece, selling for thousands of pounds—why, the kiddies in school can do better than that, specially with you teaching them, dear.'' Martha turned to radiate approval on her employer and friend. ''Things look like what they are when they've been properly taught—which is how I like to see them.''

Miss Seeton made a sudden movement, but Martha gave her no time to speak. ''And *seeing* things is what it's all about, if you ask me. Pictures, or a nice statue, I don't mind that. But when it comes to—to *eating* things . . .''

Words finally failed her. Miss Seeton, with a doubtful smile, decided it was safe to begin trying to explain. As far, that was to say, as she could. Which, she feared, was unlikely to be far, since she couldn't help but feel that there was much in Martha's point of view. Still, when one recalled that food rationing ended in 1954 . . . and allowed for the fact that a whole generation had grown up unaware of the—the respect, one might almost say, in which those who had survived the war held wholesome provender . . .

''They say it's all very clever,'' said Miss Seeton, with a faint sigh.

''Then they're mad,'' returned Martha at once. ''Painting walls with chocolate! Telling people to lick it off! Well, I should hope you've got more sense than that, Miss Emily, but there's a good few that haven't. What about the germs? Serve him right if they're all ill again—and them, too, for being so daft as doing it.''

"But that particular exhibition," Miss Seeton reminded her, "was unfortunately held in summer—not winter, as I believe was the original plan. Some muddle over dates at the gallery, if I remember aright. One can well imagine the poor man might, in the relief of having it all sorted out at last, forget that the temperature—such very large windows, for the best light . . ."

"Lick it off the walls like a heathen or eat it off a plate, if that's what you do, I've never much fancied the idea of caviar." Martha wrinkled her nose. "Smoked fish eggs? Ugh!"

Miss Seeton, whose one (conventional) taste of this delicacy had been so enjoyable that she had, unusually, taken a second helping, accepted that knowing what caviar was made of might put one off. She did not remind Martha that chickens, too, produced eggs that one could eat.

"Jelly gone mouldy on purpose!" went on Martha, warming to her theme. "Have a kiddies' party and leave the washing-up for a week, and I'd like any of your critics to tell me the difference . . ."

It was a review by the celebrated critic Meghan McKinnie in that morning's *Daily Negative* that had annoyed Martha so much that she had popped across, when it wasn't strictly one of her days, to ask for her employer's opinion in exchange for a quick dust round. As a general rule, Miss Seeton read the broadsheet *Times*, although from time to time she would glance through a *Negative* out of interest as to what case her friend, ace crime reporter Amelita Forby, might now be working on. Miss Seeton had never before thought of the tabloid *Negative* in the light of serious art criticism and, always willing to keep an open mind, was happy to oblige dear Martha by reading the article in question—even if such reading required on her part a far greater effort of concentration than normal because of Martha's accompanying snorts of irritation as she banged around the cottage with her broom.

Return of the Refreshment Rubens! the banner headline had screamed in a typeface that made Miss Seeton wince. *Brave New World At Galerie Genèvre* . . .

It was (argued Miss McKinnie) brave indeed of Antony Scarlett, the Rubens of Refreshment, to herald his return from self-imposed exile by using even more comestibles in his current exhibition than he had in the infamous "Food Poisoning Fiasco" show of the previous July. Readers (wrote Miss McKinnie) would of course recall the snarling-up of central London in the fearful traffic jams caused by fleets of ambulances ferrying those who had attended Scarlett's *vernissage*, or private viewing (the *Negative*, in an attempt to go up-market, had poached the services of Miss McKinnie from one of the drier broadsheets), to hospital for emergency admission. "Has the salmonella ghost at last been laid?" demanded Meghan McKinnie. "In the opinion of this critic, it most certainly has!"

Rubens, the *Negative* readers would also recall, had been renowned among other causes for his voluptuous and sensual depictions of the naked human form. Rubens rejoiced and encouraged others to rejoice: he celebrated the flesh and was not ashamed of that. He revelled in life: he renewed and refreshed the spirit . . . and Antony Scarlett, with his bold and imaginative use of food, the very basis of life, could rightly assume the title of a modern Rubens. "Refreshment" in Scarlett's case referred not only to food and drink, but also to his renewal, by his Art, of the very fundamentals of the human soul . . .

Miss Seeton paused in her reading to study the photographs around which the columns of print had been set and to compare them with what she could remember of Scarlett's previous work as described in the sober pages of *The Times*. She supposed one could, at a pinch, accept that a chandelier made of toffee, slowly melting in the heat from a hundred light bulbs, might be a metaphor for the fundamentals of the human *body*, since the body did eventually decay. Though probably far less stickily. But surely the greatest attribute of the human *spirit*—the soul—was that it was . . . imperishable? Immortal?

"Immaterial," murmured Miss Seeton, that most literal of souls, and read on.

Antony Scarlett had (according to Meghan McKinnie) gone far beyond his earlier, overt representations of the human form and condition towards an almost completely abstract view of the ultimate spiritual struggle. The female nude nibbled out of blocks of voluptuous blue-veined cheese; the nude moulded from slices of bread, exactly equal in weight to that of model Kristeena; the nude formed of jet-black caviar, gleaming on a background of flaming satin, should be remembered only as the juvenile seeds of what, in his months apart from the world, he had developed into a mature and satisfying philosophy. The meaning of the ultimate truth (wrote Meghan McKinnie) must of necessity be a mystery, but in the works of Antony Scarlett it had perhaps found one of its most intelligent and stimulating twentieth-century interpreters . . .

"Good gracious," said Miss Seeton, coming to the surface for air. "Dear me." She set down the paper with a sigh and shook her head. "Martha, I should rather like a cup of tea. Would you care to join me?"

"So long as you don't try telling me my fruitcake's a meta-blooming-phor for the mysteries of life, I'd love one," returned Mrs. Bloomer, grinning. "I'm right, aren't I, dear? It's all a load of nonsense?"

Miss Seeton, after a spiritual struggle of her own, ventured to suppose it really depended on the impression made by the particular work of art (however art could be defined) when one actually saw it, as opposed to accepting the im-

pressions of someone else who had. Whether or not they
were paid to offer these impressions to the general public . . .

Martha snorted. "And they pay good money for people
to write this rubbish! Fiddlesticks I said, and fiddle it is,
cheating and trickery and lies, never mind being a waste of
good food. Sausage skins! Heaps of rice all over the floor—
what about mice? Pyramids of hard-boiled eggs! Don't you
go getting Ideas, Miss Emily, chickens or no. Whatever
would Mrs. Bannet have said?"

Miss Seeton hurriedly assured her she would never
dream of doing such a thing, though she might slip up to
London to take a look at the work of Antony Scarlett,
which in its earlier incarnation she had elected to miss, but
having now read the review, which had been so different
from that in *The Times*, she was curious to know what it
was all about.

"Then I just hope it isn't catching," said Martha. "You
take care!"

Miss Seeton smiled. Dear Martha, always so anxious.
Take care? Why, she never did anything else.

There are those of Miss Seeton's acquaintance, however,
who would not agree with her.

The topography of Plummergen, Miss Seeton's adopted village, is simple. The wide, gently curving Street runs more
or less north and south to divide, at its southernmost end,
in two. The left-hand fork, as already described, narrows
into a lane running between a row of cottages (in one of
which live Stan and Martha Bloomer) and the high brick
wall of Miss Seeton's back garden as it slopes gently down
to the Royal Military Canal, built against the invasion of
Napoleon Bonaparte and now a peaceful, winding water-
way rich in bird life and much favoured by visiting artists.

The Street's right-hand fork, having become Marsh

Road, snakes its way along the edge of Walland Marsh to arrive, eventually, back at Brettenden. This town of some five thousand inhabitants lies to the north of Plummergen and (apart from Murreystone, arch-enemy to Plummergen for the past six hundred years) is the smaller parish's nearest neighbour. Three times a week—once by official decree, twice through the patriotic offices of Crabbe's Garage—a bus runs from Plummergen (five hundred inhabitants) to Brettenden for the benefit of those shoppers who cannot find what they want in the various village emporia.

Of the latter, the three most important establishments are the grocer, the draper, and the post office. All three sell groceries, confectionery, liquor, and stationery. Mr. Takeley, the grocer, has the smallest amount of floor space; Mr. Welsted, the draper, with his picture postcards and china souvenirs, caters more to tourists. The post office, run by Mr. Stillman and his wife, Elsie, has the largest floor space and the widest selection of goods. It is also most conveniently placed, being directly opposite the bus stop, and it is, therefore, by far the most important of the three most important of all the Plummergen shops.

One Thursday afternoon, the bus decanted its load of bargain-burdened Plummergenites at the post office stop and rattled off towards marshy oblivion, leaving such shoppers as had not found what they needed on any of Brettenden's market stalls to pop into Mr. Stillman's to make up the shortfall . . . and (a minor point) to catch up on any items of gossip that might have come their way during the past few hours. The six-mile homeward journey was never long enough and was far too noisy as well.

After a polite shuffle in the doorway—the repeated jangling of the bell drove the Stillmans and young Emmeline Putts quite wild—everyone who wanted to gossip was safely inside. After more shuffling as people picked up tins they didn't need and drifted in ragged groups towards the counter, it was Mrs. Spice who received the silent consensus that she should open the batting.

"You'll never guess who was next to me in the queue for Brussels sprouts today. A tin o' corned beef, please, Emmy. Tried to make out she wasn't there, mind you, but I knew it was her—not that, better make it a small one— from her picture in the paper a couple o' years back when she opened the school fête. Ta, luv. And a packet of Oxo cubes."

"Who was it," mused Mrs. Henderson, "opened the fête two years ago? Humphrey Marsh, weren't it? I wouldn't call *him* a her, not with that beard, I wouldn't."

"So what about the smock?" demanded Mrs. Skinner, who some years ago had quarrelled with Mrs. Henderson over the church flower rota. The pair had never been known to agree on any subject since. "*And* that nancy hat he wears. Them artist types, you just can't tell. Not if you know your way around at all, you can't."

"It's a berry," interjected Emmy Putts, her bosom heaving at this slur on her idol, about whom she had once watched a television documentary on the BBC. Emmy had harboured a kindred feeling towards the ultramodernist sculptor from the time of his commission by the Brettenden biscuit factory where her mother worked to create a masterpiece for their front yard. Emmy had taken it as badly as the flamboyantly bereted Marsh himself when a passing totter had carted the piece away to be melted down for scrap.

"Never mind berries," said Mrs. Spice quickly. "It was Brussels sprouts as I was talking about. Brussels sprouts— and Lady Hallbank in . . . a market queue!"

Plummergen appreciates the artistic tension of a pause as well as anyone. A gratifying chorus of disbelieving gasps followed Mrs. Spice's revelation. Mrs. Spice preened herself and examined her newly acquired tin of corned beef as if her life depended on a letter-by-letter reading of the contents label.

Prompted at last by the chorus, having judged how far she could allow tension to stretch before breaking point (and a change of subject) should be reached, Mrs. Spice condescended to spill more of the beans. Or sprouts. " 'Course it was her," she said as a few daring voices raised doubts. "Know her anywhere, like I said, for all she had a great fur hood pulled over her face—"

"A fur hood?" The doubters grew more daring. "Why," objected young. Mrs Newport, "it wasn't nowhere near cold enough for fur today. You must've bin mistaken."

"Snowed a bit this morning, though, didn't it?" came the inevitable counterobjection from Mrs. Scillicough, sister to Mrs. Newport and thus fifty per cent of Plummergen's Sibling Rivalry ideal. Mrs. Scillicough's triplets were a village byword for sheer frightfulness; Mrs. Newport had four children under five who were generally regarded as angelic. Mrs. Newport had an automatic washing machine and a tumble dryer; Mrs. Scillicough had a twin tub and a mangle in which she pinched her fingers if she didn't concentrate. It was as natural for Mrs. Scillicough to snipe at Mrs. Newport as it was for Mrs. Skinner to squabble with Mrs. Henderson.

"Call that snow?" scoffed Mrs. Newport, tossing her head in scorn.

"White and fluffy, fell out o' the sky—reckon I do," said her sister, likewise scornful. "Cold, too. And she ain't no chicken, Lady Hallbank. Your blood gets thinner as you get old." She tried not to look at the other shoppers, most of whom could give her twenty years at least. "She'll have come out afore it stopped snowing, all wrapped up, and not worth going home to change in case it started up again later, that's what she'll have done." She turned eagerly to Mrs.

Spice. "Did you get a good look at her? What were the rest of her clothes like?"

Mrs. Spice did not scruple to crush the wistful daydreams of the younger generation. "Proper mangy, that fur looks close up. You'd think with all her money she'd want summat a bit smarter, wouldn't you?"

Mrs. Scillicough's face fell. "Oh," she said. "Thinks her best's too good for mixing with common folk, does she?"

This sour suggestion, born of nothing but disillusion, at once opened the eyes of all to the shocking possibility that Mrs. Scillicough (who lived in a council house) might harbour revolutionary tendencies. Everyone experienced the same delighted frisson of fear that Mrs. Scillicough's red woollen scarf might at any minute be wrenched from her neck and used as a banner to rally the working classes against their oppressors . . . even if, when all was said and done, it was hard to imagine Lady Hallbank, so quiet and well spoken, as one who habitually ground the faces of the local poor into the proletarian dust.

Still, one could never be entirely sure. "That must be it." Mrs. Spice was a little peeved she hadn't thought of this first. "And that coat—well, if it hasn't had the sleeve patched, then I don't know a patch when I see one. *And* she'd lost a button she'd not bothered to match properly. Looked like a rag-bag, she did, without a penny to her name. I tell you, if I didn't know who she was . . . why, I would never have known it was her."

CHAPTER 3

At this point in the discussion Mrs. Flax drew breath and everyone fell silent. If the Wise Woman—the first, and sometimes the last, face the villagers saw in their lives—wished to pronounce, she must be allowed to do so. Nobody crossed Mother Flax—who helped at their birthing, laid them out at their dying—with impunity . . . except, perhaps, Mrs. Scillicough, who had been more than disappointed in the efficacy of the myriad nostrums prescribed by the witch for the suppression of the high spirits of her triplets. Mrs. Scillicough was given to sharp retorts when she thought she could get away with it, and Plummergen forgave many minor trespasses on the part of the offspring of one who had from time to time defied the Wise Woman and yet survived.

"I saw Lady Hallbank, too," said Mrs. Flax, nodding sagely. "But 'twasn't at the market. No, indeed." She surveyed her audience in a practised silence prolonged until just the right moment for the best effect.

"Fur hood and all," said Mrs. Flax at last, defying anyone to argue with her. Nobody did. "Know her anywhere, I would, after all these years." Mrs. Spice preened herself discreetly. "But," went on Mrs. Flax, wagging her choppy finger against her nose, "in all the years I've known her, there's never bin once I've seen her ladyship *going into a pawnshop* . . ."

The sensation caused by this remark was all that could be desired. In the hubbub of gasps, cries, and exclamations Mrs. Flax did not stoop to preen herself; the Wise Woman was far above such vainglory. "A pound o' carrots, Emmy," she said in level tones. "When you can shut your mouth. Catch flies, my girl, if you ain't careful."

Nobody dared to point out that in the first fortnight of January insect life was in short supply, though in the background Mrs. Stillman banged a few irritated tins around at this implied slur on post office hygiene.

Nor did anybody dare ask Mrs. Flax what she'd been doing in the pawnshop to begin with. The Wise Woman moved in her mysterious ways, and it did no good to cross them. Besides, it was possible that she just might have been passing by on the other side of the road . . .

"See what she was doing, did you?" demanded Mrs. Scillicough. Disillusioned though she might be with the aristocracy at close quarters, her disillusionment with Mrs. Flax ran even deeper. "Might have bin going to buy summat with the ticket run out, not pawning anything at all. Well?" she challenged as Mrs. Flax contrived to look wise without committing herself to a direct reply. "You didn't, did you?"

This challenge to her authority was more than the witch could bear. Let the Scillicough minx get away with her cheek and the rest of 'em would think they could, too. She drew herself up to her full height. "If you're doubting my word—" she began.

And was saved by the bell.

The collective sigh that immediately arose mingled relief and regret in equal proportions. The post office voyeuses had no real wish to watch any thaumaturgic harm being done to Mrs. Scillicough, but, if such harm as a curse (or worse) *were* to be done, they would want to be there to watch it, not have to hear about it secondhand. Still, perhaps it was just as well. Plummergen wished to go on believing in the power of Mrs. Flax and her kind, as it had believed for generations past. Let Mrs. Scillicough be the only one without illusion, and village life—village memory—was safe. Once bring the twentieth century into the darkest recesses of the Plummergen mind, and . . .

"It's growing so dark outside." Norah Blaine closed the door and stamped her feet, blowing on her mittened fingers and shuddering. "And cold—but lovely and bright and warm in here, isn't it, Eric?"

Miss Erica Nuttel—a tall and bony counterpoint to her buxom companion—inclined her equine features in an acquiescent nod. "Afternoon," she greeted the company at large. "End of the queue here, is it?"

"We wouldn't want to push in," tittered Mrs. Blaine, who could see as well as the rest that any queue there might have been had long since dispersed. Mrs. Blaine's black eyes gleamed with the thrill of gossip suspected; the tip of Miss Nuttel's nose twitched at the scent of scandal.

"Got much shopping, Mrs. Blaine?" Mrs. Flax, grateful for deliverance, was disposed to be gracious. "Never you mind my carrots, Emmy. See to Mrs. Blaine next, will you?"

"We didn't manage the bus today," said Mrs. Blaine, telling nobody nothing of which she wasn't already aware. The absence of the Nuts (as the aggressively vegetarian Nuttel-Blaine partnership is known to village wits) had been noted and debated throughout each six-mile journey to Brettenden and back. "But market prices are so much cheaper, I think I'll just take one bag of wholemeal flour, Emmy, which ought to last until next week. And a small bottle of olive oil. You won't have sea-salt, I suppose."

Mrs. Blaine—Bunny, to her friend—supposed correctly. Plummergen is only prepared to humour this precious pair so far. The ladies have lived in the village now for a baker's dozen of years, and, feeling completely at home, think themselves as completely accepted by the locals. The locals, if they chose, could tell them otherwise.

Home for Miss Nuttel and Mrs. Blaine is Lilikot, a plate-glass windowed, net-curtained modern monstrosity diagonally opposite the post office and convenient for the bus stop in both directions. The Nuts have a grandstand view of all who come or go about the village on public transport and of all who patronise Mr. Stillman's establishment, which is, as has been explained, Plummergen's nerve centre and heart. Eric and Bunny keep their fingers firmly on Plummergen's pulse; and, should they ever feel its beat is on the sluggish side, their strong community spirit can always contrive some means or other to quicken it—means usually verbal, imaginative, and involving much mental agility, as the pair leap to conclusions any reasonable person would think impossible.

Few in Plummergen would think the Nuts reasonable persons; even fewer would miss the chance of hearing whatever item of gossip they might choose to impart. As it was not, however, entirely clear whether there was indeed any nutty news to be imparted, the Lilikot ladies were waved to the front of the nonexistent queue so that everyone else could go back to dissecting the character and habits of old Lady Hallbank. The best way of making the Nuts spill any beans they might have was to ignore such hints as they might drop until they could bear being ignored no longer; and on this occasion Plummergen, understandably aggrieved that the pair hadn't gone on the bus to Brettenden market and couldn't hope to cap the revelations of Mrs. Spice and Mrs. Flax, was minded not to play unless the stakes, if revealed, should prove sensationally high.

Mrs. Flax was still in a mood to be gracious and poured coals of fire on Mrs. Scillicough's doubting head by chattering doggedly on as if the value of her evidence had never been in question. "Yes,'twas at the pawnbroker's I saw her, large as life—in a manner o' speaking, that is, for she's nought but a little thing, never mind she was wrapped up again the cold." Once more the knowing finger wagged against her nose. Mrs. Flax winked. "Or so she'd like folk to think. But it's as plain as the nose on my face she was there *in disguise . . .*"

Now was the time for Mrs. Scillicough to eat humble pie and for everyone else to start pleasurably speculating on what reasons Lady Hallbank might have for moving about her native town in this inefficient incognito. Before any of the original audience could speak, however, Miss Nuttel chipped cheerfully in.

"Hear that, Bunny? Disguise. Told you there was something a bit odd about that business this morning, didn't I?"

Mrs. Blaine, busy at the counter rejecting Emmy's offering of plain boxed salt, answered without turning her head. "Well, yes, Eric, but if she was planning to start *pawning* things, it's hardly a surprise, is it?" She coughed. "Considering."

People stirred and glanced at one another with a slowly dawning gleam of hope in their eyes. This was unexpected. The Nuts, who—both by their own testimony and according to witnesses—hadn't left the village all day, nevertheless knew about Lady Hallbank's Brettenden peregrinations that morning.

Or—hopeful hearts beat faster, eyes gleamed more brightly—did Miss Nuttel and Mrs. Blaine mean someone who lived rather closer to home?

A little woman. A little woman whose behaviour, no matter how outlandish, when considered by those who knew her, would hardly come as a surprise . . .

Lady Hallbank—together with her fur hood; her patched, button-mismatched coat; and her visit to Brettenden's universal uncle—was banished without a qualm from the thoughts of every one of the post office shoppers. Even Mrs. Spice and Mrs. Flax knew that, when the Nuts spoke in that particular way, there could be only one particular person they had in mind . . .

Miss Seeton.

And what had caused this gleeful banishment of the shade of Lady Hallbank?

Miss Seeton had overslept.

Miss Seeton had overslept: the suspicions of the Nuts, now being presented to a rapturous audience, were based on no more sinister occurrence than this. A pleasant supper the previous evening with Sir George and Lady Colveden at Rytham Hall had led to a later bedtime than usual for their guest, driven home through the starry night by their son Nigel in his red MG once he had returned from his Young Farmers' meeting. Miss Seeton took pains to leave none of her habitual yoga programme unperformed before cleaning her teeth and slipping at last between the welcoming sheets . . . but she had forgotten, as might anyone in the circumstances, to set her alarm.

Miss Seeton slept soundly, without dreaming; though had she dreamed, her dreams would have been undisturbed. As to whether others that night were undisturbed . . .

Far above the silent room, the stars in their stately saraband wheeled unnoticed around the clear midnight sky, their distant brilliance extinguished by the silver glory of the moon enthroned, triumphant, high in the winter heavens.

A stray moonbeam tipped the corner of a window and began to cross the room with a gleaming, growing motion. Specks of dust glittered in its quiet white glow. There was no other sign of movement.

The moonbeam, encountering the silvered stillness of a

mirror, leaped back to fall upon a human figure that had previously lain in shadow. No light as yet fell upon the face; the figure did not move.

The beam crept slowly—slowly—up from the tip of the outflung foot, pale and smooth in the moon's pale light, towards the knee, bent at an angle for sleeping. From the knee it began moving up to the thigh . . .

Then, all at once, there was more than moonbeam movement in the room. The pale sleeping figure slept on . . . but another pale form was there in the dust-speckled dark. A form now creeping slowly—slowly—through the shadows towards that still, sleeping shape so white, so distinct, in the moonlit silence . . .

A silence that was now no longer silent, as the shuffle of stealthy feet across the floor raised faltering echoes—so faltering that they might meld into sleeping dreams and leave them dreams, not nightmares—that did not make the sleeping figure stir.

The path of the pale, creeping form crossed that of the window-beaming moon, which for the first time flashed warning sparks from the long, thin blade in the creeper's hand.

Yet still the sleeping figure did not stir . . .

Clutching the shining sword, the creeping one crept close. And waited.

Waited for the glow of the moon to reach the centre of that still, silent figure . . .

And, when it finally did, whirled the sword arm above its head to plunge the blade, with all its force, deeper than the deepest deep into the sleeping heart . . .

For the Plummergen sleeper it had not been one of Martha Bloomer's days the day after her Rytham Hall supper. The rattling white of the milk float, the thud of the post van's diesel engine did not wake Miss Seeton in her upstairs bedroom at the back. It was only when the clock of the church diagonally opposite Sweetbriars chimed eight that, with a guilty start, Miss Seeton awoke.

Miss Seeton disliked fuss and hurry. There were several matters to be put to rights before she could leave her dear cottage to its own devices for a whole day. She would not run for the bus—hardly sensible in this cold weather, with frost still a slippery sheen on roads and footpaths. She would, when she had everything sorted out, ring Crabbe's Garage for a taxi to take her to Brettenden station for the most convenient London train.

Miss Seeton, that most retiring of English gentlewomen, had no idea that these innocent travel arrangements could be the concern of anyone but herself—that, indeed, any of her doings should be of the slightest interest. She would have been very surprised to learn that they were. She would have been still more surprised—startled, even—to learn that her decision to take a private taxi rather than the public bus, coupled with the belief that she had been seen in a Brettenden pawnshop, was to convince her neighbours that she was somehow involved in a stolen antiques fencing ring.

Or else in laundering counterfeit money—Plummergen didn't much care which. It was enough for the village to know that, according to those reliable newsmongers the Nuts, Miss Emily Seeton was At It Again . . .

As the village threw itself into joyous speculation, Miss Emily Seeton was at Charing Cross Station, about to board the homeward train. So many commuters: she had, after seven peaceful years in the country, forgotten what a crowded experience even the start of the rush hour could be. She shook the last of the raindrops from her umbrella, furled it, and set it in a discreet upright position against the wall as she sank thankfully into a corner seat, tucking her aching feet well out of the way of later arrivals, holding her bag on her knees, and finally closing her eyes. Behind their drowsy lids, the events of the day replayed themselves in pleasurable slow motion . . .

Charing Cross at midmorning is busy, but not frenetically so. It did not take Miss Seeton long to move near to the front of the taxi queue, where she was startled by a sudden swooping rush about her head by a multitude of flurried plumy peckings about her feet, as pink pigeon claws pattered on the ground in pursuit of biscuit crumbs being scattered by the small boy in the queue behind her. More pigeons whirred and cooed above in greedy chorus, preparing a swift descent to snatch more than their fair share. Fearing an accident to her cockscombed hat or to her second-best winter coat, Miss Seeton automatically opened her umbrella.

There came a whoosh, a swoosh, and the upward beating of a thousand wings as the pigeons took simultaneous flight. The air was a thunderous whirlwind of falling crumbs and feathers, and Miss Seeton's hat was blown from her head to land upside down on the edge of a kerb-side puddle and roll there in ominous spirals.

"Now, then, Tommy," said the small boy's mother, boxing her son's ears in an absent-minded way. "You just look what you've done! Go and pick up the lady's hat and tell her you're sorry."

"Shan't," said Tommy, squirming in her grasp and resisting her forceful push with a stubborn force of his own.

"Oh, no," said Miss Seeton quickly. To be the cause of a tantrum when the child's mother had the rest of the day with him . . . "No, thank you. It was entirely my own carelessness . . ." Not stopping to furl her brolly, she bent without a single click or a creak from her knees to retrieve her property before it should tip those last five dangerous inches to ultimate destruction in the waiting puddle.

She was not quite in time.

"Hop in, ducks." While this drowning tragedy was being enacted, her taxi driver had hopped out to open the door. As Miss Seeton mournfully arose, the drenched and battered headpiece in her hand, he bowed with major-domo stateliness to usher his passenger inside, stopping her only to take the open umbrella politely from her grasp and hold it over her head until she was safely out of pigeon range. He twirled the brolly at the whirling birds, furled it, feinted with it as with a rifle; then handed it to Miss Seeton with another bow, closed the door, and hurried round to his cab.

"Where to, duchess?"

"Oh, dear." Miss Seeton sighed. "The Galerie Genèvre, please . . ." She brushed the worst of the mud from the crimson felt and did her best to straighten the soggy, crumpled cockscomb; but she feared her favourite hat was now beyond repair. She sighed again.

The taxi driver chuckled. This was perhaps surprising, in the circumstances, but Miss Seeton had long known that her sense of humour was . . . well, not as robust as some. The humour of the Cockney, as her cabbie had shown himself to be, was undoubtedly robust. And if, on such a dreary day—the taxi had by now edged its way out into the rain-soaked Strand—her little mishap had made him laugh, should she begrudge the poor man some mild amusement?

"Dunno when I've laughed so much in years," said the cabbie at last, braking for a red light. "It'll be a while before them pigeons comes back to make their blasted mess, pardon my French, on our roofs and bonnets—shame about *your* bonnet, ducks, but believe me it was lost in a good cause. Forever down the car wash, we always was, and that don't come cheap." He chuckled again. "Coo, as you might say. Get it?"

After a moment, Miss Seeton got it. Politely she smiled. The amber appeared, and the cabbie turned his head to wink at her before stamping on the accelerator at the green. "Getcher there in no time," he promised. "Okay?"

London was its normal bustling self, the streets full of traffic, the pavements bobbing with umbrellas as people ran rather than walked through the storm. From time to time a brolly would be brandished to hail some passing taxi; from time to time some drenched pedestrian with less foresight than his brolly-bearing colleagues would give up the unequal struggle and slip into a shop with no intention, Miss Seeton suspected, of buying. Though in such weather one could not altogether blame the subterfuge. The windscreen wipers squeaked to and fro; the rain drummed on the cab's metal roof; the tyres hissed through puddles—Miss Seeton silently mourned her ruined hat—and threw up clouds of spray as dull and grey as the pewter clouds above.

"Gallery Geneva," announced the cabbie, making Miss Seeton jump. He pulled his cab neatly into the kerb, braked, put the gearbox into neutral, switched the wipers to slow, and turned to grin at his passenger through the open glass partition.

"Out you get, ducks." His left hand flew up and across in a motion too swift even for the sharp eyes of the retired art teacher. On the clock, the red electric figures flickered and died.

"Oh." Miss Seeton blinked. "I'm afraid I didn't quite see the fare before your meter . . ." She hesitated over the correct term. Blew a fuse? Her kettle had once done this, or at least the plug had. Or perhaps the damp had got in, although the rain had now calmed to a drizzle, so probably it hadn't. On one occasion, when Sweetbriars had been struck by lightning, the vacuum cleaner had emitted a most peculiar sound. Which could, she supposed, have happened in this case, since above the noise of the engine she might not have noticed it, though a flash of lightning would have been rather more noticeable. And she hadn't. "For," she mused aloud, "while the day is indeed stormy, it is unlikely, I think, when it is so cold, to thunder. Noticed, I mean."

"Never noticed meself, neither," said the cabbie promptly. "Stopped anyone trying to take your cab, though, eh? You have this one on me, duchess. Call it a late Christmas present—or an early one for this year, if you like. Get yerself a new titfer. Proper cheered me up, that did. Gave them pigeons something to think about, eh?"

And he had hopped out of his cab, round to the passenger door, and coaxed Miss Seeton out into the drizzle before she knew what was happening, and was gone without even waiting for a tip.

Miss Seeton stood collecting herself and blinking up at the ornately lettered legend above the door of the Galerie Genèvre. It looked most impressive. She hoped that what was exhibited inside would not disappoint: she feared that it might. Still, one must not forget that an open mind . . . Once more she sighed for the ruin of her hat, contrived to straighten it on her head into some semblance of smartness, hooked her umbrella over one arm, the handle of her bag over the other, and mounted the two low, broad, black marble steps to the gallery door.

She skidded on the top step, which was still slippery from the rain, and as she stumbled pushed the door open with a sharp thump as the ferrule of her umbrella caught against it. The attendant looked up, frowning, from his perusal of what Miss Seeton assumed was the catalogue.

"Good morning, madam." He gave her no time to catch her breath. "May I offer you a copy of Antony Scarlett's Elucidation?" He held out the leaflet he had been reading as Miss Seeton erupted into the room. It was of a pale cream shiny paper printed in dark brown ink: the chocolate influence, she supposed. "May I take your hat—your coat? Your umbrella," he said as Miss Seeton smiled her thanks and shook her head, "you must leave with me, I'm afraid."

"Oh," said Miss Seeton. This was different. A ruined hat could—would, in any case—be replaced if removed by some unauthorised person from a public cloakroom rack; a coat, likewise. But her umbrella . . .

Miss Seeton is the most modest of maiden ladies. An English gentlewoman does not flaunt herself or her possessions. She maintains a discreet silence over her financial affairs, her religion, and her politics. Above all she does not boast or allow herself any display of pride.

But Miss Emily Dorothea Seeton, spinster of the parish of Plummergen, could not help but be proud of the best umbrella of all. She had amassed quite a sizeable collection of ginghams over the years; friends, when in doubt, knew that another umbrella would always be welcome as a present for Christmas, a birthday, or some other special occasion. Superintendent Brinton of Ashford had, not a month ago, given her a splendid model in royal blue silk, with *E. D. S.* embossed in gold script on the curved leather handle. Miss Seeton was charmed with her unexpected Christmas gift . . . but it was not the first umbrella she had been given by a superintendent of Her Majesty's constabulary.

He had been promoted since the giving. Now he was Chief Superintendent Delphick of the Metropolitan Police, Scotland Yard's renowned Oracle, friend, and, unexpectedly, colleague to Miss Seeton. Seven years before, Miss Seeton was making her post-opera way along Covent Garden when she took objection to the manner in which a young man was behaving towards a young woman. Remonstrating with him as he struck his companion a violent blow, she applied the ferrule of her brolly to the small of his back, little realising that in this daring application she had interrupted the notorious César Lebel, drug peddler and hoodlum, in the act of knifing to death a known prostitute. Delphick, summoned to obtain Miss Seeton's statement, having learned she was a teacher of art, had asked her to draw her impressions of the event . . .

Miss Seeton's impressions are not always like those of

other people. As some march to a different drummer, so does Miss Seeton, on occasion, see in a different way—a very different way. She looks through and beyond what seems to be there to focus intuitively on the truth of the matter, whatever that matter might be. Her vision might appear distorted to some—indeed, to herself, for she is embarrassed by this Drawing of truths none but she can perceive, and she feels that it is somehow . . . not right. Those such as the Oracle can, with persuasion, overcome her embarrassment; can coax her to yield up the sketches and doodles her subconscious has granted to her skillful hand and her inward eye . . . and they can interpret those sketches, as Delphick did at their first meeting, with the happy result that Lebel ended up behind real-life bars Miss Seeton's instinct had sketched across his face several weeks before.

Delphick next called on the services of Miss Seeton's swift pencil when a series of child stranglings had left the Yard baffled. Once again it was the Oracle's interpretation of Miss Seeton's unique interpretation of events that led to the arrest of the culprit, for good measure adding to the bag a gang of shotgun raiders who had been terrorising local post offices for months past. Before Miss Seeton's third criminal adventure, it was decided by none other than Sir Hubert Everleigh, Assistant Commissioner, that her position should be regularised. She was therefore retained by the force as an Official Art Consultant, to be paid a regular salary and expenses as required, said expenses, more often than not, involving necessary repairs to what had long ago been dubbed her small arms: her umbrella.

Though it had been Delphick who gave her the black silk, gold-handled gamp in gratitude for her help in the Lebel case, it was Brinton who later advised her to save it for such comparatively safe excursions as taking afternoon tea with friends. Miss Seeton, visiting a London art gallery, had automatically chosen her very best umbrella from the row of clips in the Sweetbriars hall . . .

"But it was a present," she explained as the young man with the catalogue—no, the Elucidation—held out his hand for Mr. Delphick's gift. "I don't know what I would say to him if anything should happen . . ."

"I'm sorry," he said. "The word's gone out, after what *did* happen—last night—that nobody takes anything into the exhibition that could be used to damage the exhibits. Not that I think *you* would," he added as she blinked. "You don't look the type—but Miss Watson would have my hide if she knew I'd let you in the place carrying this. You should see what—well, you will, of course." He smothered a grin, wondering if the old dear would be shocked by what she saw. "Nice piece," he went on quickly, studying the hallmark. "Real gold, is it? I promise I'll take the greatest care."

Miss Seeton hovered between reluctance to allow her prized umbrella out of her sight and a pardonable curiosity as to what had happened the night before. Damaged exhibits? There had been nothing about this in *The Times*, though one did not always read every single column on every single page—especially when one was in a hurry, as with oversleeping she had been—so perhaps she had missed it. She glanced at the front page of the Elucidation the young man had thrust into her hand as he deftly removed her umbrella. Perhaps the mysterious happening would be explained—that was to say, Elucidated—here. Miss Seeton drifted along the red carpet of the entrance hall until she found a comfortable bench and sat down to read.

"The Galerie Genèvre is proud to reintroduce to the West End the work of Antony Scarlett, widely acknowledged as a modern Rubens . . ."

Miss Seeton frowned. Widely acknowledged? Not by *The Times*, to the best of her recollection. She read on.

". . . a modern Rubens who refreshes both the twentieth-century spirit and its metaphorical flesh. Rich, smooth, and deeply sensual, his chocolate creations nourish humanity at its every level . . ."

Miss Seeton muffled a sigh and shook her head before stopping to wonder whether this behaviour wasn't perhaps a little . . . ungracious. After all, she hadn't yet seen the exhibits. Perhaps the new-look Antony Scarlett did indeed deserve the reputation of a modern Rubens, even if honesty and her vague memories of his earlier work would suggest that he probably didn't. Genius, by definition, was surely unique. Inimitable. And who would wish to be a second-rate, imitation Rubens when, with sufficient genius, one might be a first-rate (if indeed he was) Antony Scarlett? She skimmed the rest of the paragraph, already weary of what was being said by—with relief she reached the bottom of the page—Genefer Watson. Not a critic of whom she had ever—oh. Genèvre, of course. She should have realised. Well, one could hardly expect an unbiased opinion from the owner of the gallery . . .

She turned the page. A photograph of a brooding Antony Scarlett headed a further—she flicked through—six pages she felt she really could not bear to read in detail, the more so because it seemed they had been written by Antony himself. Her eye caught various phrases to make her shake her head again. "The contrast between formal and inherently informal values of perception . . . an ironic and uncompromising tightrope stretched by his art between coherence and incoherence . . . consistent, yet clearly unsettling logic of life . . . clarity of childhood's vision transformed by the growing self-knowledge of an adult . . . exuberant profundity . . . powerful paradox . . ."

Miss Seeton sighed gently for a third time. One must at all costs keep an open mind, she reminded herself . . .

CHAPTER 4

"I suppose it *could* be blackmail, sir." Detective Constable Foxon of the Ashford force had just been listening to his superior break a confidence.

The information divulged to Brinton by his bank manager had posed something of a puzzle for the superintendent over the past few days. In the rare free moments when he wasn't busy with the many cases officially on the books, he was to be observed in a brown study, scribbling on bits of paper he would shove in an unmarked folder if anyone drifted too near his desk. At home he brooded over his meals. At work he had almost (though not quite) lost his appetite for peppermints, and on those occasions when Foxon annoyed him he had refrained from throwing even an empty packet at the lad.

Foxon, who had hopes of making detective sergeant one day, deduced that his superior was either ill or worried. He considered Brinton's ruddy face, his brisk step, his far from tremulous voice. Not ill, then. Worried? Trouble at home? Mrs. Brinton was some ten years her husband's junior, but there had been no rumours of anything . . . untoward, thought Foxon as he chewed the top of a ballpoint pen and frowned. Money troubles? Well, hadn't everyone, after the season of statutory good will and present giving? Wait a bit, though. There'd been that morning when Old Brimmers had come in late, and someone had said he'd spotted him trotting up the steps of the City and Suburban Bank . . .

It was when Foxon came to work wearing a purple tie with a yellow floral pattern and Brinton didn't even groan that the young man knew drastic action must be taken. Instead of crossing to his own desk, he pulled out the visitors' chair in front of his superior and sat firmly down.

"Go away," Brinton had said without looking up from what looked like yet another anonymous piece of paper.

"No, sir." Foxon shook his head gently as Brinton, scowling, looked up and thrust the paper into its cardboard folder. "Not until you tell me what's up."

"Up?" The scowl turned to a glare. "You mean with me? There's nothing *up* with me, Foxon. What the devil do you mean by saying there is?"

"Of course there is, sir." Foxon jabbed a finger at the cardboard folder. "And that's the evidence—whatever it is. You won't tell me. And you've never been this—this cagey since I've known you, sir. It makes me nervous." As Brinton glared even harder at him, Foxon nodded. "Honest. I haven't the foggiest what you're doing, but I can't concentrate on what *I'm* doing if I'm waiting for the explosion and it never comes because you're . . . bottling it up. It's been three days now. The suspense is killing me. Look, sir," he continued as Brinton continued to glare, "they say two heads are better than one. Why don't you tell me what's been going on? Then I can relax and get back to solving nice ordinary crimes without worrying about you and yours."

"Crimes?" Brinton, who had been building up to a fair-sized explosion as Foxon talked, suddenly subsided with another scowl. "Not guilty. I haven't been dipping into the petty cash, lad, if that's what you're suggesting.''

"Perish the thought, sir.''

"Right.'' The superintendent sighed. "I mean,'' he said, as if continuing a lengthy discussion, "it's not as if we're even sure there's been a crime committed in the first place. Or crimes. Not really . . .''

"We, sir?'' prompted Foxon.

"My bank manager and me.'' Brinton sighed again. "No, I haven't been embezzling or uttering forged notes or anything like that. But Jestin's worried, Foxon, and he's got me worried, too. He told me about it when I dropped in the other day—asked my advice, and I . . . didn't have any. Never come across this sort of thing before. Never mind *you* being unsettled—how d'you think I felt? This is my manor. I'm supposed to know what's going on here. A bank manager does and I don't.''

Brinton hesitated. He made up his mind. "Well, if I can't trust you after this long, lad—but I'll have your guts for garters if I ever find—''

"Cross my heart, sir. Scout's honour.'' The Old Man was starting to sound his usual self again; it'd been worth the risk of a rollicking. "Not a word. Uh—about what?''

"I suppose it *could* be blackmail, sir. Couldn't it?''

Glumly the superintendent nodded. "It could—but it's not exactly the logical answer, is it? I know most of these people, Foxon. Jestin gave me their names, though I'm not telling you.'' His features twisted in a wry grimace as his hands closed about the cardboard folder. "I'll keep the youngster's confidence that far, at least.''

"Fair enough, sir. You know 'em.''

"Right. The whole bunch is honest-to-goodness backbone of England, salt of the earth—gentry, some of them. Not the sort to have secrets they'd pay hundreds— thousands, one or two of 'em—to hush up if some unscru-

pulous blighter found 'em out. Yes, I know,'' he said as
Foxon tried to speak. ''I've jumped through the same
hoops, laddie—and so has Jestin. 'The most surprising
people,''' he quoted. ''But—so many of them? More or
less at the same time? Men *and* women? I want to know
what it's all about and stop it before it gets any worse. We
don't want another suicide, Foxon.''

''Did she leave a note, sir?''

''No, she didn't, poor old duck.'' Brinton sighed again.
''We haven't a single clue about why she did it.''

''Oh.'' Foxon sat up. ''As for having a clue, sir, and old
ducks, I don't suppose . . . ?''

Brinton drew in his breath with a hiss. ''No,'' he said
flatly. ''Whatever it is—if it's anything at all—I want her
kept out of it, Foxon. Her—and her umbrella—and her
whole blasted village. I like the peaceful life, I do. And if
you do, too, you'd better not breathe a syllable of this to
Miss Seeton. Because if you do, I swear I'll . . .''

To the uninitiated, it might seem strange that Superintendent Brinton should object to his junior's oblique proposal
that Miss Seeton might become involved in his current
mystery. The elderly spinster was, after all, in technical
terms a colleague. She had assisted the police, in the most
innocent way, with their enquiries on many occasions over
the past few years.

And there's the rub. Perhaps not quite so innocent. Not
in the dictionary sense of ''harmless,'' that is, though there
could never be any serious doubt that the lady was ''not
guilty (of crime).'' Guilty of imposing a strain on people's
nerves, yes; guilty of causing raised blood pressure in those
who had dealings with her and her notorious umbrella. And
yet . . . guilty? Once more, the dictionary definition poses
more questions than it answers. ''Criminal, culpable;
having committed a particular offence . . .''

Miss Seeton offends without intention. She has no idea that her innocent—yes—actions may have such remarkable results. It has already been explained how her *innocent* prod in the back of César Lebel led to the latter's arrest for the Covent Garden stabbing. What was not mentioned in that brief explanation was the subsequent partial breaking of a society drug ring. Nor was the associated murder, suicide, drowning, gassing, shooting, car crash, abduction, and embezzlement: none of which, her supporters protest, could seriously be considered Miss Seeton's fault.

Her detractors—yet many of those who detract still find much to praise—point out that Miss Seeton was, well, *there*. Involved, no matter how innocently. She might not have meant to stir things up, but she did.

And does. They were not wrong who once described her as the Catalyst of Crime, something that induces a change in others without itself undergoing change. Whatever tempest may embroil those about her, Miss Seeton remains resolutely unembroiled. The question nobody has been able to answer after seven eventful years is, does Miss Seeton raise the tempest, or is she herself, like others, tempest-tossed?

Superintendent Brinton was no more able to solve this riddle than anyone else. He lived, however, a lot closer to Miss Seeton than, for example, Chief Superintendent Delphick of Scotland Yard. Plummergen was on his patch. If MissEss (as the Met's basement computer insisted the lady's retainer cheques should be addressed) ever showed signs of Starting Up Again, Brinton would demand more than the statutory four-minute warning. The local man, Police Constable Potter, had his standing orders. If anything—anything—remotely untoward in the neighbourhood of Sweetbriars or The Street or the village as a whole should happen, then Potter must advise the superintendent, whether at night or on his days off or (Mrs. Brinton had boggled at

this, but being a policeman's wife understood the urgency)
on holiday. And at once.

The superintendent's response to Foxon's mischievous—
miss-chievous?—suggestion of approaching Miss Seeton in
the matter of the impoverished old-age pensioners had been
automatic. Just letting off steam, as Foxon knew well—
because, obviously, until they had some better idea of what
was going on, their hands were tied. The Misguided Missile, as she'd been called, could not—thankfully, need
not—be asked for help. Brinton and the Ashford force
could rest easy in their beds. PC Potter would make no
unsettling reports . . .

Superintendent Brinton would have been considerably
unsettled had he known that, even as he abandoned his
Pauper Pensioners problem and returned to his official
workload, a press conference was being held in London.
Ignorance is deemed to be bliss; knowledge, somewhat par-
adoxically, is said to be power. It is open to question
whether Brinton would have felt better or worse, more con-
tented or less powerful, for knowing that even a distance
of fifty miles might not necessarily be beyond the Seeton
Danger Range covered by PC Potter's standing orders . . .

Time would show whether this knowledge was to be
vouchsafed to him or not.

Miss Seeton had never been especially fond of sweet stuff.
Wartime had been no great hardship to her. When rationing
for confectionery was finally ended in the 1950s, she had
not been one of those who rushed out to buy chocolate in
such quantities that the system had of necessity been
swiftly, if temporarily, reinstated.

This wasn't to say that she found sugar, in its myriad
forms, unpalatable. While she liked her tea weak and plain,
not strong and syrupy, she would spread jam on her toast
in preference to marmalade. She had a weakness for Bat-

tenburg cake, that pink-and-yellow chessboard sponge
wrapped in marzipan—and for gingerbread—and for a certain brand of chocolate biscuit . . .

She had not realised until she stepped into the exhibition
proper just how overwhelming the flavour and the scent of
chocolate could be.

And the sound.

The first exhibit to catch Miss Seeton's eye was a huge,
circular, low-lying vat in the middle of the floor, from
which came a startlingly musical sequence of plops, blops,
gurgles, glubs, and pings. Miss Seeton consulted her catalogue—she begged its pardon, the Elucidation—to learn
that the vat contained milk chocolate at just above blood
heat and that the three invisible jets at the centre of the vat
sent up their triple fountain of chocolate spray, Prince of
Wales Feathers fashion, to bounce off a triangular mirror
of electro-polished stainless steel. *Primaeval Nurture and
Modernity: A Paradox.* Miss Seeton found herself thinking
of porridge in a saucepan and after a few minutes moved
on, humming under her breath, to the next exhibit.

Resting on top of a tall Perspex cylinder was a large
cardboard box, coated on the outside with silver paper. The
open lid faced upwards. Another stainless steel mirror, of
faintly embryonic shape, hung at a ridiculous angle—Miss
Seeton blessed those years of yoga that meant tilting her
head to one side didn't make her feel giddy—to reflect the
interior of the box, which was dark brown and smeary in
stripes the Elucidation advised were plain chocolate mixed,
for better smearing, with coconut oil. *Containment of the
Degenerate Self.* Miss Seeton had seldom felt less degenerate in her life.

Paper Clip was a long—very long—and thin stretch of
what might almost have been chocolate wire without a single bend or kink. Another of Antony Scarlett's paradoxes,
Miss Seeton supposed. Its companion piece, *Filing Cabinet,*

was no more than three cubes of chocolate set squarely one on top of the other. "Modern life," trumpeted the Elucidation, "has lost its way in the labyrinth of bureaucracy." Had it? Miss Seeton considered the Income Tax and sighed.

Before *The Life-Force Reappraised*, Miss Seeton halted for a long time. This was partly from interest, but more from relief that the piece had been arranged near an open window: it would be a long time, she thought, before she would wish to eat a chocolate biscuit again. Perhaps Antony Scarlett had begun to feel the same way, for *Reappraised* was constructed—it was the only word—of rounded heaps of eggshells, illuminated between and from beneath by pale blue fluorescent lights. "The vacant sterility of Being thrown into cold relief by an unseen power whose Power is more than seen." Oh. But the eggs, fortunately, didn't smell, and there was a refreshing, if a trifle chilly, breeze from the window . . .

Wandering from exhibit to exhibit, consulting the Elucidation after her initial guesses had invariably been proved wrong, Miss Seeton began, in an odd way, to enjoy herself. The exhibits themselves were . . . interesting; one had always to keep an open mind . . . but the comments of others walking round the gallery were more than interesting. Miss Seeton's sense of humour, as has been remarked, is far from robust; but she has a dry appreciation of the absurd and a genuine clarity of vision Antony Scarlett and his iconoclastic ilk perhaps (that open mind again) do not.

"Awe-inspiring." A young man of aesthetic appearance gasped in front of a bunch of bananas on whose skins Antony Scarlett had drawn, in purple ink, a series of numbers and abstract squiggles, the whole suspended on a gleaming brass chain from a stainless steel plate in the ceiling. *Futility and Decay*. "Oh, doesn't that speak *volumes*?"

The equally aesthetic young man at his side—how Oscar Wilde would have adored them—fervently agreed that it did. Miss Seeton, who had never suffered from a hearing deficiency in her life, waited for a moment, decided there was more vocal sprightliness in the Oxford English Dictionary, and moved on. Different generations . . .

She was farther now from both window and door than at any point in her progress around the gallery. Red light glowed in a relentless tunnel—*Facilis Descensus Averno*, though Miss Seeton had never envisaged the descent to hell as being down a stainless steel tube dotted with dabs of white chocolate—and drew her ever onwards. The smell of chocolate and decaying fruit (the infrared-spotlighted slices of apple comprising *The Mother of All Is to Blame* had been floating in their stainless steel bowls for a week) was overwhelming.

But as she emerged from the tunnel, Miss Seeton felt for the first time that her steps were being guided; felt that there might, after all, be some power—though she wouldn't care to speculate what kind—in Antony Scarlett's work one could not dismiss out of hand as (she rather feared) mere self-indulgent bombast.

Here, at last, was the *pièce de résistance* of the Rubens of Refreshment: the first representation of anything like a human form Miss Seeton had yet seen, lying massive and, yes, surprisingly graceful in its smooth white contours on a bed of—inevitably—scarlet satin, artistically rumpled to catch every point of light from the mirror-ball revolving slowly overhead.

"Very potent," observed a man with moustaches Salvador Dali would have envied and a malicious gleam in his eye. "Wouldn't you say?" And the young woman hanging on his arm sniggered happily as she joined him in gazing at the front of the reclining figure, which lay in a sleeping position, one arm bent to support the head, one leg bent at the knee.

As the pair tittered together before drifting away, Miss

Seeton contemplated the well formed and rippling muscles
of the sculpture's—the moulding's—back. Consulting the
Elucidation, she discovered that the white chocolate nude—
Desires of the Heavenly Flesh—was an exact replica of The
Artist himself, moulded in his studio over several laborious
days during which, for perfect authenticity, he had con-
sumed his own body weight in chocolate—to the last
ounce. Miss Seeton couldn't help wondering whether he
had eaten anything else in between his frantic bouts of scoff-
ing and (if not) what the effects on his digestion had been.
Or even if he had. The young. So much more enthusiastic
about their work than prudence might advise . . .

Miss Seeton moved round to the front of the sleeping
figure. She stopped. She stared. She saw what the Dali
Moustache and his giggling girlfriend had seen . . .

The midriff of the desirable, heavenly chocolate body
had been pierced by some sharp instrument that, it seemed,
had then been twisted in a disembowelling motion before
being withdrawn and—Miss Seeton blinked—applied to
the figure's genitals. Which had been cut off.

Miss Seeton shook her head. Such a waste. The figure,
from the rear, had displayed a gentle, flowing grace proving
that Antony Scarlett—besides being a fine figure of a
man—had some natural sense of form and balance, of line
and harmony he would have done well to develop in the
classical style that was now, after all, so old-fashioned it
could have been hailed as avant-garde, with Scarlett the
leader of a new artistic movement. But such wanton damage . . .

On a plain white saucer, a sad little mound of melted
white chocolate marked, Miss Seeton supposed, the remains
of the artist's confectionery genitalia. Beside it there was a
notice scrawled in Antony Scarlett's favourite purple ink.

''Some might view what has happened here as wanton
damage to a work of Art. I, the creator of the Work, accept

it as a statement of one (albeit anonymous) individual's response to the piece, and as such I must consider it contextually valid. For this reason, I have no intention of carrying out what some might call repairs, but others might rightly condemn as a falsification of the basic artistic truth.''

Oh. Miss Seeton hid a smile. She thought it far more probable that Mr. Scarlett was tired of eating chocolate . . . undoubtedly a valid response, given the number of pieces in which he had used the stuff.

''You find it amusing?'' Evidently she hadn't hidden her smile sufficiently well. ''I, on the other hand, Miss Seeton, find it depressing.''

Miss Seeton blinked. She turned. She smiled. ''Why, Mr. Szabo! How pleasant to see you again after so long.''

Ferencz Szabo bowed, one plump hand on his pink silk waistcoat. As a compliment to Miss Seeton, for whose good opinion he had a high regard, the Bond Street dealer moderated his Hungarian accent—carefully lost when he became a British citizen; as carefully cultivated when he realised it was a professional asset—to a minimum. ''Miss Seeton, the pleasure is all mine. To find in this—this puerile farrago someone with common sense is a delight. Allow me to take you out for lunch to celebrate our escape. Am I right to assume that you have already seen the rest of the exhibits?''

Miss Seeton confirmed his assumption. She twinkled at him. ''A little bread and cheese, perhaps,'' she suggested. ''I doubt if my appetite for anything . . . exotic will return for some time yet.''

Ferencz patted his corporation—yes, perhaps he was somewhat plumper than the last time they had met—and sighted. ''Had I but your strength of will, Miss Seeton . . . but there, dieting is for the determined, which I freely confess that I am not. Apart from my determination to be away from here as soon as possible, that is. You will allow me to escort you?''

Miss Seeton gladly gave her permission, and the two were about to leave when she turned to look once more at the nude *Desires of the Heavenly Flesh*, and the wanton damage—for so she must regard it—done by that anonymous commentator. She sighed. Such a waste, indeed.

''The only piece worth coming here for,'' said Ferencz, following her glance. ''Which is not to say much. But, as a gallery owner myself, I could say very loudly that I wish the wretched Scarlett had cared less for his damned contextual validity and more for common sense.'' He tucked Miss Seeton's arm under his own and proceeded in stately fashion towards the door.

''There are those, you know,'' he whispered gaily as they walked, ''who see the destruction of the digestive areas as somebody's Statement''—the emphasis was withering—''on the food poisoning débâcle at Scarlett's previous exhibition—a hint that Revenge,'' he said in melodramatic accents, ''is on the cards.'' He gestured dismissively with his free hand. ''They could well be correct, although that does not matter except insofar as, were I the young Scarlett, I would be wary whose invitations to dine I accepted in the near future.'' He and Miss Seeton exchanged friendly smiles.

''No,'' he went on, ''what really matters, Miss Seeton, is the nonsensical satisfaction this foolish youth evidently feels about the affair and the way his response may influence others. Has it not occurred to him that he and his fellow artists, and the owners of the galleries where their work is displayed, are—in the light of this deplorable damage for which no one has yet been brought to book—now wide open to any amount of . . . of blackmail a certain type of mind might conceive?''

It was, thought Miss Seeton, perhaps the most valid comment anyone at the Galerie Genèvre had made all day.

Even as Mr. Szabo and Miss Seeton contemplated the genius (or otherwise) of Antony Scarlett, Miss Genefer Watson, nominal owner of the Galerie Genèvre, was deep in conference with her sleeping partners about that self-same genius. As the two friends left the exhibition in pursuit of a light lunch, Miss Watson and her conferring colleagues began to have the glimmerings of yet another idea to boost publicity . . .

Publicity for the Galerie Genèvre was sorely needed. Initial critical response to Antony Scarlett's return to the London art scene had been mixed. While there were those who had praised his bold change of direction from the natural to a more abstract style, others deplored it, saying that the white chocolate moulding of his naked form was the best part of the show, and the rest, roughly speaking, was self-indulgent rubbish. Even the nude, significant though it undoubtedly was, must likewise leave the artist open to the charge of self-indulgence. It was (said some) a mere echo of the bread, cheese and caviar nudes of his earlier period—with one obvious exception. He would have made his point (whatever it might be: opinion was sharply divided) with greater force had he used not a male but a female body.

Where were the delicious (in more ways than one) curves of Kristeena Holloway, his former model? Did Scarlett's new rejection of the individual symbolise a wider rejection of the burgeoning women's liberation movement? Did the substitution of Scarlett for Holloway express hitherto unrecognised Communist sympathies? On the other hand, Holloway was a well-known women's prison. Did Scarlett, in his symbolic denial of Kristeena's right to exist, wish to express reactionary condemnation of the Red prison system and (in his more abstract pieces) of the treatment of political dissidents behind the Iron Curtain?

And so on and so on. Everyone who went discovered different meanings and different levels of meaning; everyone enjoyed arguing with everyone else about What It Meant . . .

Everyone who went. The trouble was that after the first few days there hadn't been many who did, including critics. Even the damage done to *Desires of the Heavenly Flesh*, telephoned at first light to every Art Editor in the land, failed to arouse any interest, despite a concentrated attempt by Miss Watson to promote the incident as a serious political gesture on the part of the Communists, the Fascists, or (a last, desperate throw) the Women's Liberationists. Antony Scarlett groomed himself in preparation for interviews about this Contextually Valid Artistic Vandalism with radio, television, and newspaper reporters . . .

And nobody had thought him worth interviewing.

Antony was annoyed. He felt that he was being slighted. Had he not already that week allowed himself to indulge in an Artistic Temperament, storming up and down the street wringing his hands and delivering in loud and impassioned tones a grandiloquent oration on the Oppressive Torment of the Struggling Creative Soul, and the convenient proximity of the River Thames?

The film and television crews, sensitively alerted by Miss Watson to this display, had preferred the spectacle of a Member of Parliament bravely informing the cameras that she would stand by her husband, despite his confession that he had committed adultery with each of the household's last five au pair girls . . .

Thus matters had become desperate. Genefer Watson, as we have seen, had spent a day in urgent consultation with her partners: who had, in the end, between them concocted yet another Idea—which, they were sure, was a corker. The Galerie Genèvre announced its umpteenth press conference and this time spiced its announcement with dark hints that the Reputation of Britain might well be at stake. A dastardly plot to undermine the nation's psyche would be revealed by one who had suffered from perhaps its earliest manifestation . . .

And the gallery was packed. The press, television, and radio had elbowed and jostled their several ways to the most favourable positions. Genefer Watson, looking anxious, kept consulting her watch and sighing. Antony Scarlett did not appear. A series of questions from the floor about his likely state of mental health went studiously unanswered, firing speculation to fever pitch. (The initial questioner had received a down payment in cash and the promise of a bonus to be calculated according to the number of spontaneous questions subsequently asked.)

Twenty minutes after the appointed hour, the main door to the Galerie Genèvre was hurled open. Antony Scarlett— eyes flashing, hair wild—strode into the room in a swirling black velvet, red satin-lined cloak, brushing aside hysterical demands from Genefer (and, of course, the reporters) as to where he had been, how he was feeling, and what was the matter.

"I," began Antony Scarlett, "have been wrestling with myself." There was no time to ask who had won. "It has been a long, laborious encounter. I have . . . suffered." His face writhed in remembered suffering. "I have been riddled with doubt and uncertainty. I have been torn in two"— here he flung out his arms—"on the horns of a spiritual dilemma the like of which few artists in recent years have had to endure." He rolled his eyes to the ceiling, as if seeking advice from the spirit of any artist, recent or otherwise, who might be flitting about the neighbourhood. "Should my personal inclination, I asked myself, be allowed to triumph? Should I yield gracefully—submit to the

selfish desire of the Artist for that peace of mind, that freedom from anxiety so necessary to the creative process?''

Again he flung out his arms in a far from peaceful gesture. Reporters in the front row instinctively ducked as
black velvet billowed over their heads, and forgot to make
their half-formed comments on Antony's previous claims
that anxiety and its associated mental restlessness together
served to induce that spiritual tension so essential to the
Creative Mind.

''But,'' went on Antony Scarlett as the billows subsided,
''I have made my choice, difficult as it was—and I have
not chosen the craven path of peace.'' His chest swelled as
he drew himself up, deepening his voice to a growl. ''I am
no coward and I am resolved. I shall not yield! I shall not
flag or fail. I shall go on to the end . . .'' Some of his audience wondered whether he also proposed fighting in the
fields, the streets, and the hills; but again they had no time
to put the question to him.

''I will not be intimidated!'' boomed Antony Scarlett.
''We British are renowned throughout the world for our
hatred of bullying and for our love of fair play. I do not
point the accusing finger at any one nation—any one individual—in particular, but I say to you all that I, a red-
blooded, true-blue Englishman, will not allow this—this
shameful attempt to intimidate me to deter me from entering the Stuttaford Competition, to do so! I appeal to you
all—I appeal to everyone who means to try for the Prize—
that no matter what the provocation to abandon your entry
might be, you must never surrender! This is a free society,
and we rejoice in our freedom. England will not stomach
tyranny, whether it be political, ethical, or artistic! It has
been tried in the past—it has failed in the past, and so it
must fail today!''

His voice was growing hoarse. He shuddered, flung out
his arms once more, then gathered himself and the folds of

his cloak for the final verbal assault. "Maybe my claim will sound immodest—but I believe that I speak for England." He threw up his head, his eyes gazing into a Union Jack infinity. "Where one man leads, others are bound to follow. I will be but the first to set an example by starting the fight against those Philistines who would suppress the free competitive spirit, the spirit of equal rights, of equal chances for all . . ."

At this point the speaker's eloquence was drowned out by the cheers from more than several journalistic throats and the thunderous clapping of forty pairs of hands.

Genefer Watson, part owner of the struggling Galerie Genèvre, hid a smile of satisfaction as Antony Scarlett took his bow—and bowed again—and again.

For some reason she had the impression that the wolf wouldn't for much longer be licking the paint from her door . . .

CHAPTER 5

The thunderous applause in London found an echo fifty miles away in the heavy mutterings of genuine thunder trapped in clouds above the Kentish skies. Pedestrians in Brettenden's busy streets cast anxious glances to the brooding greyness above and walked a little faster to their destinations or slipped into providential shops until the worst of the storm should be over; shopkeepers whose properties had been flooded in the last heavy downpour rushed for the buckets and mops they had hoped would not be needed again before the insurance claims were sorted out. Drivers, peering through the sudden gloom, switched on lights and wipers as the first chilly drops began to fall.

A small, slim female figure wearing galoshes, a tweed mackintosh, and a preposterous hat put up her umbrella, tilting it over her face as the wind dashed vicious needles of sleet against, then through, the thin fabric. She fluttered her way among the few brave souls who had not sought cover and came to the edge of the pavement, where she dithered on the kerb waiting for the flow of traffic to ease, and while she waited repeating to herself the litany she had learned long ago at school and which she had always taken such pains to impress upon her pupils.

"Look right, look left, look right again. If all is clear, cross the road." She looked—and kept looking, her head flicking from side to side, the cockscomb hat giving her the appearance of some tiny, exotic bird.

The cars kept coming. The sleet fell harder and more like hail. The wind grew stronger. The little lady with the umbrella shivered as cold air whipped about her ankles and icy trickles filled her galoshes to puddle nastily around her toes. She looked right, left, right again . . .

There was a lull in the traffic as someone farther along the road stepped on the zebra crossing. No cars came from that direction; those coming the other way slowed to a halt and formed a queue. The umbrella made its cautious progress down from the kerb to pass between the throbbing front bumper of one queueing car and the puffing exhaust of another. A knee-level smoky stain on the tweed mackintosh was immediately washed away as the wearer stepped into the sleet from the shelter of the metallic vehicular sandwich to the empty half of the road . . .

Empty for just a few moments more. The people on the pedestrian crossing were safely across. In waiting cars, hand brakes were released and accelerators gunned. The queue of stationary traffic turned into a steady, flowing stream. Windscreen wipers lashed along with the sleet . . .

Which lashed its way around the fabric shield of the lady with the umbrella, stinging her eyes, making her start. The brolly slipped from her feeble grasp. Wildly clutching, she lost her balance—stumbled—and fell . . .

Into the path of an approaching car whose driver simply could not stop in time.

On the desk of Superintendent Brinton, the telephone rang. The superintendent glanced over to Foxon at the other desk.

"I'm out. Unless that's someone confessing to the armed hold-up at the jeweller's, I don't want to know."

Foxon, muttering under his breath about dogsbodies and exploitation, picked up the extension. "Mr. Brinton's office . . . Yes, it is." His voice changed. "Yes, it is! What's happened? What's wrong? Calm down now, like a good girl, and tell me all about it."

Brinton's attention, which had been on the point of returning to his files, now focused on his junior. The lad might be a wow with the ladies—though Brinton couldn't imagine what they made of his peacocky taste in clothes— but he'd never been one to let his private life interfere with his work. Offhand, his superior couldn't think of a single occasion when any of his girlfriends had rung him at the office. He might go through the odd giddy spell, but Foxon was basically sound. Professional. He was putting in for sergeant any day now. Whoever this was on the blower, she must be something special . . .

Foxon's superior wondered glumly if this uncharacteristic call presaged another little chat with Percy Jestin about an extension to his overdraft. Wedding presents didn't come cheap. If the lad asked his advice, he'd tell him to wait a few months for the warmer weather—unless, of course, there were good reasons for the girl to be in a bit of a state. You couldn't expect a baby to wait to suit the convenience of another bloke's bank balance . . .

"Look, love, you're not making much sense." The eavesdropping Brinton's eyes popped. It'd be "sweetie" next. He'd never thought he'd live to see the day. "Take a deep breath," advised Foxon, "and try again. Slowly. Now I know you're upset—but I need to know *why* you're upset if you want me to do anything about it, which I suppose you do or you wouldn't have phoned me here." With a rueful, though (to Brinton's surprise) far from apologetic grin to his superior, he addressed the telephone sternly.

"You've phoned me at work, and the super's pretty strict about wasting police time. You don't want me busted back to uniform, do you? Well, then,'' he continued as the telephone squawked at him in an agitated soprano. ''Take a good, long breath and try again. Slowly,'' emphasized Foxon, himself speaking more slowly to drive the message home.

The telephone, after a few moments, appeared to heed his instruction, for he did not speak again for some time. His face, as he listened, grew grave. He did not ask questions; he let her, whoever she was, speak without interruption. He frowned and made a few jottings on his blotter; he nodded and jotted some more. Once or twice he glanced across at Brinton, although the superintendent could make nothing of his junior's expression. In the end, as the telephone ran out of hysterical steam, he spoke.

''You were quite right to ring me,'' he said. ''I'm glad you did—no, really, I am. You try not to worry about it any longer, though that's easier said than done, of course. I'll tell you what!'' It was as if inspiration had suddenly dawned. ''I'm flattered you think I've got all the answers, but I haven't, you know. It needs someone with experience—someone like the super.'' Brinton let out a startled yelp, which Foxon studiously ignored. ''Would you mind very much if I asked for his opinion? They say two heads are better than one, and—''

The lad hadn't been joking. This was too much. Brinton snatched up the phone on his desk. ''Now see here, miss, if young Foxon's trying to involve me in his personal business, I can assure you—*what?*''

''Mrs.'' repeated the telephone loudly in his ear. ''Not miss—I'm a respectable woman, I'll have you know!''

Brinton groaned. Not a shotgun wedding, then—which would've been bad enough—but seduction. Adultery. There would be a court case—an irate husband yelling about loss of conjugal rights—yards in the local paper, maybe even the nationals if things on the world front were a little slack—he'd have to kick Foxon out for bringing the force into disrepute, when the lad would've made a damned good sergeant some day . . .

"Hang on." Brinton gaped at the telephone, which was still haranguing him in a stern soprano—no, not soprano. Not now that it had calmed down a bit. It was a contralto—a mature, not to say elderly, contralto. "Hang on!" bellowed Brinton. "Madam," he added, a grim suspicion having formed in his mind. He shot a furious look at Foxon, who was grinning. "I swear I'll kill you one day, laddie," he said.

"Don't you talk to him like that!" scolded the telephone at once. "Threats and curses—a fine example for a young man at the start of his career!"

"If he goes on the way he's started," returned Brinton, "he won't have a career much longer, Mrs. Biddle." He saw Foxon grin again and was assailed by doubt. "Er—it *is* Mrs. Biddle, isn't it?"

"Not miss." The elderly contralto still sounded indignant. "I married Biddle a full year before my eldest was born, I'll have you know, and a better husband never drew breath. Poor Addie!" Indignation gave way all at once to lamentation. "If only she'd had a good man to look after her . . . It's dreadful—dreadful, poor soul. But there," the woman said in brighter tones, "I'm sure you'll find out what's wrong, Mr. Brinton, and help my grandson put it right." Brinton could not meet Foxon's glittering eye. "It's wicked," went on Mrs. Biddle. "At her age, to get in such a state and not one of us knowing, and us thinking we were her friends . . ."

The contralto was quavering now, and Foxon rushed into the tremulous breach. "I told you before to be a good girl and stop worrying, Gran. You've done your bit and told me, and in a minute I'm going to tell the super, and then it'll be official business, so you won't need to bother your head with it anymore. In fact, you mustn't. Mr. Brinton gets dead stroppy with amateur detectives poking their noses into official business—don't you, sir?''

"I damned well do," he growled. "So if he's got all the details of . . . uh, your statement, how about letting us get on with it, eh?''

"Bless you, Mr. Brinton." Mrs. Biddle's relief was obvious. "I can't tell you how grateful I am—and I'll be off up the hospital the minute it stops raining to tell Addie to stop being such an old silly. Poor soul!" And, with a few grandmotherly admonitions for Foxon, she was gone.

The superintendent looked that irrepressible young man straight in the eye and breathed deeply several times. "Whatever it is, laddie, I don't want one word about Miss Seeton. *Amateur detectives*, indeed! And trying to make me think . . . Well, never mind. Just tell the tale and make it short. I won't need the details at first. I know your gran— she isn't one to make a fuss about nothing—and, by the look of you, you didn't think it was nothing from the minute she started talking."

"No, sir." Foxon was now completely sober. "Once she'd stopped, well, babbling, it did sound . . . serious, sir. One more for the files, if you ask me."

Brinton sat up. "I'm listening."

"My gran's a tough old bird, sir, as you know, and she's not the only one around these parts. That generation, they took on Kaiser Bill and won: they aren't the sort to give up without a fight. But that's apparently what this Miss Addison—Adelaide Addison, of all the daft names—has gone and done. Been starving herself to death, it seems, without a word of complaint." He paused. Brinton looked at him. He went on: "Got knocked down by a car in Brettenden this morning, ended up in hospital with a broken leg. And they say she's nothing but skin and bone, sir, and can't have eaten properly for months, according to Gran.''

"How does she know? No—daft question." Neighbours in Brettenden were . . . well, neighbourly. "Women's Institute? Some church group? The milkman?"

"Sort of the latter, sir. One of Gran's bingo cronies lives next door to Miss Addison, and she was the one the hospital rang about cancelling the milk and taking care of the cat. You know the grapevine when it's just ordinary gossip, sir. Something like this . . ."

"Fair enough. Mind you, if she hasn't eaten for months, I'll bet the moggy has. Milk? If that poor old girl's been short of the ready, it won't have been the cat who starves— they can catch their own. Free. You could be right, Foxon. This is probably another for the files. It's a pity the banking rules on privacy are so strict . . ."

"From what Gran says, Miss Addison didn't much hold with banks. Seems her dad fell out with his manager in eighteen ninety-something and never trusted another of 'em to the day he died. Daughter's the same, honouring her dear papa's memory by being a real money-under-the-mattress type. But she hasn't been burgled—I'd swear to that, sir. Even if she hadn't reported it—and from what Gran says she's the sort who'd be on the blower at once—the neighbours would have known. Which means Gran would know. And she's never breathed a word to me, sir, any more than she did just now."

"It's a pattern." Brinton, who as Foxon spoke had been delving into the heaps of documentation on his desk, pulled out the cardboard folder in which he had shoved his random ruminations on the Pauper Pensioner problem. He opened the folder and leafed through its contents. "We've almost a dozen cases here, Foxon, and my instincts tell me it's just the tip of the iceberg. There's some devilry going on we know nothing about, and the victims, poor old souls, are keeping their lips well and truly buttoned. If this Miss Addison of yours is any different, I'll be surprised."

"My gran's a . . . persuasive woman, sir."

"To quote you, Foxon, she's a tough old bird. It won't be easy to stand up to her—for this Addie to keep her secret—but I'll bet you a tidy sum she manages it somehow. That whole generation . . . well, you said it yourself."

Foxon nodded. He scratched the tip of his nose with his ballpoint pen, leaving a smear of blue ink. "There could be hundreds of them, sir. I mean, statistically—if we only get to hear about the more, uh, obvious ones . . ."

Brinton scowled. "They've survived two world wars and a depression. And now, when if anyone's earned the right to take things easy they have, they end up on the breadline. *Below* the blasted thing, if they can't afford to eat and're dropping in the streets from starvation." His jaw set in a grim line. "I'd love to get my hands on whoever's to blame . . . but how? We haven't a clue where to start looking for the blighter. I can't see anything any of the—the victims have got in common beside the fact they're old. More women than men, but that's another statistic: in the natural way of things, you get more widows than widowers." A lifetime's experience of human nature made him add, "Except when the odds've been helped along a bit by people who can't be bothered to get divorced. Many a good woman's realised too late the soup didn't quite taste the way she made it . . . But that's not the problem here."

"No, sir." Foxon had been thinking. "How about if we sort of put the word round discreetly for doctors and so on to keep an eye open for old folk who aren't as chipper as they used to be? For no obvious reason, I mean. And to let us know, and we could try a bit of—of friendly persuasion, sir." He straightened his fluorescent tie and smirked. "I couldn't guarantee getting much out of the old gentlemen, of course, but . . ."

"But the ladies like you—heaven knows why." Brinton rolled his eyes to the ceiling. "I suppose it might work."

He favoured his subordinate with an appraising glare. "If we picked the ones with the strongest nerves and the darkest sunglasses—unless you want to tone yourself down a bit, that is." He was sidetracked down a mental path he had often, though never out loud, travelled before. "What do you do if you have to go to a funeral? Cover yourself with a long black cape or hire something more in keeping?"

"Scrounge off my brother, sir. We're about the same size, apart from the shoes, and he works in a bank."

"Your brother's a suit-and-tie merchant? Must be a changeling. Hey!" Brinton's eyes grew bright. "A bank? Not—"

"No, sir, sorry. He's in Southampton, anyway. He'd be no use to us, or I'd've suggested it before."

"I suppose you would. Even someone with your horrible taste in clothes can't be entirely lacking in common sense." Brinton reflected for a while, then began to muse aloud. "You know, it could just work, at that. I doubt if they'd tell me, because that would make it too official. If they haven't complained so far about whatever-it-is, they're not likely to if a superintendent asks 'em about it. But a youngster like you . . ."

"You'd be a youngster, too, sir. Comparatively speaking. If you don't mind my saying so."

Brinton grunted. He jabbed with the tip of his pencil at his blotter, brooding. He sat up. "We can have a word with Doc Wyddial," he decided. "That woman keeps her ear to the ground, and being a police doctor she'd be more inclined to be . . . a bit less confidential than some of the others if we tell her what's worrying us. She won't mind bending her Hippocratic oath in a good cause—and old-age pensioners being blackmailed or whatever into starvation's one of the best causes I can think of. I hate bullies, Foxon," said the man who could hurl peppermints faster—

and harder—than anyone else in the young constable's experience. "And if the old folk can't stand up to the bullies by themselves, then us coppers've got to do it on their behalf!"

The superintendent would have been very much surprised to learn that, even as he uttered his battle cry, one elderly lady of his acquaintance was being bullied in a way she had never, in all her sixty-something years, known before.

Miss Seeton had planned to work in the garden. Her invaluable handbook, *Greenfinger Points the Way*, had recommended for the first half of January that a little light pruning would do the apple trees and roses no harm. She could take cuttings from carnations and pinks or could think about begonias. It would help (advised *Greenfinger*) if she pricked over the bulb beds or started forcing her rhubarb using upturned buckets with the bottoms cut off. Miss Seeton, who had serious doubts about her ability to wield metal-cutting implements with any skill, had resolved to leave the technical niceties to Stan: but she would have been happy enough to potter away at other outside jobs, if only the weather had been kind.

It had not. The forecast had predicted rain; the wireless announcer had not misrepresented the situation. Miss Seeton gazed through her sitting-room window at the sodden green mass of her lawn and beyond it to bushes and trees whose bare branches, spangled with raindrops, seemed decked in necklaces and tiaras of exotic, liquid diamonds. The diamonds swelled—merged—broke into a thousand shimmering shards and fell to earth, there to dance in merry puddles that, spilling over, formed rivulets running in sinuous slow motion down the gentle slope to the canal at the bottom of Miss Seeton's back garden.

Miss Seeton felt sorry for the chickens, who so disliked

the damp. Stan, of course, had ensured that the roof of the hen-house was thoroughly waterproof, but it might be several hours before the rain stopped and they would wish to venture out into the open wire run. This weather was really better suited to ducks. Which, as she recalled from her reading, gave larger eggs. But which would perhaps confuse all her recipe books, and which, she believed, had a much stronger flavour. But which would be . . . interesting, especially living so close to the canal.

Miss Seeton considered ducks. Wild waterfowl, such as wigeon and golden-eye, scoter and shoveller and gadwall, were no strangers to one who, since her retirement, had become a keen bird watcher. The domesticated duck was, however, a different matter, though, like their undomesticated cousins, they had such pleasing names: Khaki Campbell (which inspired visions of a Scotsman wearing a kilt of cavalry twill) and Aylesbury (a town she had never visited); Buff Orpington (which reminded her of Kipling's celebrated remark about standing steady) and Muscovy (how fortunate that here it was only sleeting, not snowing).

"Napoleon's retreat from Moscow," murmured Miss Seeton with a shiver. It had been Russia's weather, not her military, that had defeated the Corsican egomaniac. Miss Seeton recalled other, more recent, maniacs with delusions of world domination and shivered again before scolding herself. So dismal, when ducks were such . . . comical birds: quite unlike geese, which could be so fierce and whose eggs were even larger. But which made excellent watchdogs, if that was the word. "Ancient Rome," mused Miss Seeton, recalling long-ago lessons about the night attack on the Capitol by the Gauls, thwarted by the cackling of the sacred geese. "Goths," said Miss Seeton, "and Huns and Vandals . . ."

She had no idea that a genuine twentieth-century vandal was even now preparing to knock on her door.

The unexpected thumping made her start. Most people, after all, used the bell. She supposed that in the gloom of the rain-filled day the bell-push must be in shadow. Which meant it could not be a friend or acquaintance who knocked, as they would have known where the bell-push was. And it would be discourteous to be tardy in responding to the call of a stranger . . .

The thumping was repeated before Miss Seeton had jumped to her feet and begun hurrying down the hall. She clicked her tongue. One did not care to make premature judgements, particularly when the weather was so gloomy, but it was a little brusque, if not discourteous, of whomever was outside to have allowed her such a short time to leave the sitting room before knocking again . . .

And again—or almost. Miss Seeton, slightly out of breath, snatched open the front door just as a fisted hand was preparing to deliver its third impatient salvo.

"Oh!" said Miss Seeton, moving hurriedly back as the fist quivered in front of her. "I do beg your pardon."

"Ugh," said the man—yes, a stranger—on the doorstep. Or—perhaps—not a stranger. There was something about him that was vaguely familiar: something about the stance, about the eyes in their deep, wide sockets above that nose with the high arch and flaring nostrils . . .

"I," announced the stranger, "am Antony Scarlett." Miss Seeton blinked. Of course! But before she could speak, the Rubens of Refreshment hurried on:

"You are something of an artist yourself, they tell me." The tone in which he repeated this tale implied that he did not hold the opinion of others in very high regard.

Blushing, Miss Seeton replied that, while she had heard of Mr. Scarlett—had, indeed, visited his exhibition only the other day—she would not care to place herself in the same category. (This, she felt, committed her to nothing while being absolutely truthful.) She wondered who had done so, for she feared that person had misled him. "A teacher, that is all, and retired—evening classes, some private pupils; and I occasionally help out when Miss Maynard or her mother is unwell—the local school, you know."

"I don't," said Antony Scarlett. "I have never heard of an art school in Plummergen—but it is of no importance," he said as Miss Seeton attempted to explain her relationship to the village's deputy head and its junior mixed infants. "You say you have visited my exhibition?"

Miss Seeton nodded without speaking. If only he didn't ask her what she thought. She could still hear the caustic comments of Ferencz Szabo as they lunched together at the Savoy (light omelettes, fruit salad, and black coffee); she hoped Mr. Scarlett wouldn't connect her with the withering—and, one had to admit, for the most part justified—observations written by Mr. Szabo in the Visitors' Book before they had left the Galerie Genèvre.

"Then you know my work," said Antony Scarlett. "You are aware of its importance—of its relevance to modern life." He flung out his arms in a gesture that sent drops of rain pearling from the black folds of his cloak—not velvet, in such weather, but a surprisingly sensible gaberdine with, of course, the inevitable scarlet lining. He did not wait for a reply. "And," he hurried on, "since you are aware of my credentials, you cannot, of course, refuse to let me enter to put my proposition to you, Miss Seeton."

Miss Seeton blinked again. They had not been formally introduced. How . . . ?

"They told me in the bakery." Scarlett had caught her puzzled look and interpreted it correctly. "Most helpful," he added. "A delightful lady; delightful." Mrs. Wyght, who ran the bakery and tea room diagonally opposite Sweetbriars, was indeed a friendly and helpful soul, though Miss Seeton couldn't help musing that a Mrs. Pink, a Mrs.

Black, or a Mrs. Greene would have been regarded with equal favour.

She was becoming whimsical; Antony Scarlett was growing wet. And impatient. "A proposition?" enquired Miss Seeton, politely stepping aside to usher her visitor into the house. "I fear you may have been misled over my . . . small talent, Mr. Scarlett. As I thought I explained, I retired several years ago, and—"

"No, no, nothing like that!" The hall was too narrow for the full-blooded flourish, so Antony waited until they were safely in the sitting room before flinging out his arms and filling the air with a warm red-silk glow. "I ask for your help, Miss Seeton—for your cooperation. No, for your sacrifice in the cause of art as a memorial to the spirit of a truly remarkable man!"

A faint bell chimed in the recesses of Miss Seeton's memory. As yet, it did not sound a warning, though perhaps it should have done; but Miss Seeton seldom thought the worst of anyone, even when there was cast-iron evidence that worse than the worst had been done—or was about to be done.

As now.

"Miss Seeton, I want you to sell me your cottage," said Antony Scarlett.

Miss Seeton hadn't yet asked her guest to sit for fear she must answer to Martha for the effects of wet gaberdine on feather cushions. Out of courtesy she had herself therefore remained standing, but she sat down now with a vengeance. She dropped on the nearest chair and stared, speechless, at the tall caped figure who had made such a monstrous suggestion.

"I must have this house," said Antony Scarlett as Miss Seeton continued to struggle for speech. She tried shaking her head, but the movement didn't communicate itself to the artist, who was waving his arms again as he warmed to his terrible theme.

"The Stuttaford Prize," he announced, "will be awarded for an original work of art paying the greatest tribute to the memory of Sir Andrew Stuttaford, the Victorian plutocrat and philanthropist. Now, how did the man make his money, Miss Seeton?" Miss Seeton was still trying—and failing—to croak out her refusal; but Scarlett did not notice her silence as he swept on with his explanation.

"Stuttaford made his money in the tea, tobacco, and chocolate trades. He set up the foundation when his best clipper sank within sight of land—sank in water, Miss Seeton!" This was said with an air of triumph Miss Seeton failed to appreciate. "This house, your house, the house soon to be mine, stands on a corner where three roads meet—the triad, the triangle, the balance of life—and it stands near water—water once used, I am told, as a means of transporting commercial goods . . ."

"Napoleon," Miss Seeton managed to gasp as Antony swooped in an expressive circle around the room, gesturing first to the invisible Street and Marsh Road outside, then towards the bottom of Miss Seeton's garden and the Royal Military Canal. "Hitler!"

"No!" cried Antony Scarlett, revolted. "Miss Seeton, I am no tyrant, no philistine destroyer who tramples on free thought—my aim is to restore the weary spirit, the jaded palate of the soul! I am an artist—I create, I inspire! The Rubens of Refreshment, who glories in the richness of the liberated life—so they call me, and so I am! You have seen my exhibition—you are an artist. You, of all people, must understand!"

He gave her no time to reply, but swooped in another circle, his arms outstretched in a universal embrace. Miss Seeton flinched as the cape's heavy hem swung past her nose. "I," said Antony Scarlett, "would celebrate the glo-

rious achievements of Sir Andrew Stuttaford by buying
your cottage and transforming it into a three-dimensional
memorial to the man—yet, even as Sir Andrew is remembered, so will those who remember be forced to remember
that, even as he, so must they perish and decay, like this
house . . .''

"Glp?'' cried Miss Seeton, in a horrified squeak.

Antony Scarlett, still oblivious to her mood, perorated
onwards. ''I shall buy this house. I shall bring huge vats
of molten chocolate and pour the contents into every
room—rooms around which I will have already, in carefully selected places, set an assortment of smoking
paraphernalia: matches, pouches of tobacco, and, above all,
pipes. The humble clay, the churchwarden, the meer-
schaum—and the briar. A multitude of briars. You see the
symbolism, Miss Seeton? It is vital—exquisite—perfect!
This cottage, Sweetbriars—chocolate, tobacco pipes . . .''

Miss Seeton saw and was aghast. Antony Scarlett was
not. ''The rooms,'' he went on, gloating, ''will be entirely
filled with chocolate, and once it has set, a trio of workmen
will demolish the house with pickaxes, brick by common-
place brick, from roof to cellar! What remains will be a
perfect, paradoxical marriage of art and architecture—this
house in a reverse, in a negative form—not Sweetbriars,
but Briars Sweet! Exposed for a year to the elements, the
chocolate will slowly melt and decay, trickling its way towards the canal along which, throughout the centuries,
weary cart-horses dragged barges laden with the merchan-
dise that made Sir Andrew rich . . .''

Miss Seeton shrank from the wild fire in his eyes, from
the violence of his destructive vision manifested as a dull,
red gleam. A maniacal gleam? The border between genius
and madness was said to be very thin. From her own
knowledge, and with the words of Ferencz Szabo still blis-
tering her ears, she could not in all conscience call Antony

Scarlett a genius. Which left—well, the other. What was the correct way to deal with a madman? One was, she believed, if all else failed supposed to humour him. But to humour him she would have to agree to sell her dear cottage, and nothing on earth could induce her to do that. Not yet, at any rate, although once she became unable to live here, perhaps—if, that was, she in fact ever did. Dear Cousin Flora had been ninety-eight when she stopped living in the cottage and had only stopped then because she died.

What would Cousin Flora have said to Antony Scarlett when he told her he wanted to knock down her house? Miss Seeton, seated in Cousin Flora's own cottage, with so many heirloom ornaments, pictures, and pieces of furniture about her, felt her courage starting to return. She knew what Cousin Flora would have said.

"Ridiculous," she said, as Antony swooped in one final symbolic circle and turned again in triumph to face her. "Ridiculous," repeated Miss Seeton, rising to her feet on legs that hardly trembled and not caring if he thought her discourteous. "I have no intention, Mr. Scarlett, of selling my house. Absolutely none. And especially since all you wish to do is—is demolish it. You will have to find somewhere else to—to build your . . . chocolate paradox." She bit back another "ridiculous" just in time.

She cleared her throat and drew herself up to her full five-foot-nothing in her slippered toes. "And now, if you will excuse me, I have things to do."

As Antony had been oblivious to Miss Seeton's earlier perturbation, so now was he oblivious to her hints that he should depart. All he had heard was her refusal—which he did not think discourteous, but ignorant. Philistine. He had been deceived in his opinion of her: those who said she was an artist had been wrong.

"I do not see," said Miss Seeton rather sharply, "that I can be held to blame for what other people tell you. And,"

she added more gently, "perhaps you misunderstood. Or
didn't listen properly." Oh, dear. Did that sound rude?
"As, of course, would be understandable, if, that is to say,
you were . . . overexcited at having found what you believed to be a suitable location for your work."

"But it is!" cried Antony, latching on to the one phrase
that might indicate a weakening on her part. "This house—
this site—is perfect, Miss Seeton! I must have it. There is
nowhere else that will do!"

"There will have to be," Miss Seeton told him. It was
so much easier to be brave when standing up: and his eyes,
when one faced them squarely, did not gleam with quite
such unnerving fervour. "There are other canals in England," she said as Antony began to pace the floor and tear
his hair in the authentic Thwarted Genius manner. She held
her breath as he flounced past certain china ornaments on
the radiator shelf, but she uttered no reproach beyond:

"In the eighteenth century, before the railways . . ." No,
one should not allow oneself to be sidetracked, fascinating
though one's leisure reading always was. "Might I suggest," said Miss Seeton, who really didn't want to appear
disobliging, "that you purchase a good atlas—I believe the
Ordnance Survey is excellent—and search through it for a
similar configuration of roads and waterways to the one you
believe you require?"

She did not add her suspicion that he would find it as
hard to persuade the owners of whatever house he eventually chose to sell it as he had found the persuasion of
herself. If not more so. "And now," she said again, "you
must excuse me. I have things to do."

"No!" cried Antony Scarlett in a voice of thunder. His
reluctant hostess winced, but stood her ground. "I will
not—cannot—be cast into the howling desert darkness
when I have found here the one and only oasis!"

"It is broad daylight," said Miss Seeton, that most literal

of souls. "And still raining." Through years of teaching she had learned that it was inadvisable to allow children's tantrums to get out of hand.

Children? Why . . . yes. No wonder she had ceased to feel any great alarm. Antony Scarlett, ranting and raving about the place in that exaggerated fashion, had suddenly seemed no more than an overgrown child, about to indulge in a sulking fit because he couldn't have what he wanted.

Well, he couldn't. "Well, you can't," said Miss Seeton. "Buy my house, I mean. And if you don't run away—that is, if you don't leave now, I . . ." Antony had settled on the hearthrug, and Miss Seeton's eye was caught by the watercolour hanging on the wall above the fireplace. It was one of her own: a bleak, windswept moorland under stormy skies, powdered with snow she had pastelled later at the request of dear Superintendent Delphick, of whom it had been a fanciful likeness. *The Grey Day.*

"I shall be forced," concluded Miss Seeton, inspired, "to call the police."

CHAPTER 6

In Ashford, Superintendent Brinton was feeling pardonably pleased with himself and his team. After a tip-off, a dawn raid had successfully netted the already suspect, but as yet unproven, gang behind a whole series of armed robberies in high street shops: a father, his two sons, and his youngest daughter's boyfriend. All four men, plus the daughter (who had beaned Detective Constable Foxon with her bedside lamp as he tried to apply handcuffs to her sleeping companion) were currently in police cells, trying to fabricate—that is, to recollect—their numerous and complicated alibis for the benefit of their exhausted lawyers.

"That shirt doesn't help. You still look horrible." Brinton looked up from his desk to grin ferociously at Foxon as that young man made his entrance after a quick trip home to rectify at least part of the damage done at dawn. "But the tie could be worse . . ." Then he remembered. He sat up straight. "Foxon, what the hell are you doing here?"

"Horrible, sir?" Foxon contrived to look wounded in the spiritual as well as the physical sense. "I'd call it on the tasteful side, myself." He did not respond to the hint that he was technically on a day's sick leave suffering from concussion, but dropped into the chair opposite his superior and returned the latter's grin, though—in deference to his burgeoning black eye—with less ferocity.

Brinton sighed. "So much for sending you round to charm the old ladies. One look at your tasteful gear and your ugly mug and they'll be talking to the police, all right—but it'll be on the other end of a three-nines call. We don't want you scaring the witnesses into fits; we want them spilling the beans nice and easy. Well, they won't, not until you and that shirt've . . . faded a bit. You look horrible," he reiterated, "and you'll look more horrible still before you're done."

"Sorry, sir."

Brinton grunted.

"She moved a bit faster than I was expecting."

Brinton rolled his eyes.

His subordinate brushed a feeble hand across his brow. "Here's me," he lamented, "struggling back to work when by rights I ought to be in bed with an ice-pack on my head—"

"Shuttup, Foxon." The command was automatic. Even as the younger man launched into his lament, the superintendent was fishing in the "in" tray for his Pauper Pensioners folder. "If it's ice you want, shove your head out of the window. It's cold enough out there to freeze—"

He stopped, conscious that the comparison he had been about to make might not be appropriate for a senior to use in front of a junior officer. His junior grinned. "Do you know, sir, I found out the other day what it really means? And it isn't rude at all. It's all to do with the old-time Navy and cannon balls. Apparently they used to stack 'em on deck to be ready for action, in a pyramid held together by a brass frame called a monkey. And when the temperature went too low, the monkey would shrink and make all the balls roll out. They were made of iron, you see, sir, and

iron and brass have different . . . uh, they expand at different rates. And, uh, shrink,'' he finished as the inevitable
objection could be seen on Brinton's lips.

''Amazing.'' The superintendent rolled his eyes. ''Useless, but amazing. Children's television, was it?''

''Admiral Leighton, sir. I bumped into him when I was
over in Brettenden checking that jeweller's statement, and
you know how cold it was the day I was there. We got
chatting, and—well, he told me.''

''*He* didn't look as if he was starving to death, did he?''
Brinton had retrieved his Pensioner file and was poised to
open it. ''Hale and hearty, I hope? Still got the twinkle in
his eye?''

''And the ginger in his beard,'' Foxon readily confirmed.
''Whatever's been going on with the old folk, it hasn't
reached Plummergen yet—sorry, sir,'' he said as Brinton
winced at this light-hearted reference to Miss Seeton's village. ''And I don't suppose the Admiral'd thank me for
counting him among the pensioners, even if he is retired.
He's all there and a bit more, I'd say.''

''So would I.'' Brinton opened the file. ''Unlike some
poor wretches—this Miss Addison, now. She's out of hospital, they tell me, and the district nurse'll be popping in
every day to make sure the old girl gets at least one decent
meal. A close friend of your gran's, is she?''

Foxon knew who he meant. ''I'd say close enough for
our purposes, sir.''

''Yes, but they aren't really ours.'' Brinton glared at him
across the open folder. ''They can't be, because there's
been no official complaint. This is . . . a spot of private
work. A hunch of a case when there isn't a case, if you
know what I mean.''

''Got you, sir.''

''But *I* haven't got you. You're off sick today, laddie.
And of course I can't tell you the best way to recuperate—

I'm no medical expert—but if you felt well enough to pop round to see your old grannie—take her out for a drive on such a nice sunny day . . .''

Both men glanced through the window at the pouring rain and glanced away again quickly. They kept careful custody of their eyes and suppressed their separate smiles. ''Yes,'' said Brinton, ''a nice drive in the country—the fresh air's bound to be good for your headache . . .''

''Right, sir.''

''Right.'' Brinton slammed the folder shut and scowled at its closed cover. ''I haven't a clue what to tell you to look out for. Anything wrong's about the best I can manage. Use your initiative, laddie—and don't put the wind up the old girl if you can avoid it. She'll be feeling bad enough to start with, having that shiner of yours staring her in the face. Proper rogue and vagabond, you look. If your gran doesn't vouch for your good character, heaven help us; she probably won't even let you in the house.''

''I'll do my best, sir.'' Foxon eased himself out of the visitors' chair, adjusted his jacket, and straightened his distinctive kipper tie. ''See you tomorrow, sir?'' he said and was gone.

Use his initiative. Well, he was a copper. That's what coppers did in the general run of things, and if they were detectives they used even more. Foxon thought he didn't do too badly, on the whole—though he wasn't sure what Old Brimstone would say when he found out how much *initiative* his junior meant to use. Even if he'd more or less put the idea in his head in the first place by jabbering on about Rear Admiral Leighton. Still, by the time he presented his report, it'd be too late to do anything about it . . .

About *her*.

Whistling only once he was well out of earshot, Foxon bounded from Brinton's office down the corridor to the car park at the rear of the station. Not being officially on duty, he took an unmarked vehicle and didn't bother letting Desk Sergeant Mutford, letter of the law or not, know he'd taken it. Old Brimmers could sort everything out if questions were asked.

One of the many questions the superintendent had not asked was whether Foxon was going to his grandmother's by the direct or by the scenic route . . .

The young detective constable threaded the car through the complexities of Ashford's traffic system until the thinning houses of the residential area gave way to fields and farmland and the signpost informed him that he was travelling along the B2070. He passed through Bromley Green and negotiated the crossroads at Hamstreet; he went under the swinging cables of the electricity pylons and gave way to a vehicle coming in the opposite direction on the narrow bridge over the Royal Military Canal. He took the fork for Snargate—turned left and north on the B2080—crossed the railway line and the canal for a second time . . .

By this roundabout route, Foxon accomplished his arrival at the southern end of Plummergen without anyone in any of the shops to the north noticing that he had arrived.

He was taking a risk, of course. Miss Seeton might be out, and if he went looking for her he was bound to be spotted. And that wasn't the only risk. He knew as well as Old Brimmers, or the Oracle, that once MissEss and her brolly were on the case, you could never be sure what would happen next. But it wasn't her brolly he wanted so much as her . . . presence. She was good with people: and not just children, either. Maybe it was because it was hard to take her seriously in those awful hats she always wore. They made you smile; they put you at your ease.

And who better to put a sick, elderly lady at her ease with an unknown, villainous-looking young man than another elderly lady? He and Miss Seeton weren't exactly strangers. They'd once spent the night together, in the most innocent way, in a deserted church. And she'd ended up saving his life by dropping things—that umbrella again— on the head of the thug who was pursuing her up a ladder, after having coshed her companion senseless, with intent to return and finish the job properly once he'd finished Miss Seeton. And she'd, well, finished him. For which Foxon, once he'd come round, had been more than grateful.

He pulled the car up to the kerb; switched off wipers, lights, and engine; and prepared to be grateful again.

With his head bowed against the rain, he scurried up the short, paved front path to Miss Seeton's door and rang the bell. He waited. She did not answer. After what he judged to have been two tactful minutes, he rang once more.

Still no answer. She must be out—yet surely not shopping, brolly or not, in such weather? He rang a third time and, when there was still no reply, was struck by an idea.

She'd been kidnapped before; she'd been attacked before in the privacy of her own home. He couldn't think of any current reason for the bad guys to be after her, but with MissEss you could never be sure. He'd better scout around the back for broken windows or other signs of violence so the super could be warned to start looking . . .

It was as he made his way down the passage between Sweetbriars and the high brick wall separating it from the narrowed Street that he saw the oblong of light shining on that wall. It was yellow—electric—barred, as if coming through a window. The kitchen window, he knew.

On tiptoe, Foxon crept the last few feet and peered into Miss Seeton's kitchen . . .

He observed Miss Seeton in person, making herself a cup of tea with every appearance of calm. She was alone; she seemed unharmed, though a slight pucker between her brows might hint at some mental perturbation. With raindrops running down the back of his neck, Foxon wisely waited for her to complete her manoeuvres with the kettle of boiling water, then rapped on the glass to attract her attention.

Miss Seeton looked up. The pucker between her brows was now a frown. She saw Foxon's waving hand and smiling face, blinked, and suddenly smiled back at him through the speckle of raindrops obscuring her view. She hurried to the back door and let him in.

"Mr. Foxon! What a delightful surprise—but, oh, dear, you're soaking wet, and I suppose it's all my fault." She gave him no time to reply. "And your poor eye—have you bathed it properly? Would you like some salt water and cotton wool? It won't take me long."

"No, I'm fine, thanks. Just a bit damp, but you know me, tough as old boots. Honestly, I'm fine," he insisted as she studied him in silence for a while, then nodded.

"Let me pour you some tea to warm you: I always make enough for a second cup, and I'll top up the pot as well. It was very rude of me, I know, but really it seemed the best thing to do, in the circumstances. And a few biscuits? Some cake? Thank you, yes—that cupboard." Miss Seeton was happy to allow him the pottering privileges of an old acquaintance. "Any of my friends, of course, would know that if I didn't come to the door they would find me out here or in the sitting room at this time of day. So far, thank goodness, he doesn't seem to have thought of that, though I fear it may only be a matter of time." And, as she poured the tea, she sighed.

It was usual for those associating with Miss Seeton to need to unravel certain complex trains of thought before they could come to any understanding. After seven years, Foxon was as good as most at reading between the lines.

And especially in the circumstances that had brought him here. "Someone keeps bothering you?" She was elderly; she lived alone; she had money, he knew—her police income, her pension—that might make her a suitable victim. She was on the skinny side to begin with: it wouldn't show . . . but he'd never thought of MissEss as the sort to give in easily, and he'd never doubted her common sense or her courage. Still, there was always a first time.

"Someone keeps bothering you?"

Miss Seeton blushed. "I don't like being rude, but when he won't take no for an answer—of course, I haven't let him in the house again, after dear Sir George so kindly explained to me about trespassing—but I find raised voices so disagreeable. He will *boom* at me. And with that black cloak of his—like Dracula, so foolish and theatrical—he makes me think of Stendhal. *Scarlet*, you see, *and Black. Le Rouge et le Noir*. Of course, I don't speak French," she added hastily, not wishing to seem pretentious. "And when I saw you I ought to have realised, for you weren't wearing one, only with your head down against the rain when I looked through the window . . ."

"You were keeping out of his way?" He'd leave asking *whose* way until later. Whoever he was, Miss Seeton didn't sound too scared of him.

Miss Seeton was still musing on Stendhal's famous novel. "I doubt, you know, if his motives are either religious or genuinely spiritual. Or military," she added with a twinkle. "But then," she conceded, "he is young and still making his way in the world. Without much talent, I fear." She shook her head and twinkled again at her guest as she handed him the biscuit tin. "They say that every little helps, don't they? Publicity and so on." She sighed. "Which if one wants it is beneficial, I suppose. But *I* have no intention, as I keep trying to tell him, of helping the foolish young man by allowing him to buy my house and fill it with chocolate and knock it down—"

"To do *what?*" Foxon, poised to bite into a plain digestive biscuit, allowed astonishment to overcome both etiquette and hunger.

"Knock it down," repeated Miss Seeton and explained.

"He's mad," said Foxon as she came to the end of her tale. "Stark, staring bonkers."

"A little . . . overenthusiastic, perhaps." Miss Seeton's instinctive pedagogic approval of enthusiasm must, as ever, be tempered by a gentlewoman's innate disapproval of excess. "Or merely fashionable. Modern art . . . But, as we know, fashions change." The prospect seemed to please her. "With luck, it may not be long before some other idea occurs to him for the competition, and then he will stop appearing on my doorstep for good."

"Yes, well, until he *does* think of something else, you just carry on not letting him in the house, MissEss. With these nutters, and you here on your own, you can't be too careful."

"I am fortunate in my friends," said Miss Seeton gently. "It is kind of you to be concerned, but I assure you there is no necessity."

"Other people aren't so fortunate," Foxon said, grateful for the lead. "Which is really why I came to see you today, Miss Seeton . . ."

"Not for some first aid?" enquired Miss Seeton with another studied look at her visitor's battered countenance.

"Oh, I got in a slight argument with a lampshade. It lost." Foxon grinned to show her again that he would survive, then sobered. "No, why I'm here's because . . . well, it's a bit complicated, but . . ."

He knew, of course, that he could rely on Miss Seeton's discretion. Were he to tell her every detail of every victim's bank account (if known), he was confident she would repeat those details to nobody else. Money, politics, and religion: the likes of MissEss just never talked about them; and she wasn't one to gossip, in any case.

But it was more because Brinton had no idea he meant to take Miss Seeton along with him to talk to Addie Addison that Foxon hesitated to elaborate on the reasons for his visit. His superior's ignorance—and the feeling that if he wanted MissEss to do her stuff in her own particular way, then the less he told her, the better. Not that he'd know what to make of her sketches (if she did them) the way the Oracle always seemed able to do; but he could have a damned good shot at it. And even if it didn't work, which knowing his luck it probably wouldn't, it'd still be an elderly lady putting another elderly lady at her ease, which, fond of the old girl as he was, he couldn't say his gran was all that good at doing, friend or not. When you'd just come out of hospital you needed rest and soothing, not someone bossing you about telling you how silly you'd been and that you ought to eat three square meals a day; she'd just nip round with a duster and the broom to make things nice for you and ask if there was any shopping you wanted. Gran Biddle's tongue, even her nearest and dearest had to say, wasn't so much hung in the middle as completely freewheeling, like the rest of her. Perpetual motion—and then some.

"A bit complicated," said Foxon slowly. "Let's just say I'm taking my gran to see a friend of hers the other side of Brettenden. This friend's a bit under the weather, and I think a little of your common sense, Miss Seeton, would, uh, help to keep the peace."

Miss Seeton blushed for the compliment, then smiled. "You want someone to talk to while your grandmother and her friend are chatting, of course. I am flattered, Mr. Foxon, that you should consider me a suitable companion . . ." The twinkle was back in her eye. "One whose presence will not give rise to any family pressures." Foxon blinked. It was the one argument he hadn't thought of. "When one is still in the early stages of one's career," Miss Seeton went on, "it is quite conceivable that one should lack the inclination to settle down, although one's relatives sometimes fail to understand this. Not every young man is as fortunate as dear Nigel Colveden."

Foxon grinned. "Yes, but his dad gives him a hard time if he dates anyone more than twice, I know. Drops hints about top hats and speeches—drives Nigel wild."

"Sir George's teasing is meant in the kindest way, as I'm sure Nigel knows. His father has always had an eye for a pretty girl and of course is happily married himself. It's only natural he should wish his son to be similarly happy. But it is equally natural that, at the age you young men are, there seems no great urgency to marry." This was said with complete innocence; Foxon took it in the spirit in which it was said.

"You're quite right, Miss Seeton. My gran's always on at me to find some nice girl and get married, but I want to put in for sergeant before too long." *Use your initiative.* "I'm glad you don't mind being used as . . . camouflage. You don't, do you?"

"I shall enjoy my little excursion and the company," said Miss Seeton firmly. "It will be a great pleasure to meet Mrs. Biddle at last—and a change of scene, in weather like this, is always welcome. I believe I will take my sketchbook if you don't mind."

Foxon assured her that he didn't mind in the least.

Once he'd introduced them, Foxon popped the two ladies in the back seat of his car, saying how much it would impress Miss Addison with the quality of her visitors if they came sweeping up to the house driven by a chauffeur. Mrs. Biddle chuckled; Miss Seeton smiled. So tactful. Mrs. Biddle, as the family matriarch, must expect to take precedence; but Miss Seeton was an invited guest. The etiquette was tricky. For herself, she wouldn't mind at all sitting alone in the back, but Mr. Foxon evidently thought it best to avoid any little difference of opinion by treating both his passengers the same.

Not for one minute did she suspect Foxon of wanting to give her time to become comfortably acquainted with his grandmother so that there would be less chance of her feeling uncomfortable with Miss Addison. Her remarkable talent for seeing to the heart of things might be suppressed by the effort of making perpetual courtesies and stilted small-talk. He wanted her at her ease; he wanted her instincts to be given full rein, not to be held back.

Mrs. Biddle was certainly not holding back. Always a chatty soul—even Martha Bloomer, of whom it was often said that she must have been born in midconversation, would have come a poor second in a prattling contest—she appreciated any new audience, especially one so willing to listen and to make polite reply as occasion required.

"Yes, poor Addie. Skin and bone, she was—nothing but skin and bone." Mrs. Biddle, of whose skin there was a more than ample covering on the well-fleshed bone, clicked her tongue. "The hospital said she couldn't have had a decent meal for weeks, silly girl, but they've been feeding her up, and she's got the district nurse now she's out, though it's not the same as having your friends pop in to see you, is it? Strangers round the place, I mean—no offence, dear." A plump hand hastily patted Miss Seeton on the shoulder. "I can't seem to think of you as a stranger, being as my boy's told me so much about you, not to mention what I've read in the papers, of course."

Miss Seeton sighed quietly; Foxon winced. While having earlier given her a brief character sketch of Miss Seeton, he had obviously failed to convince his grandmother that not everyone had the high regard for press coverage readers of the tabloids might suppose they did.

"I fear," murmured Miss Seeton, "that the newspapers

do tend to exaggerate.'' She considered her dear friend
Amelita Forby of *The Daily Negative*. ''It makes a—a good
story, of course, which is their job, but one should always
take these things with a—a generous pinch of salt. Several
pinches,'' she added rather mournfully.

''Mum's the word, dear, if that's the way you want
it.'' Mrs. Biddle patted her on the shoulder again. Who
would've thought the Battling Brolly'd be so . . . well, shy?
World famous, she was, but you'd never know it to look
at her—mind you, it took some nerve to wear a hat like
that—or to hear her talk. Might be anyone's old auntie,
really. Nice and quiet and restful: do Addie a power of
good. Mrs. Biddle was not entirely unaware that her bracing
personality could sometimes overpower those less robust
than herself.

'' 'Course, she never was all that strong,'' she said aloud.
''Never seemed to have that much gumption, neither, always on the quiet side. Never one to let you know what
she's thinking—but then she don't moan all the time about
her aches and pains the way some folk do. I wouldn't have
worried half so much about her tumbling herself into hospital like she did if it hadn't been for Philly Byng the other
day, swallowing all them pills and doing herself in, and the
very last person you'd expect. Depression, they called it—
and her always bright as a button until recent! These doctors don't know what they're talking about, do they?''

Whatever Miss Seeton's reply, Foxon did not hear it.

He was too busy wondering what Brinton would make
of Gran Biddle's unexpected mention of the late, suicidal,
Miss Philippa Byng.

CHAPTER 7

"She and Addie knew each other from the old days, you see," Mrs. Biddle was saying as Foxon finally surfaced from his wondering. "Good pals for years, they were, only they fell out over something . . ." Maud Biddle's tone showed how dearly she would love to know what the cause of that falling out had been. "And then it's cross the street rather than talk to her, dear, when both of them you'd think would have more sense. Years it went on, would you believe?"

Miss Seeton, while deploring the sad breaking of a long-held friendship through what must surely have been a simple misunderstanding, could.

"And then she opens the paper one day to read Philippa Byng's killed herself, coroner's inquest and everything they had. Balance of the mind disturbed, they said, and thin as a rake besides. Shook Addie Addison up something cruel, it did. But that," said Mrs. Biddle, "wasn't more than a week ago, and they say she's been starving herself for as long as Miss Byng, if not longer. Which, seeing as they weren't speaking to each other and I don't believe in mind-reading, it's a funny coincidence, isn't it?"

Miss Seeton, who shared Mrs. Biddle's disbelief, agreed that it was. In the front seat, Foxon, his face hidden from those in the back, grinned with relief that the conversation had been grandmother-led in exactly the direction he'd hoped it would go.

"We must be almost there," he said, seeing in the mirror how Mrs. Biddle agreed with Miss Seeton's agreement and the pair regarded each other with approval. It was an unlikely friendship, if you went by the book: but MissEss got along with all sorts of people in that happy-go-lucky innocent way of hers, and Gran Biddle was a law unto herself. He crossed mental fingers as his physical fingers flicked the indicator for the turn into Miss Addison's street, and sent up a short prayer that his gamble would soon pay off.

"That's the house, on the left. She's let the place go," observed Mrs. Biddle. In a lesser woman her tone might have been thought smug. "I'd hardly have known it. The gate could do with a good lick of paint—and there's a hinge coming loose. And for all that asphalt drive looks new, the grass came through in great clumps, see? And I wouldn't care to say whether she cut the lawn at all last year, and if this was my garden, I'd do something about the weeds, I really would."

"Well, she's got a broken leg right now," said Foxon. "Which is why we're here, to cheer her up. So we *won't* mention mowing the lawn, hoovering the carpets, or digging the garden, will we? We don't want to upset her."

"That's what friends are for," came his grandmother's ambiguous reply as she fumbled with the handle of the car door. "You and Miss Seeton can have a nice chat with poor Addie while I fix us a cup of tea and find out where she keeps the keys to her shed. We wouldn't want to make extra work for you and your friends, lad, having burglars think the house is empty and they can break in when they feel like it and help themselves. You never know," she added darkly, "if that's not the sort of thing wouldn't send poor Addie after Philippa Byng as quick as wink."

She grumbled all the way up the drive about the state of Miss Addison's garden. Miss Seeton silently agreed with her, while accepting that not everyone was as fortunate in matters of fitness (her yoga, so beneficial) and domestic help (dear Martha and Stan) as she. Foxon, whose horticultural expertise was such that if told tulips bloomed in July he would believe it, repeated his warning about not upsetting Miss Addison by reminding her of the many jobs about the house she hadn't, for whatever reason, managed to do. So busy was he with his little lecture that, without thinking, he mounted the steps in front of his grandmother and rapped on Miss Addison's door with the all briskness of the professional caller.

"Manners," snapped Mrs. Biddle, but was then sidetracked by a knot of groundsel in what should have been a weed-free bed and marched across to root it out. Miss Seeton, whose trained eye was even quicker than her new friend's, watched with wistful approval, but deemed it discourteous to move from her place two steps lower than Foxon at the door.

"Somebody's coming," Foxon said. "Dot-and-go-one, by the sound of it. That'll be the crutch. Amazing what they can do with broken ankles nowadays."

"Indeed, yes." Miss Seeton remembered long-ago visits to hospital for the benefit of air-raid victim acquaintances in their monumental plaster casts and the splints bulging with cotton-wool padding. "Strapped bandages and a type of lightweight plastic cast are used now, I believe, for less serious injuries. So much more pleasant for people to be able to convalesce in their own homes. One makes such faster progress."

Miss Addison's progress to her front door was far from

fast, but she arrived in the end. There was a rattle at the latch, and the door swung slowly open.

"Oh." The faded little lady now revealed gasped as Foxon's smiling face met her gaze and he prepared to introduce himself. "Oh, no! No!" One hand supported her against the jamb; the other, trembling, swept the aluminium elbow-crutch up from the floor. "Go away!" shrilled Miss Addison and poked her visitor in the chest. "Leave me alone!"

The thrust was so unexpected that Foxon leaped backwards down the steps, in his fall bumping against Miss Seeton, who, with yoga-nimble reflexes, contrived to hop sideways out of range, flinging out her arms to keep her balance. Her handbag, bulging with sketchbook, pencils, and other essential paraphernalia, plopped straight to the ground. Her umbrella, more streamlined, flew several horizontal feet before yielding to gravity and plummeting, ferrule first, to land quivering in the black asphalt of the drive like some sinister silken arrow.

"Addie!" screeched Mrs. Biddle, brandishing her bunch of groundsel from the flower bed. Miss Addison's eyes swivelled in the direction of the screech. "Adelaide Addison," cried Mrs. Biddle, stamping to the bottom of the steps, "what on earth do you think you're playing at?"

"Maud!" squeaked Miss Addison, aghast. "Oh, Maud—you mean it's—it's all right?"

Mrs. Biddle dropped the groundsel, plucked Miss Seeton's umbrella from its sticky black confinement with one sturdy wrench, and strode up the steps to confront her friend at the top. "A fine way to greet visitors, I must say," said Mrs. Biddle. "Here's me got my grandson on his day off to bring me over to see you, and you try to give *him* a broken ankle, if not worse! Never mind Miss Seeton"—with a brisk nod, she handed the brolly back to its owner—"that's been brought here special on account of you always liking pictures, and her being an artist my boy's known for years, so we thought you'd like to meet her. But if pushing people down the steps is all the thanks we get, we'll be off this very minute and leave you to yourself.''

Miss Addison gulped. ''Oh,'' she said meekly. ''Oh, Maud, I'm so sorry. I didn't . . .''

''You didn't mean it.'' Foxon bounded back up the steps to give his anxious hostess the full benefit of his smile. ''We quite understand that it must have startled you, opening the door to find a pair of complete strangers outside, with you not being in the best of health, if you don't mind my saying so. How about taking my arm, Miss Addison, and I'll help you inside to sit down and rest your ankle, and Gran can do the honours properly?''

Ten minutes later, Miss Addison was sipping tea from one of her best sprig-patterned cups and asking Miss Seeton's expert opinion of the age-dark oil of her grandfather over the mantelpiece and of the dainty watercolour of her dear grandmother beside the sofa. Mrs. Biddle was clattering happily in the kitchen, running taps, slamming cupboard doors, and giving conflicting orders to Foxon, who grumbled that he couldn't cope with more than one thing at a time, and if he had known what it would be like doing her a favour he'd have gone to work after all.

Not even his grandmother could guess at the enormous grin of satisfaction he was trying not to show. Miss Seeton was performing as required without even realising it; she'd be dashing off one of her doodles next, the way Miss Addison was chattering on about pictures and portraits and how she'd done a bit of sketching when she was young, and how she supposed it was like riding a bicycle, which you never really forgot. MissEss wasn't one to ignore a hint. She'd let the poor old girl have a go, then she'd show her, ever so politely, where she wasn't getting it quite right. And the next thing'd be a full-blown Drawing, which with luck and a following wind might just explain—among other things—why this Addie had been so scared when she opened her front door . . .

"And while we're about it," said Mrs. Biddle, "you can run the mower across the lawn, if it's not too wet. And if it is, you can help me with some more of the weeds."

Foxon sighed. What he suffered in the cause of justice. "It's rained a lot these last few days," he said hopefully. "Won't it be bad for the soil to have me tramping about all over it with a mower? And I'm a sick man," he added, pointing to his empurpling eye. "I shouldn't go bending with a shiner like this."

"The Foxons were always slackers," returned Mrs. Biddle. "When your mum said she wanted to marry your dad, I warned her if she wanted anything done she'd spend the rest of her life nagging if she didn't do it herself. You get in there right now and find out where Addie keeps the shed key while I finish this floor."

Sighing, Foxon skipped out of the path of the approaching mop and headed for the sitting room. On the threshold he paused. Ten out of ten. MissEss had fished her sketchbook out of her bag, and Miss Addison was squinting across at the hideous clock on the table next to a bunch of ratty dried flowers and scribbling with a borrowed pencil on a nice blank page.

Foxon coughed. "Excuse me, Miss Addison." She looked up, wide-eyed, from her scribble. "We thought we'd do a spot of work outside while we were here—tidy the garden, you know the sort of thing. Weeds," Foxon said, gesturing with as much confidence as he could muster. He wouldn't pull up a sausage unless Gran gave her Bible oath it wasn't supposed to be growing where it was, which he'd always understood to be how you defined a weed. The Foxons could work just as hard as the Biddles-by-marriage—even if they needed supervision in certain areas.

"Outside?" faltered Miss Addison. In her thin fingers, the pencil began to shake. "Work? Oh, dear—no, really, I would so much prefer it if you didn't. That is," she continued, rallying, "it's very kind of you, but I don't want to put you to any trouble, and in any case there's nothing outside that needs doing. Not really."

"Adelaide Addison!" Mrs. Biddle, her floor finished, had arrived to lend force to Foxon's argument. "How you can sit there saying that, I don't know."

Adelaide gulped. She glanced from Foxon to Mrs. Biddle and back. She lowered her eyes to the sketch she'd had so much fun drawing and looked up to meet Miss Seeton's sympathetic gaze. "Oh," said Miss Addison after a moment. "Oh, yes. Yes—thank you. I'm sure it will be all right."

"All right?" Brinton glared at his junior colleague as the verbal report, over which Foxon had puzzled for most of the previous evening, reached its conclusion. "I'd say some people are easily satisfied." He jabbed with an irritable finger at the page from Miss Seeton's sketchbook where it lay on his blotter. "D'you think *this* looks as if everything's all right?"

Foxon contrived a hurt appearance, then caught Brinton's eye and decided he'd better come clean. "That's the reason I showed it to you, sir. The only reason, really. I, uh, wasn't going to tell you I'd taken MissEss along with me unless she came up with the goods—you know what she's like about, uh, not being able to perform to order—but, well, she did. Once I'd got her safely home and she asked me in for a cup of tea, that is."

"More tea?" Despite the gravity of the moment, Brinton had to chuckle. "You must have been drowning in the stuff."

Foxon applied a rueful hand to the small of his back.

"Gran had me mucking about in that garden for what felt like hours, sir. Believe me, I needed all the fluid replenishment I could get—besides, I thought it'd give Miss Seeton another chance, seeing as she hadn't come up with anything while we were at Miss Addison's. And she did," he repeated, indicating the apparently innocuous white page on its bright pink background. "Didn't she?"

"She did." Brinton sighed. "Of course, we can't tell just what she's come up *with*. I've always said you need a translator when Miss Seeton starts her infernal Drawing . . ."

Frowning, he stared again at the picture. "Infernal" wasn't such a bad word, come to think of it. There was a hint of something—something devilish about all this. It wasn't so much that the place seemed . . . out of proportion, but . . . "I suppose this *is* Miss Addison's house?" he demanded, wondering whether he wished it to be so or not.

Foxon hesitated. "I wasn't sure either to begin with, sir. Sort of House of Usher when you first look at it, isn't it? But the—the basics are there—right number of windows and doors, and the garden and so forth—only she's made them so . . . distorted. And there's an atmosphere . . . much gloomier than a few rain clouds, only I can't for the life of me tell you why . . . but in any case, it's not so much the house that strikes you, is it, sir?"

Brinton grunted. It wasn't. While the gables were more steeply arched, the beams more darkly black, the pitch of the roof sharper, the windows blanker and more staring— the phrase "hollow-eyed" sprang unbidden to his mind . . . while the doorway was more narrow and unwelcoming— almost repellant—than in a normal house, it was on the driveway leading up to that abnormal house and on the bare-branched tree—a tall, cruel-spiked thorn—beside it on which the artist had expended her most detailed skill.

"When she gets Seeing in that cockeyed way of hers . . ." muttered Brinton, shaking his head. "Is she tell-

ing us the old girl's on the breadline? Money doesn't grown
on trees—perhaps that's what she's saying. There's been
a—a wicked wind blown those bank notes off the branches
and splashed them all over the path in . . ." An uneasy note
entered his voice. "In—funny patterns . . ."

"A regular blizzard," agreed Foxon with a shudder that
had nothing whatever to do with memories of gardening in
the January cold.

Brinton did not hear him as he peered more closely at
the path in question. "Yes, those're bank notes all right—
and that damned block pattern rings a faint bell, though I
can't . . ." He looked up to see Foxon miming similar be-
wilderment. He returned to his study of the picture. "You
can see the Queen's head in every one, can't you? And—
and all laid out, dammit, in nice neat aitches as regular as
you please . . ." He shook his head once more. "H. H. H
. . . it doesn't make sense, Foxon. A for Addison I could've
understood, but . . ."

"Search me, sir."

Brinton hardly noticed the reply. "And as for the old
dear herself on the step . . . Was she *really* as skinny as
that? She's practically a skeleton—her face is a skull, for
heaven's sake! That's not a . . . happy face, Foxon. And I
don't suppose for a minute it's because of the busted leg.
Talk about—about empty expressions and hollow
eyes . . ." The superintendent wouldn't have called himself
a fanciful man, but for a moment, looking at Miss Addison
as portrayed by Miss Seeton, he felt that he was following
her tragic gaze into the bitter bleakness of infinity. He shuddered, sighed again, and scratched his head as he became
brisk.

"Yes—well. You've had longer than me to think about
this, laddie. What d'you make of it?"

Foxon frowned. "The house is just . . . wrong, sir, and I
don't know why. And I can't make anything of Miss Ad-

dison except that she's . . . wrong, too, sir. Creepy—and
again I don't know why, except that money *must* come into
it somehow. MissEss has taken so much care with the bank
notes . . . And I'm seriously puzzled by the block paving
drive. I mean—Miss Addison didn't have blocks at all, just
a cheap coat of asphalt cracked up by the frost. When
MissEss, uh, dropped her brolly, it went into the stuff like
a knife through butter. It would have bounced off those
blocks like a—like I don't know what, sir.''

Brinton tore vaguely at his hair. ''You don't know and
I don't know. Neither of us knows how to make sense of
Miss Seeton the way the Oracle does—but there's such a
thing as professional pride, Foxon. We can't keep running
to Scotland Yard every time there's an odd bit of scribble
we don't like the look of . . .''

Foxon thought this a masterly understatement, but was
too conscious of the difference in rank to do more than
murmur that the sketch, indeed, was not very nice.

''Nor's what's been going on,'' appended Brinton, wagging his finger. ''Whatever it was—*and still is*, laddie.
While you were gallivanting among the buttercups yesterday, I had a word with Doc Wyddial.'' Thankfully averting
his gaze from the sketch, he waved the cardboard folder in
the air. ''She wouldn't go into details, but she did admit
she's got more than one elderly patient on her books who's
on the undernourished side. And she thinks it's the same
for other doctors in the area.'' He tore at his hair again,
observed Foxon's grin, and subsided. ''Shut up and let me
think.'' Foxon duly shut. He'd tried his own spot of thinking and he hadn't much liked his thoughts. He wondered
whether Old Brimstone would think the same way. He
rather suspected he might . . .

''Listen,'' came the command at last as Brinton picked
up the telephone. ''I'm going to have another talk with
Percy Jestin at the bank.'' He paused. He put the receiver

down. He scowled. "But first," he said slowly, "I think I might just have a tactful word with the coroner . . ."

He had it. He asked questions and received guarded answers. He made notes and compared them to the contents of the cardboard folder. On the extension telephone, Foxon listened and tried to understand.

"The scenes of the crime," said Brinton, brandishing a fresh sheet of paper under his subordinate's nose. "If," he added, "there *is* a crime, which we still don't know for sure—but we have our suspicions. Right?"

"Er . . . right, sir." Foxon, whose suspicions had been aroused by more than one circumstance, massaged the small of his back with a thoughtful hand and had little need to contrive the accompanying wince. Brinton glared at him. Foxon coughed. "Strong suspicions, sir. But . . ."

"But?" snapped Brinton with another glare.

Foxon chanced it. "Well, sir, scenes of the crime have to be, uh, visited. I remember how you had me and MissEss stake out the church at Iverhurst in that witchcraft business a few years ago, and—"

"And somebody coshed you." Callously, Brinton shrugged. "So this time you've got a black eye. Never stay in one piece for more than half a minute, you don't. What d'you want me to do about it—buy you a tin hat or a personal insurance plan?" Then he frowned and scowled at the sheet of paper. "Ugh. Come to think of it, if Miss Seeton *is* going to start up her old tricks again—why I told you to use your blasted initiative I'll never know . . ."

"All she's done is Draw, sir," Foxon reminded him gently. "Enough to show us you were right about it being, uh, suspicious. Worth investigating."

"Worth investigating a dozen or more times over? That's how many we've got here, if scenes of crime is what they are, which we still don't know for sure, and I'm damned if I know how we'll find out. The sad and sorry fact is there aren't any old dears left, not at these addresses, which is the only reason we've got them. Doctors still have their Hippocratic Oath to worry about, remember.''

"Even Doc Wyddial? I thought—a police surgeon . . .''

"Yes, well, since I first asked, she's done her best to twist a few arms and she's asked a sight more questions than I'd have got away with, but you can't blame them for keeping quiet, I suppose, about the ones who're still with us. Which means every single person whose name's on here''—another brandish—''is either dead or gone. Two Accidentals that were suspect suicides the coroner was too kind-hearted to upset the friends and relations by recording—not that the relations were close, but it's the principle of the thing—and one Misadventure who basically starved herself to death, nobody knows why, except that she was broke like the rest when the Social Services people started poking about. One is a long-stay patient in hospital after a fall and nobody in the family willing to look after him, and two more got parked in homes of one sort or another . . .''

As Foxon coughed, Brinton scowled again at the paper he still held. "It's the same old story. None of these has— or had—what anyone'd call close family, same as the ones Jestin at the bank has got so hot and bothered about . . .''

"And, sir," prompted Foxon as his chief fell silent. The two words were uttered with such an innocent air that Brinton's fingers itched for the peppermints.

"And," said Brinton, resisting with difficulty the urge to throw things, "one of the places they got parked was— is . . .''

An unholy grin began to materialise on the countenance of Detective Constable Foxon.

Superintendent Brinton drew a deep breath. "Doctor Knight's place in Plummergen," he finished with a shudder. "Yes, I know," he said as the grin split Foxon's face from ear to ear. "I know! And I *know* that if the worst comes to the worst, we can always ask Miss Seeton to go along for a chat and a Draw . . .

"If," he reiterated heavily, "the worst comes to the worst . . . which it hasn't done yet, not by a long chalk." He brightened. "Miss Seeton has played her part, laddie, confirming there's been something . . . out of the usual going on. Now it's up to us to find out what it was—and still is, to judge by your recent jolly hollyhocks experience."

Foxon winced, but now it was the turn of Brinton to grin. He surveyed his battered subordinate thoughtfully. "That shiner of yours, laddie, is a really revolting sight."

"Honourable wounds of battle, sir."

Brinton rolled his eyes to the ceiling. "Anyone might think the local villains had arranged it on purpose to put me off my work—and we can't have that." His eyes returned to the young man opposite. "Now, if I didn't know the canteen better I'd send you along for a pound of steak and a bowl of ice cubes, but as all they'd give you'd be a slice of old boot and an earful, that's not the answer. Is it?"

"No, sir?"

"No," said Brinton, absently pushing the sheet of paper across his desk. "What *is* the answer is . . . fresh air. New horizons. Take your mind off things and stop giving me a pain just with looking at you." The paper drifted over the edge of the desk as Foxon's hands came up to catch it. "Why not," suggested Brinton, staring at the ceiling again, "have yourself an afternoon off to see the sights?"

"As well as I can with one black eye," murmured Foxon, a bare half-decibel above inaudibility. "An afternoon off? Why not indeed, sir?" he said aloud, glancing at the paper, folding it, and thrusting it in his jacket pocket. "I fancy a change—if you're sure you can spare me, that is."

"I can spare having to look at that ugly mug of yours,

believe me, my lad. If I don't see it again before tomorrow morning, that'll be quite soon enough. Go on—scram.'' And Brinton buried himself in his paperwork without looking up again to bid his subordinate goodbye.

Had the superintendent done so, it would have been his last chance to see Foxon with his one black eye for some time to come.

CHAPTER 8

Foxon slowed the car into a bend. Visit the scene of the crime. Get a feel for what'd been going on. Well, it wasn't the first time Old Brimmers had tried something of the sort, but it promised to be a lot less risky on this particular occasion. And a hell of a lot less spooky, he hoped, even taking into account Miss Seeton's skeleton sketch of poor Adelaide Addison. But there was spooky and spooky. Like he'd told the super, he hadn't forgotten how he and MissEss had waited together in the deserted Iverhurst church in the middle of the night until he'd nodded off to sleep, then woken up to find the place lit by candles and full of devil worshippers, some of whom had been a damn sight more devilish than others. If he tried, he could still feel the bump. Miss Seeton, bless her, had saved him from far worse, climbing up that ladder and dropping stuff on chummie's head until he'd received a much harder, and more lethal, bump than the one he'd handed out.

He trod on the accelerator. An empty church at midnight was one thing. A dozen or so empty houses in broad daylight would be another kettle of fish altogether. Foxon grinned. Fish. Unofficial, of course. Old Brimmers wasn't

sure, for all he tried to sound it. Without the docs and the
bank and the coroner willing to swear, though he supposed
they would if anyone came up with a good reason why they
should, there was no proof—not unless you counted
MissEss's Drawing, and that was more a hint than hard
evidence. What hard evidence he'd get from staring at
houses he had no idea, but it was worth a try. Nothing
confidential about going down a road and stopping to admire the view, was there?

Going on foot, not on wheels. You couldn't admire the
view when you were driving a car, even an unmarked one,
and you had more chance of seeing . . . whatever there was
to see if you looked slowly. Better to leave the car somewhere out of sight, just in case there might be anyone to
recognise it . . . though as the owners of said houses had
left them (one way or another) several months ago, whoever
had bought them, if they had, probably wouldn't have
enough of a guilty conscience to get the jitters if anyone
stopped to take a quick gander over the garden gate. And
if they had . . .

Foxon, flicking the indicator and slowing the car to the
kerb, shook his head. Conscience, maybe, in the plural?
Conspiracy? He applied the brake in both the physical and
the metaphorical sense. No, it did seem a bit far-fetched to
suggest the old folk had been hounded into poverty and
beyond by a gang of overimpatient homeowners. The market, for heaven's sake, was buoyant enough if you went by
the number of estate agents' boards with *Sale Agreed* or
Sold adorning front fences up and down every road he'd
travelled. He climbed out of the car and locked the door.
He'd thought at first the houses on Brimstone's list would
still be empty, but second thoughts showed him they most
likely wouldn't. He began to walk slowly down the road.
More of a conspiracy if they were, perhaps. A network of
safe houses for crooks on the run? Ditto for an as-yet-

unknown charity for retired tramps? Ditto of builders, eager to buy at a cheap price, do up, and sell at enormous profit?

Foxon scratched his head. This last might not be such a barmy idea. Adelaide Addison's house, with a lick of paint and some plumbing repairs, wouldn't be at all a bad place to live if you could find someone—his bones still ached— to sort out the garden. And plenty of people were really keen on gardening . . . Foxon's grin acknowledged Miss Seeton, her umbrella in one hand, a trowel in the other, as she flashed upon his inward eye wearing gumboots and a green felt hat with a jaunty feather.

Feathers. Foxon jumped as a bird, squawking, flapped out of the hedge when he slowed his walk to a saunter and casually leaned against the gate-post to tie his shoelace. He tipped an imaginary hat in gratitude. Only natural for his gaze to follow the bird as it headed away from the distur- bance towards the safety of the house. He nodded to him- self. Another nice place. Potential, he believed they'd say it had, his theoretical builders. On the shabby side now, but with gables, dormer windows, quaint patterns of tile over- hanging the brickwork, stone steps leading up to the pan- elled door from the gravel drive curving its way between shrubbery and flower beds bordering a lawn with only a few worm-casts dotted about to look untidy . . .

Instead of Miss Seeton with her umbrella, it was Martha Bloomer, domestic paragon, who now appeared with a broom. Foxon grinned. The worm-casts were not long for this world.

Neither was Foxon. Martha Bloomer vanished in a sud- den shower of fireworks, and sickening darkness enveloped him in an irresistible embrace.

Brinton's charge that Foxon had been frolicking among the flowers of spring might have been an exaggeration, but not a gross one. Even in the middle of January there were usually flowers of some sort to be seen in Kent, the southeast Garden of England.

Miss Seeton, heading back from the shops with her basket over one arm, her brolly over the other, was in no hurry to reach home. From time to time she would pause to peep admiringly over some neighbour's fence into her front garden. (In Plummergen it is rarely the men who do the gardening; most work on the land during the day, and the last thing they want is to see any more earth than they need during their hours of relaxation.) Miss Seeton admired neatly edged lawns, hand clipped where mowers would have compacted rain-soaked soil. She saw snowdrops and cyclamen, irises and aconites, periwinkles and hellebores and sarcococcas, with their haunting, heavy perfume and their dainty cream blossom.

Was she reminded more of vanilla or of honey? Miss Seeton breathed deeply, inflating her lungs in the approved yoga fashion, from her diaphragm down. She exhaled slowly, then inhaled again, savouring the distinctive bouquet. Yes. Something . . . exotic. Rich. Mysterious . . . and faintly oriental in its aroma, teasing the taste-buds as well as the sense of smell. All at once Miss Seeton had visions of myriad eastern houris, clad in diaphanous garments and floating veils, bearing cups of spiced chocolate and trays of sickly, sugared Turkish delight.

Chocolate . . .

Ah. Shaking her head, Miss Seeton resumed her homeward journey. What a pity one had suddenly remembered—

"Miss Seeton!"

Oh, no. No, surely not. One's imagination had simply conjured up an unpleasant coincidence when—

"Hello there, Miss Seeton!"

Oh, dear. Not imagination, but a true coincidence—and very far from pleasant. Yet one could hardly pretend not to have heard: the voice was so very loud. Sadly Miss Seeton stopped walking, squared her shoulders, and turned to look back up The Street at the figure of Antony Scarlett as it strode, cape flapping, arms gesticulating, towards her.

"Miss Seeton!" boomed Antony for the third time, drawing closer. "What a splendid coincidence!"

A gentlewoman knows when to bite the bullet. One could hardly be expected to smile in welcome, but . . . "Indeed, yes, Mr. Scarlett," said Miss Seeton, inclining her head as far as politeness demanded and no farther. "Good morning." On the handle of her umbrella, her basket-bearing hand clutched for reassurance. Really, it was ridiculous to feel . . . intimidated, but there was no doubt the wretched man's visits were growing rather more than tiresome. There were some children who never seemed to know when enough was, well, enough. Not, of course, that Mr. Scarlett was a child. She would remember the advice of Sir George and kind Mr. Foxon and refuse to allow him indoors . . .

The handle of the basket dug into her forearm. Except, of course, that it would become inconvenient to stand for too long outside the house—and one could hardly slam the door in his face. Miss Seeton, while in no way afraid of Antony Scarlett, was severely embarrassed by the imminent necessity of being rude to him. Blushing, she stood her ground and wondered just how firm she would have to be.

"Miss Seeton, I see that you have been toiling about the shops and are heavy laden. You must allow me to escort you home." Antony thrust a hand through the folds of his cape to reach for the basket. Miss Seeton, slightly startled at his irreverent rewording of holy writ, took a backward step and held firm. Antony stepped after her. "I insist, Miss Seeton. It will be a pleasure!"

"Thank you, Mr. Scarlett, but there is really no need to trouble yourself. I am more than halfway home now, and the basket is not in the least heavy."

"No trouble, Miss Seeton, I assure you. Please." Once

more the hand on the basket; the automatic backward step.

"Thank you," said Miss Seeton, "but no." No trouble to Antony Scarlett—but certainly to herself and certainly no pleasure. One could not accept the escort of a gentleman only to dismiss him on the doorstep of one's house. Courtesy would compel her to ask him inside, and, once there, he would be almost impossible to dislodge.

To uproot. Miss Seeton, with lingering memories of her garden musings and their oriental bias, had a sudden vision of Antony looming over her as a giant, all-shadowing tree. A upas tree. She blushed. How rude. Yet—she sighed—how, well, apposite. Java, where these trees grew, was undoubtedly eastern. And there was no doubt in her mind that Antony Scarlett, while certainly not pernicious, was something of a nuisance. She wished he would leave her alone. She feared she would have to invite him indoors. She did not want him to carry her basket home . . .

"No," said Miss Seeton again with a shake of the head. "It is very kind of you, but I . . ." She blushed. "I have other errands to run, which may take some time." She could always pop across to the bakery for the bread she hadn't planned to buy until tomorrow. "I would not wish to take up any of *your* valuable time in—"

"My time?" cried Antony Scarlett with an expansive gesture that made the whole world a mass of swirling black and red. Miss Seeton, blinking, took another step back. "My time," boomed Antony, "is entirely at your disposal, Miss Seeton! It was only to see you that I came to this—this benighted village in the first place! Can you suppose I would be here for any other reason than to ask—to beg—to beseech you to change your mind?"

This insulting assurance provoked Miss Seeton to a far sharper retort on Plummergen's behalf than she would ever have ventured on her own. She drew herself up to her full

five-foot-nothing, took a deep breath, and stared Antony
Scarlett firmly in the eye.

"Then I regret," she said, sounding not the least regret-
ful, "that you have had a wasted journey, Mr. Scarlett. I
have told you more than once that I have no intention of
selling my house, and I have not changed my mind. You
may insist that it is the perfect place to construct your—
your chocolate absurdity." Miss Seeton was now so irritated that she did not blush for this rudeness. "I, on the
other hand, consider Sweetbriars the—the perfect place for
me to live. Good morning."

With a nod she turned to go. Antony's hand shot out
again. As she turned, it fell, not on the basket handle, but
on the umbrella. The folds of the cape eddied and enveloped. There was a clatter as the umbrella slipped from Miss
Seeton's arm to the ground. Automatically Miss Seeton
ducked to catch it.

So did Antony. But, while several decades Miss Seeton's
junior, he did not have the benefits of yoga to assist him.
The brolly was safe in its owner's grasp, and she was rising
to an upright position again as Antony was still on the way
down. There came an unpleasant wickery clump as his chin
met the rim of Miss Seeton's shopping basket.

"Oh, dear," said Miss Seeton with a guilty blush.

Then her heart sank as she realised there was now nothing she could politely say or do that would prevent the
arrival of Antony Scarlett on the doorstep of her cottage.
And—which was worse—inside. Good manners demanded
that she at least offer him a cup of tea; he would start to
boom and bluster about the location of the canal, the bridge,
and the corner of The Street and how it would be a Philistine act for her to continue to deny him the chance to
create his masterpiece . . .

"Oh, dear," said Miss Seeton again, and she sighed.

•   •   •

The frequent visits of Antony Scarlett to Plummergen, and his pursuit of Miss Seeton, did not pass unnoticed around the village. Speculation was, as ever, rife. Antony—with his cloak, his booming voice, his expansive gestures—was so much a contrast to Miss Seeton, with her muted tweeds and soft-spoken gentility, that there could be no doubt in the mind of anyone that there was Something Going On.

The more discerning gossips had not failed to remark how after each of Antony's visits Miss Seeton always seemed for a while somewhat *distraite*. In true Plummergen tradition, there were at least two different schools of thought as to the cause of her condition, but general opinion was coming round to the idea that the man Scarlett must have some hold over his elderly acquaintance—a hold he chose at intervals to exercise for sinister purposes of his own. Blackmail was mooted as one possibility; dope peddling another. The fact that Antony had made the purported reason for his visits more than audible had been dismissed as an overobvious attempt at bluff. He wanted to buy Sweetbriars just to knock it down? He must be mad to suppose anyone could believe a thing like that: or he must be mad to suggest it. Either way, he was mad. Which all artists were, weren't they? And, of course, notorious for their illegal habit.

Miss Seeton taught Art. Antony Scarlett had an exhibition on in London, hadn't he? And he hadn't been down to Kent until after she'd gone up to Town to see it, had he? There you were, then. Either he kept coming to bring Miss Seeton her regular fix, as they'd arranged, and charging her more for it each time, which was why she was looking more and more fed up when he'd gone again, and why she'd gone pawning stuff in Brettenden hoping nobody would see her; or else she was supplying to him (a post office shopper asked how she got her supplies and was mocked for missing the obvious), and he was refusing to pay the money she demanded, which was why she looked fed up because he was bigger than her and could easily intimidate her as criminals invariably did.

In fact, as has been shown, he could not. Since their first unfortunate meeting, Miss Seeton had bitten the bullet and invited the man into her home only on the one occasion necessity in the form of a bruised chin had forced upon her. She had not, however, allowed him to browbeat her, even as she poured tea and apologised again for her carelessness in the matter of the dropped umbrella. His next two attempts to persuade her to sell her house in the interest of Art—although Miss Seeton feared it was more in the interest of the Stuttaford cheque for fifteen thousand pounds—had been thwarted by a prudent retreat into the kitchen (one day when it was raining) and the garden (on another when it was not).

Antony Scarlett had stalked the pavements of Plummergen, flaunting himself in his silk-lined cape and trying, in his search for the elusive Miss Seeton, to strike up conversations with people who scuttled in the opposite direction when they saw him coming, which in a village with only one street was not difficult. On the journey to and from Brettenden, he sat noticeably alone on the bus. It was the policy of Genefer Watson that her latest discovery should demonstrate true artistic disdain for worldly comforts by eschewing such expensive luxuries as the motor car, unless driven and owned by someone else.

On one occasion Antony made the mistake of asking Nigel Colveden, who had pulled up outside the post office to run a quick errand en route to Brettenden, for a lift in his MG. Nigel had heard from his parents (consulted by Miss Seeton as to the legal position regarding unwelcome guests) of Miss Seeton's continued persecution by the would-be purchaser of her home, and returned him a dusty answer before leaving him blinking as he roared off in a cloud of furious exhaust, quite forgetting his promise to buy stamps. Rytham Hall believed in supporting local industry where possible. Stamps bought in Brettenden, while fiscally just as valid, would have been somehow disloyal.

Antony's cape swirled in the slipstream. He said something ungracious as a piece of grit bounced up into his eye. Something loud. Crude. Profane. Blasphemous . . . and audible on both sides of The Street.

"Well, really!" Mrs. Blaine turned to Miss Nuttel, her plump hand frozen in midopening of the post office door. From above came the last echoes of a jangling bell. "Eric, did you hear?"

The jangle had warned those inside the shop that new arrivals were imminent. The presence of Antony Scarlett on the other side of the road had been noted; it had been the sole topic of discussion among a huddle of persons so keen to theorise that they had allowed their attention to drift from what was happening outside. The sudden roar of Nigel's departing engine and the subsequent roar from Antony had shown them, too late, that vigil should have been maintained. The sight of the Nuts, who must have witnessed the entire incident, in the doorway immediately stilled wagging tongues and pricked expectant ears.

"Nasty piece of work," said Miss Nuttel, closing the door and following her friend through a crowd of people all trying hard not to listen. "Quite see Nigel wouldn't want him in the car, even six miles. Sinister."

"Well, yes," said Mrs. Blaine. "Only it's too unlike Nigel, don't you think? To be so very disobliging, I mean. If he was on his way to Brettenden in any case, I can't see what harm it would have done to offer the man a lift."

"No?" Miss Nuttel shook her head sadly. "Trouble with you, Bunny, is always thinking the best of people."

This intelligence startled Mrs. Blaine almost as much as it astounded everyone else. Modestly blushing, Bunny begged to be enlightened. Why should—how could—her benevolent regard for her fellows be considered a handicap?

Miss Nuttel sighed. "Risky," she said. "Very. Didn't dawn on me before, but . . ."

"But what?" gasped Mrs. Blaine, blackcurrant eyes widening in horrified apprehension. "Oh, Eric . . ."

"That cape," said Miss Nuttel, jerking her head towards the window through which Antony Scarlett might still be observed, magnificently glooming at the bus stop. "Visits Miss Seeton, too." She paused to allow another horrified gasp to burst from Bunny's lips, which were turning pale. "See what I mean?"

"Oh, Eric," quavered Mrs. Blaine, shuddering. Clearly she saw. Others listening did not, but nobody cared to ask. They had a feeling they would not care for the answer.

"Red lining," said Miss Nuttel, driving the message home with relish. "Hate to say this, Bunny, but it reminds me of—well, of . . ."

"Blood," said Mrs. Blaine in a thrilling whisper. "Oh! It's too, too dreadful . . ." She clapped a hand to her brow and tottered to the nearest counter, against which she leaned, breathing heavily. "Oh! Oh . . ."

Such a reaction to Miss Nuttel's remark was thought extreme, even for a notoriously fervent vegetarian. Shoppers crowded close for the ultimate grim revelation some of the quicker wits had begun to guess.

"Yes," said Miss Nuttel, herself turning pale now that the dread word was spoken. She threw an anxious glance at the vegetable rack where parsnips and swedes rubbed shoulders with cauliflowers, potatoes, and leeks. "No garlic—thought as much. Lucky we grow our own." She turned to the cheeses on their marble cutting slab, presided over by Miss Emmeline Putts. "Garlic's the only thing, they say. Come over later. Let you have some."

Emmy stared. "M-me, Miss Nuttel? What would I be

wanting with garlic? My mum does all the cooking.''

''Oh, Emmy!'' Mrs. Blaine let out her palpitating breath in an exasperated sigh. ''Can't you *see*? It's simply too awful—we can't let you remain at risk without doing something to try to save you—it's what neighbours are for . . .''

''Be all right for a few days,'' said Miss Nuttel in what were meant to be reassuring tones. ''Full moon's when you've got to take most care. No harm in being prepared, though.''

''F-full moon?'' Emmy was still trying to work it out as others about her shuddered and made the age-old gesture of protection. It was left to Mrs. Blaine to set about enlightening the youngest unwed female present.

''Why, surely it's too obvious, now Eric has pointed it out—such sacrilegious language, and so blatant—why that man keeps coming here. Wanting to see Miss Seeton is just a blind, as if we couldn't guess with such a ridiculous story. Casing the joint—isn't that what burglars call it? That's what he's doing. But—but he's not a burglar, Emmeline, even if he is on the lookout. He's—''

''On the prowl,'' interposed Miss Nuttel. Mrs. Blaine, darting an irritated look in Eric's direction, after a second or two accepted the amendment.

''On the prowl, Emmy. For young girls like you. Everyone knows that's what they need . . .''

''Vampires,'' said Miss Nuttel, in case anyone had still failed to grasp the point.

Emmy Putts, scattering cheese and sheets of greaseproof paper in all directions, fell in an appalled swoon facedown across her marble slab.

CHAPTER 9

"I haven't brought you any grapes." Superintendent Brinton seated himself heavily at the bedside of Detective Constable Foxon and glared at the figure before him, wilting in its regulation hospital cocoon. "Or flowers." He paused. "I'm giving some serious consideration to that tin hat we talked about, though."

Foxon regarded his chief through not one, but two black eyes whose blackness was emphasised by the pallor of his face and the snowy folds of the bandage about his forehead. "Might not be such a bad idea," he muttered feebly.

Brinton snorted. "A bad idea," he growled, "is having one of my officers suspected of being an escaped lunatic, of all things. What the hell were you playing at? I told you to go and look at the scenes of the crime, not get yourself arrested by some overzealous citizen who's terrified you're going to lay about you with a meat axe."

Foxon groaned. "It was *him* laid about *me*, sir. I don't think my head will ever stop aching." He closed his eyes—which didn't take much effort—and groaned again.

Brinton was unsympathetic. "Your head aches? Well, it can't be addled brains, because the way you've been carrying on you haven't got any. Capering down the pavement grinning and waving and pulling ridiculous faces—what d'you expect the man to think? A complete stranger drapes himself over the gatepost and leers into the bushes, and he's not supposed to worry? You were damned lucky Buckland answered the nine-nine-nine call as quickly as he did. Another minute or two, and you'd have been mincemeat.''

His words echoed strangely in Foxon's muddled brain. He forced his eyes open. ''Meat axes and mince, sir? You said steak last time. You want me to try vegetarianism?''

''If I thought it'd improve your chances of making anything like a decent career in the police I'd force-feed you carrots myself, but you'd still be more donkey than detective by the end of it. However . . .'' The pleasantries were over. ''They tell me you'll live. Concussion doesn't kill. But has it affected your memory at all?''

Concussion might not kill, but its lack of focus can render its victim careless of life and limb. ''I remember everything going black,'' volunteered Foxon, ''just as I was watching Martha Bloomer brush worm-casts off the lawn.''

''What?''

''After Miss Seeton waved at me with her umbrella,'' said Foxon. ''And a trowel. The garden needed a bit of attention, you see . . .''

''Er—yes,'' said Brinton, who thought he did. The lad was rambling. So much for learning how many of the houses he'd had time to check before the Abinger bloke had gone into panic overdrive and belted him. And so much for medical science saying there was no lasting damage. If Foxon'd got Miss Seeton and her blasted brolly permanently stuck in his mind, so to speak, then forget about making a detective—he'd be so confused he'd be useless as a traffic warden, for pity's sake, and as for point duty . . .

''Yes. Well.'' The superintendent tried to sound cheerful. ''I'll leave you to sleep it off, shall I? I'll pop back to the station and have a word with Mutford. What that man doesn't know about the invalidity rules could be written on a postage stamp.'' Desk Sergeant Mutford was a staunch member of Brettenden's Holdfast Brethren, a small but influential sect noted for its rigid adherence to the letter of biblical and (where the two did not collide) secular law.

Foxon's sluggish brain had at last caught up with his ears. ''An invalid, sir? Me?'' He began struggling to free himself from the double manacles of sheet and blanket clamping him to the bed. ''Oh, I'll be out of here in no time. Honest. I mean, it's not as if I'm not used to it.''

Brinton eyed him warily. The lad was sounding a little more back in the real world. ''I suppose,'' he conceded, ''you could say that's true. What's a bump on the head between friends for a bloke with a skull as thick as yours?''

''A couple of days and I'll be fine,'' promised Foxon, freeing one arm to wave it in a gesture emphasising good health, high spirits, and devotion to duty. ''But,'' he added, wincing, ''I dunno about 'between friends,' sir. This character who clobbered me. What have we got on him?''

Brinton stared. ''Nothing, except that he overreacts a bit when sinister blokes with black eyes lurk outside his house. Which I'd call a pardonable error, in the circumstances, though I can understand you wouldn't. Why should you think we'd have anything on him? You might not care for being clobbered, but in some ways this Abinger wasn't acting unreasonably, and we've no call to suppose he makes a habit of assaulting perfect strangers. And it isn't exactly good for the image of the force to do him for accidental arrest or mistaken identity, if that's what you had in mind.'' The familiar savage grin appeared. ''Look at it this way, lad. If we throw the book at him—well, two bops don't make one right, do they?''

Foxon essayed his own grin, but his heart wasn't in it as past and present mingled in bewildering disorder in his

mind. "He's . . . got a guilty conscience, sir." Brinton
looked at him.

Foxon tried to nod, but could only wince. "He must
have." It was not easy to marshal his thoughts into some
logical sequence, but he did his best. "I mean—for Buckland to have got there so soon, the bloke must've already
dialled nine-nine-nine . . . so why didn't he just wait for reinforcements? I wasn't going anywhere."

"You certainly weren't once he'd finished with you—
er, sorry." The lad had sounded so much better all at once
that Brinton had forgotten how sick they'd said he was.
"But he wasn't to know that, was he? Look at it from his
point of view. He's new to this area. He didn't know—
though he damn well does now—how efficient a force
we've got. He says he had no idea how long it would be
before anyone responded to his three-nines, so he thought
he'd better hang on to you until they did. It's all perfectly
logical, laddie . . ."

Foxon eyed his superior as balefully as he could through
swollen eyelids. "And you don't believe it either, sir."

Brinton hesitated. He shrugged. "Guilty consciences
come in all shapes and sizes. Maybe he's just twitchy about
an unpaid parking ticket somewhere, or a traffic offence."

"You said *he* said he didn't know I was a copper,"
Foxon objected, so indignant that he neither winced nor
groaned as he sat bolt upright in bed. "And even if your
idea's right, he was happy enough to call us when he
wanted me out of his hair. Something smells wrong here,
sir. Dunno what it is, but I reckon Abinger could bear a
spot of checking."

"I hope you're not planning to start a private vendetta,
Detective Constable Foxon."

"Come off it, sir. You should know me better than that.
'Specially when it was all your idea in the first place."

Now it was the turn of Brinton to be indignant. Just

because he might, in moments of stress, in the privacy of the office, hurl the odd missile at his junior—

"What?" cried Foxon, feeling that assorted peppermints and paperweights dodged over the years were being played decidedly down.

This did not mean (went on Brinton) that he had given his blessing to more or less unprovoked attacks on said junior, or on any other officer, by unauthorised personnel following his privileged example. The general public (he maintained) had no business taking the law into their own hands: the law was the responsibility of the police.

"And the safety of my officers," he concluded, "is the responsibility of me. You're right, laddie," he said as Foxon tried to grin. "Abinger could bear looking at."

"Which is what I meant," Foxon said, "about it being all your idea in the first place, sir. For me to go looking at the scenes of the crime, I mean. I dunno what else has been going on, but in my book bashing me on the head's a crime. Couldn't we ask . . . er, someone at the Yard to run Abinger through that basement computer of theirs?"

"Someone with the initials A. D., I suppose, although what Chief Superintendent Delphick might say about wasting police time I shudder to think."

"He might say thank you," Foxon said. "For all we know, Abinger's been on the Wanted list for years." He closed his eyes and smoothed a gallant hand across his bandaged brow. "If anyone offers me the Police Medal in gratitude for devotion beyond the call of duty, I won't say no, sir."

"You sound perkier by the minute, heaven help us." The superintendent pushed back his chair: he had just spotted a starched and silver-buckled uniform heading in his direction with a purposeful look in her eye and an ominous metal tray in her hand. "But you've done enough thinking for the day. I don't want your death from brain fever on my conscience, talking of consciences. Assuming you've got a brain in there under all that bandage . . .''

And he was gone before Foxon could either register even the slightest protest or demand police protection against the syringe of startling proportion that now appeared in the starched one's hand.

"Don't hover, Buckland." Brinton stabbed a pencil towards his visitors' chair. "Sit down. Whatever your sins may be, they haven't yet been found out. You're not on the carpet, you're helping me with my enquiries. Sit down!"

PC Buckland sat. He coughed. "How's the invalid, sir?"

"He'll live. Not too happy with friend Abinger, though. Thinks he's worth a look. You're the panda man around that area. What do we know about him?"

"Er—them, sir. He's married," offered Buckland after a moment.

"Was it the husband or the wife who beaned young Foxon with a brick?" Brinton glared. "Or whatever it was," he added as Buckland looked uneasy. "Well? Did she join in raising merry hell on Foxon's noddle or just help to raise the alarm?"

"Er—neither, sir. She was shopping when it happened, as far as I can make out. Surprised as anyone when she got home and found out what'd been going on."

"So the wife's irrelevant in this particular context. Abinger wasn't . . . protecting her honour because she wasn't there at the time." The superintendent sighed. "Unless there's something you're not telling me, Buckland."

"Like what, sir?"

"Like have you ever been called to that address in the past, for a Domestic? Does he thump her? Noted for his quick temper, maybe? Jealous? Unstable? Just the type to bash first and ask questions afterwards?"

Buckland, who as a serving police officer had seen more than most, was still a little shocked at this suggestion. "They seem very happy together, sir. She's rather nice-looking, in a quiet sort of way. Doesn't work, though they haven't got any children. He's some sort of bank executive, I think." Brinton's ears pricked at this, but Buckland was now in full flight. "Started doing the place up almost as soon as they moved in once Mr. Pontefract died—you remember, sir, the chap who tried that snack bar idea in Plummergen and went broke."

"Bits 'n' Pizzas. I remember." Brinton tried to close his mind to the uncomfortable coincidence of Miss Seeton, albeit by proxy in the form of her village, making yet another appearance in the case—if, he reminded himself, a case it was. "I forget what happened to him afterwards, though."

"They tried a Bed and Breakfast, sir, him and his wife." Buckland, who had kept devoted company since the age of five with the same young lady he had met in his first week at primary school, sighed quietly. "She only stuck it for a few months, then pushed off with a travelling salesman—one of the customers, too." He shook his head. "Talk about 'for better, for worse'!"

"Yes, well." Brinton did his best not to sound scornful, but it was hard. "There's 'for richer, for poorer' to take into consideration, too. Some women like the high life and get a bit stroppy if they can't have it anymore. And when you're married, lad, you'll know how touchy a woman can get about her kitchen, never mind the rest of the house, if their old man suddenly decides to invite a load of strangers to stay the night day in, day out. Starting with the builders," he added, with grim memories of how his wife had found the idea of a fitted kitchen, on paper, appealing: and how she had gone home to her mother after a week of argument, dust, and sandwiches at every meal.

"Oh, they got a fire certificate without any trouble, sir.

Staircases and access and—and stuff like that—and the plumbing was all sorted out, too—and the parking. You know how the emergency services complain if there's too many cars clogging up the roads."

Brinton rolled his eyes. He did.

"Mr. Pontefract," Buckland continued, "had asphalt laid all over the front for parking, so these new people, the Abingers, one of the first things they did was have the whole lot took up and a lawn put back, with a gravel drive. It was one reason they got the place so cheap, sir, all the money they knew it'd cost to get it back to being just a—a house again."

"A successful banker wouldn't need the extra cash from a B and B," said Brinton thoughtfully. "Yet he can't have had that much cash to play with or surely he'd have bought a house that didn't need any alterations straight off."

"Perhaps," offered the sheepish Buckland, "he didn't want to . . . er, upset his wife by asking her to do it." He turned pink as Brinton eyed him sourly. "Bed and Breakfast, I mean, sir. I mean, after Mrs. Pontefract . . . he might have been, well, superstitious. Or something."

"Bankers aren't superstitious. Folk who mess about with money all day have got to be level-headed or they go under." Brinton frowned. "And a banker gets preferential rates on his mortgage . . . which we can assume this Abinger didn't, for the same reasons as before. Odd. I hate to say it, but Foxon was right. Our bop-happy friend could do with checking. I wonder if it's too late to phone the Yard?"

He decided, in the end, that it was not. Once he had ascertained that his subordinate had no idea which bank had the dubious pleasure of employing Patrick Abinger, but that he thought it was in London, Brinton threw Buckland out of the office and exhorted the switchboard to find an outside line as soon as possible, if not before.

The tinny voice in Brinton's ear soon connected him to

the office of Chief Superintendent Alan Delphick, where
the telephone was picked up by Sergeant Bob Ranger, six-
foot-seven, seventeen stone, and afraid of nothing.

In normal circumstances, that was to say. But . . .

"Good evening, sir." Bob's cheery tones were for once
tinged with apprehension. "I, er, hope there's nothing
wrong . . ."

Bob had been at Delphick's side on that momentous occasion seven years earlier when Miss Seeton first appeared
on the criminal scene. He had been puzzled and amused by
her then; he had been baffled and impressed after her second appearance; and by her third his feelings were such
that when his then fiancée Anne—daughter of Plummergen's Dr. Knight of nursing home fame—had adopted her
as an honorary aunt, he'd been happy to go along with the
idea. What had started as an expedient measure to justify
the whisking of MissEss from under the noses of a group
of thugs had become something more. Bob, like his wife
Anne, was fond of Miss Emily Dorothea Seeton. Aunt Em.
And unexpected telephone calls from the superintendent of
police in charge of the district where she lived did nothing
for the peace of mind of Aunt Em's adopted nephew.

"Wrong?" Brinton knew very well the way Bob's mind
was working. "Relax, she's fine. I only wanted a bit of
info, if you've got it, on some people who've just moved
into the area—and I don't, for once, mean Plummergen. As
far as I know, Miss Seeton's living a nice peaceful life
minding her own business and not stirring up trouble for
anyone else—which is just the way I like it."

"Me, too, sir," Bob assured him in relief. "Same here."
His chuckle echoed through fifty miles of electric wires to
deafen Brinton's ear. "So what was it you wanted to
know?"

It was as well for his peace of mind—and Brinton's—
that they had no idea of the truth.

• • •

When they were on speaking terms, Emmy's best friend
was Maureen, who worked—or, to be more accurate, was
employed—at the George and Dragon. Plummergen's favourite hostelry (Prop. C. Mountfitchet) stands beside the
church at the southernmost end of The Street just before it
narrows and divides in two, directly opposite the bakery—
and diagonally opposite Sweetbriars. As they were currently speaking, once Emmy had milked her sensational
collapse for every last ounce of drama it contained, she had
no hesitation about phoning Maureen to give her the latest
intelligence concerning the goings-on between the owner
of Sweetbriars and the sinister Antony Scarlett.

The roar of Maureen's Wayne's Kawasaki motorbike
was a familiar sound to everyone in the village as he either
dropped his lady love off at the start of her daily round or
collected her at its finish. Not only was it familiar: it was
loud. Doris, head waitress and right hand to Charley
Mountfitchet, always knew when Maureen was arriving
some minutes before she arrived. Should the girl be late
(which she all too often was) the Kawasaki Early Warning
System gave Doris ample time to position herself on the
George's front step to deliver a pithy and forthright lecture
on punctuality, which the rehearsal of several years had
made a model of its type.

"Beats me, Miss Seeton." Doris had advanced from her
usual place to exchange a few words with the neighbour
from over the way on an early trip to the shops. "I mean,
how long is The Street? Why that lazy young madam can't
walk here on her own two feet I'll never know."

Miss Seeton had often wondered the same thing herself—the small council estate where Maureen lived was at
most a mile from the George—but felt she could say no
more than that not everyone had a partiality for fresh air
and exercise. People were, after all, different. Some tired

more easily than others, and since Maureen worked so . . .

Miss Seeton's natural honesty here must curtail the rest of this charitable observation. An arthritic tortoise moved faster than Maureen on even a normal working day, as everyone in Plummergen knew. Perhaps (offered Miss Seeton now) it was one of the few opportunities the young couple had to be . . . well, alone together; and she was sure Maureen must appreciate Wayne's gallantry in driving to and from Brettenden each day simply to suit her convenience. Such little attentions would, she supposed, make all the difference to the progress of a courtship.

Miss Seeton's long teaching experience had given a certain clarity to her speaking tones, although a gentlewoman does not raise her voice any more than she must. She spoke her final words to Doris just as the black-leather-clad figure of Wayne steered the motorbike off the road on to the grey asphalt in front of the George. A booted foot kicked downwards, there was a minor upward jerk, and the Kawasaki was on its rest, its engine idling. Miss Seeton, beside a frowning Doris, beamed her approval. In his own way, Maureen's Wayne had quite as much in him of the Galahad as dear Nigel Colveden.

Wayne turned to assist Maureen down from the pillion. Doris, whose stern and watchful form had hidden that of the smaller Miss Seeton, moved forward to deliver her customary reprimand. Maureen hopped off her perch, removed her crash helmet, and shook out her hair in readiness.

"Look here, young Maureen," began Maureen's exasperated supervisor and colleague. "This really isn't good enough, you know, specially when we've got guests. I had to do Mrs. Ogden's breakfast myself, and I'll have your wages docked if it happens again. I'm sure I don't see why—''

Miss Seeton, whose views on punctuality were as firm as those of Doris—to be punctual is to be polite—had nevertheless to hide a smile as Galahad Wayne kicked the motorbike rest upwards, revved the engine, and took off in a roar of exhaust with which not even the scolding voice of Doris could compete. Which was probably the idea. Still smiling, Miss Seeton prepared to take her leave. One would not wish to be thought an eavesdropper on what was likely to be an embarrassing scene. More embarrassing for Doris, of course, than for Maureen. The younger woman's blissful and voluntary deafness to all instruction was a village byword, while the indignity of being ignored . . .

"Aow!" Maureen's shrill scream as she finished shaking out her hair pierced even the roar of the disappearing Kawasaki and caused Doris to abandon the tirade she had just resumed to clap her hands to her startled ears. The sudden appearance of Miss Seeton, hitherto concealed behind the statuesque severity of the head waitress, had done more to galvanise Maureen's reflexes into action than any amount of nagging could have achieved.

"Aow! Aow!" Maureen shrieked again, her eyes wide with fright as she looked at Miss Seeton, who had been reminded by the shrieks of nothing so much as the wartime air raid siren's high-pitched, penetrating howl, and was wishing the memories conjured up would go away again.

"Aow! Naow!" Maureen had caught Miss Seeton's change of expression and redoubled her efforts, fearing what it might betoken. "Naow! Naow!"

Doris pulled down her hands and wound back her arm for one sturdy box of Maureen's ears as the best cure for the frenzied state into which the girl was working herself all too quickly: yet not so quickly that Maureen didn't guess what might be about to happen. With one last shriek of denial—against what, neither Doris nor Miss Seeton knew—she turned to run—Maureen, running!—across the asphalt car park into the George.

"Maureen, stop it this minute!" commanded Doris. Miss

Seeton, with her wider experience of juvenile hysteria, knew that the command was in vain. In her senseless panic, the silly child could hear nothing. She must be stopped before she did herself or others any harm. In one movement Miss Seeton dropped her shopping basket and snatched the umbrella from her arm. She scuttled after Maureen's flying, arms-akimbo form and lunged forward, the crook handle poised like some quaintly curved spear to pinion its prey about the upper arm. Miss Seeton tugged as Maureen stopped in her tracks, frozen with terror. Maureen, her shrieks silenced, was forced to turn.

She took one long, wide-eyed look at Miss Seeton's face no more than an arm-and-a-brolly's-length away . . .

And fell with a muffled groan in an appalled swoon face-down upon the grey asphalt of the car park of the George.

When Charley Mountfitchet heard Maureen's screams, he was put in mind not of air raids, but of pig killing. Since Plummergen farmers have always taken their beasts to authorised slaughter-houses, he thought the noise worth investigating. He was halfway out of the door when the screaming girl began her swooning descent to oblivion and was at her side in good time to assist Doris and Miss Seeton as they disentangled the latter's umbrella and set about a gentle slapping of Maureen's pallid cheeks.

"Best take her inside," proposed Charley, scooping up his unconscious employee as easily as he would heft a beer barrel from its cellar rack to the tap-room pump.

"Too many late nights, that's what it is," muttered Doris to Miss Seeton as she helped the latter collect her scattered belongings. "Can't burn the candle at both ends, not for long you can't, and I've told her so many a time. But would she listen?"

"The young," observed Miss Seeton, "are sometimes so

uncomfortable—impatient—with the idea of physical frailty, are they not?''

''Think it'll never happen to them. Huh,'' said Doris, the voice of experience. ''Give it time.'' She rolled her eyes in the direction of Charley and his burden, now vanishing through the George's front door. ''No need to bother any-more, thanks. You get on with your shopping.''

''Well—if you are sure,'' said Miss Seeton doubtfully. One had no particular knowledge of first aid in the sense of being trained, but so many years of dealing with school-girls had certainly resulted in a knowledge of what one might call the basics. Loosened collars and the application of a moderate amount of cold water, for instance . . .

''And we'll burn a feather or two under her silly nose,'' said Doris cheerfully. ''She'll be fine.''

''Yes, indeed. Like the candle,'' said Miss Seeton with a smile. ''Though only one end, of course.''

With another smile and a nod, she was gone before Doris could work out what she meant. Which—as Doris herself remarked to Charley Mountfitchet once she'd followed him inside—was nothing unusual, was it? Just so long as the shock of watching Maureen go into hysterics hadn't turned the poor old lady's mind, that was to say.

All Charley had to say was ''feathers.'' Bearing in mind the likely sensibilities of the George's overnight guest, he had whisked with his fair burden through the foyer to the kitchen, where he had dumped the girl on the table and was energetically fanning her with a tea-towel. A watcher might have seen her eyelids start to flicker as the colour crept slowly back to her cheeks.

Doris giggled. ''Oh, aren't I the daft one? Yes, I'll get a duster from the cleaning cupboard. We can spare a feather or two.'' It wasn't as if Maureen made much use of them. The girl generally sneezed and asked someone else (mean-ing soft-hearted Dogsbody Doris) to do the high corners and cobwebs. "Matches," added Doris, poised to hurry off dusterwards. "Candles!" And she giggled again with relief that the shock of all the fuss and bother hadn't really turned poor Miss Seeton's m—

"Candles?" Maureen, finding herself laid out as a virgin sacrifice, sat bolt upright with a shriek that had Doris clapping her hands to her ears. "Naow!" screamed Maureen, struggling. "Let me gaow! Help! Help!!"

"Don't!" cried Doris.

But the warning went unheard above the screams. She shot out her hand to grab Charley's arm as it wound back to box the girl's ears and was about to box them with her own free hand when the screaming stopped as suddenly as it had begun. Maureen's face was as white as it had ever been. Her eyes met those of Doris and were once more wide with horror as visions of the Black Mass floated before them.

For a moment, nobody moved; nobody made a sound.

Then, with an indistinct gurgle, Maureen closed her eyes and fell back into her swoon.

CHAPTER 10

Superintendent Brinton's long-standing orders to Plummergen's PC Potter were that Potter should immediately advise his Ashford superior of any untoward occurrence in the vicinity of Miss Emily Dorothea Seeton.

Potter knew his Plummergen. He was also more than well acquainted with Brinton's temper. Mountains out of molehills were a local speciality and hardly untoward in the routine scheme of things. PC Potter had far more sense than to waste the superintendent's time, or risk his own skin, by reporting to Ashford either the current village speculation that Miss Seeton's latest enterprise might be the procuring of young and innocent females for the benefit of a London-based vampire, or the hysteria said enterprise was starting to generate in such impressionable persons as Emmeline Putts and her friend Maureen.

Brinton's blissful ignorance of the latest Plummergen brouhaha meant that when the superintendent set out on his own scene-of-the-crime inspection, he did so with no more to worry him than whether he, like Foxon, might not have his purpose mistaken by some nervous householder. Two cases of concussion and four black eyes in the space of

three days would be mathematically undesirable for the mo-
rale of the force. The boy had gone in an unmarked police
vehicle: he, Brinton, would be driven by the uniformed PC
Buckland in a regulation panda.

"We'll start with the Abinger place," he instructed,
strapping himself into his seat belt as Buckland prepared
for the off. "Just because the Yard hasn't come up with
anything yet doesn't mean we needn't try making the
blighter feel a little uncomfortable. Bashing cops over the
head is something we don't want to encourage, Buckland.
Let him and his neighbours get the idea we're keeping an
eye on him, and it might just stop anyone else following
his example."

"Right, sir." Buckland had been more worried about his
friend than he had cared to admit, although Foxon's natural
chirpiness had begun to surface by the end of last night's
hospital visiting hour, and there were rumours he might be
released later that day. "Abinger's, then where? Round the
other places poor old Foxon never even got to?"

Brinton scowled at the sheet of paper in his hand. He
hesitated. Buckland politely stayed his hand on the ignition
and his foot on the pedal. Brinton cleared his throat. "Well,
more or less the same, with just one new place. Doc Wyddial put me on to it this morning as a—as a possibility, she
said. Might not be anything at all to do with this business—
apparently he's neither starving himself to death nor flat
broke like the rest—but we asked for info on things that
don't seem quite right, and when another doctor over the
border mentioned it at some medics' get-together, she
thought it, uh, didn't. Doesn't."

"Over the border, sir?" Buckland's attention, now that
he had set the car in motion, was on the road ahead, but
he could still think. "You mean . . . Sussex?"

"I don't mean Bonnie Scotland, lad—and before you
ask, no, I haven't talked to Inspector Furneux. We're only

going to look at an empty house, for heaven's sake. It's not one of your cross-border raiding parties breaching professional etiquette left, right, and centre." Brinton, who still wasn't sure the whole thing wasn't a mare's nest, had no wish to make a fool of himself by involving his opposite number in the Sussex constabulary any earlier than he must.

He cleared his throat again. "Seems some old chap this side of Hastings was beaten up about six months ago, only according to the doc it wasn't a burglary as such—nothing pinched, no vandalism, just—just personal spite, and they never found who did it. He ended up in a home—a really posh place, not Knight's—suffering from loss of memory." He coughed. "And it hasn't come back, so nobody knows quite how or why it all happened. But the whole affair seemed so pointless—doesn't make sense . . ."

Like the other cases, he reminded himself as Buckland slowed the car for the turn into Abinger's road.

As Foxon had done, Brinton and Buckland took careful note of the gables, dormer windows, tiling and brickwork, and curving gravel drive of the house previously owned by the late Mr. Pontefract, now the property of Patrick and Lucy Abinger. A net curtain in the front window twitched, but there was no other sign of life. Even the worms seemed to have abandoned their under-lawn excavations, for the grass was muddily green but unsullied by mounds of earth.

"Miss Addison next," said Brinton, quite as baffled as he'd been before he came, but not giving up yet. Buckland muttered something about damned-if-he-was-doing-the-garden-for-her, which Brinton chose not to hear. The car rumbled on its way with Brinton brooding in the passenger seat.

At Miss Addison's house they pulled into the kerb behind a sturdy vehicle Buckland soon identified as belonging to the district nurse: a plaster-cast inspection was suggested as the reason for the visit. Brinton grunted and climbed out of the car without saying whether he agreed or not. Buckland maintained a discreet silence as he followed.

"Gate needs painting," remarked Brinton after a few uneasy moments, unconsciously echoing Gran Biddle. "Drive's suffered some frost damage, too. It'll cost some money to put that right, though I suppose the old girl won't be using her car for a while, with a broken leg."

"No, sir," said Buckland absently. He was looking at the drive and frowning. "Surely that's new," he murmured to himself. "And it's not as if the winter's been all that cold. Wet, yes, but . . ."

Beside him, Brinton stirred. "Let's get on," he said. One minute he'd suspected a conspiracy of overkeen housebuyers; now it was importunate motorists after low-mileage cars. "We've half a dozen more addresses to check before the light goes. Buckland, stop daydreaming!"

"Sorry, sir." He didn't altogether sound it. There was something on his mind—at the back of his mind, refusing to come forward. Something that wasn't—like the super'd said before—quite right, although . . .

"Buckland!" roared Brinton from the panda; and Buckland wisely sprinted down the pavement without a backward glance at the house of Adelaide Addison.

As they drove away, it was not only the occupant of the passenger seat who was, this time, brooding. Buckland's honest brow, like that of his superior, was furrowed deep in thought. Anyone given to the practice of atmospheric incision could have perfected their art inside that panda car.

The third house turned out to be a bungalow, almost invisible under a shroud of heavy-duty fluorescent plastic while a gang of large and muscular men clumped up and down ladders carrying boxes of nails and hods of pantiles to repair the battered slate roof.

"This one's sold," Brinton roused himself to say, unnecessarily. Buckland nodded. The estate agent's board might have gone, but there was no mistaking the frenzied activity generated by a new homeowner demanding instant perfection. The lorry parked nearby carried bags of cement and planks of wood as well as roofing materials. There were drifts of sawdust interlaced with whitewash footprints going in both directions along the asphalt drive, on one part of which an enormous pile of paving stones had been erected.

"I hope those are reconstituted," muttered Brinton, his crime-prevention instincts coming to the fore. "The real stuff costs a small fortune, so if that's what they are, the owners'll be damned lucky if the whole lot hasn't walked by the end of the week."

"Less noisy than gravel, sir," said Buckland. "No frost damage, either."

"Just don't spill yoghurt on them," growled Brinton as they headed back to the car.

Buckland shot him an anxious look. "Er . . . I think that was whitewash, sir. Paint of some sort, anyway."

"What? Oh, that." Brinton emerged from his abstraction to grin a rueful grin. Mrs. Brinton, on a recent visit to the dentist, had picked up some overambitious home improvement ideas from a women's magazine. Her husband liked gardening no more than did Detective Constable Foxon and sadly foresaw a long, strenuous, and yoghurt-ridden spring ahead for the Brinton ménage. "No, it's what they paint statues with to get 'em to grow moss just like real old stone. A couple of years and you'd never know it was just powdered marble and resin under there, I'm told." He sighed. "What will they think of next?"

"Next, sir?" Buckland had only caught the tail end of his superior's musing. "Right." And the car set off at a brisk speed towards household number four.

Dull pebble-dash walls and uncurtained windows looked down upon an overgrown front garden. Shabby asphalt, frost-pitted and potholed, wound between scruffy flower beds to a double-doored garage in which broken panes of glass were mournful eyes surveying desolation.

"Vandals," growled Brinton. "Probably hasn't even been reported, if the place is standing empty. We don't stand a chance of catching the blighters if the public doesn't cooperate—but do they listen?"

Buckland, for one, wasn't listening. He was staring at the broken-windowed garage and frowning. "She hasn't got a car," he said. "She never drove, even before her busted ankle, according to Gran Biddle. I wonder . . ."

Brinton blinked. Light was beginning to dawn. He might be imagining things, but . . . "These places we've been checking," he said slowly. "Apart from the fact some poor old soul used to live there and doesn't anymore . . ."

"Yes, sir?" The tone of Buckland's response seemed to suggest that he, like Brinton, might have begun to see the light. The superintendent let out a quiet sigh.

"Of course we'll look at the other addresses," he said slowly. "To make sure. But before we do, if you'd care to wager a small sum on what else they've all got in common, I'd be happy to take you on . . ."

PC Buckland was shaking his head. "No bet, sir," he said firmly. "I think," prudence made him add. "Not until we've seen the rest of the list, anyway . . ."

"Then let's get going," commanded Superintendent Brinton. Whereupon they got.

Plummergen, on the whole, is conservative at heart. The villagers view change-for-the-sake-of-change with suspicion. A smooth-tongued commercial traveller had, however, with some difficulty talked Mr. Stillman's wife Elsie into trying a different brand of tinned pineapple chunks at a Special Introductory Price, and the relative merits of "Juiceo" and "Ananas" were being enthusiastically debated as the Brettenden bus, with a squeal of brakes, pulled up at the stop outside the post office.

Ears pricked; conversation faltered. People forgot what they were saying and moved from the display counters in the middle of the shop towards the window and the half-glazed main door. Taller shoppers, longer in the leg and with bags and baskets over their arms, barged and elbowed their unfair way to an even better view than their shorter, disadvantaged sisters. As far as anyone knew, everyone who had gone into Brettenden earlier that day had already returned. For the bus to stop meant that somebody had requested it to do so: somebody who was most likely a stranger.

The rubber doors of the bus thudded open, and a figure materialised in silhouette on the platform. A collective sigh of deep satisfaction confirmed to all inside the post office that nobody who saw the figure recognised it. Her. Despite the mufflings of a heavy tweed overcoat and the fact that only the back was visible, the figure must surely be female. Conservative Plummergen could not conceive that any normal man would dare to flaunt such glorious, waist-length auburn locks in public.

"Coo! That hair's never real," said an envious Emmy Putts, who had stolen a march on the rest by mounting the aluminium steps Mr. Stillman kept behind the counter for less popular items on the top shelf. Balancing on tiptoe, Emmy scowled over the heads of everyone else at that lustrous red-gold mane as its owner, still with her back to those watching, continued (so the watchers assumed) to address words of thanks and farewell to the bus driver. "Out of a bottle, that's got to be. Coo . . ."

"Or a wig," someone said sharply. It was never forgotten in certain quarters (meaning those households with female inhabitants of qualifying age) that Emmy had not once (which was bad enough) but twice been crowned Miss

Plummergen as an artificially long-haired blonde when her everyday appearance was that of a short-haired brunette.

"Not natural, anyway," said someone else pacifically.

Although people could have argued with this, nobody did: the redhead in the overcoat was collecting her belongings with the air of one about to leave the bus, and it was more than likely she would be in their midst within half a minute. Any stranger who visited Plummergen seemed to find the post office irresistible, and no worthwhile debate about the business of said stranger could take place in a mere thirty seconds. They would wait until she'd gone and enjoy themselves all the more with the luxury of unlimited time.

"Might be from the films," said Emmy, more envious than ever as she hopped off the aluminium steps and folded them away. She and the George's Maureen shared a rapturous daydream of Discovery by some passing producer who, instantly recognising their talent, would whisk them from humdrum Plummergen to Hollywood of a thousand thrills. "A star," mused Emmy as she twirled the handle of the bacon slicer, "like Greta Garbo, come on holiday in secret and wanting someone to—to be a double . . ."

Nobody managed to do more than snigger at her before the redhead was, as they had anticipated, off the bus . . . and, rather than entering the post office, with an elegant swaying motion was walking southwards down The Street.

"Well!" said Mrs. Skinner as the tawny mane vanished from sight. "Well, I never!"

"Poor soul," said Mrs. Henderson, seizing the chance to out-comment her rival, who had seemed lost for words. "Poor soul," she said again in doom-laden tones. "Ah, they were right, young Emmy, to give you that garlic, for you see it's worked, hasn't it?"

"But—" began Emmy. Her protest was ignored.

"They've had to leave you alone, and all thanks to the

Nuts for it, that's what I say.'' Mrs. Henderson looked round in triumph at her audience, nodding in sympathy with sentiments as yet unspoken but understood by all.

"Left *her* alone,'' said Mrs. Skinner, recovering quickly, "but there's young Maureen to be thought of, too, remember. With working at the George, she'll be in need of a warning once that one,'' she said with a jerk of her head towards the vanished tawny, "starts trying to—to draw her into her toils, which is what she's sure to do seeing as she's baggage in her hand and no other place to stay. You ought to be on the phone to her right now, young Emmy, before it's too late.''

"Maureen's safe enough *now*,'' said Mrs. Henderson as everyone nodded in sympathy with this point of view. "Why should they want *her* when there's her friends to protect her and make it more difficult? Always want the easy way of it, they do.''

This argument on the side of practicality gained a second round of approving nods. Mrs. Henderson smirked. She lowered her voice to a thrilling whisper. "Easy for them,'' she said, "to draw poor innocents into their toils, like it's plain they've already done with that one''—she jerked her head in imitation of Mrs. Skinner—"because she's a stranger and don't know any better. But you and Maureen, Emmy—*you* already know, don't you? About keeping well away from that Dracula man and from Miss Seeton . . .''

The George and Dragon's busiest times were generally spring and summer, when Charley Mountfitchet played host to a steady stream of honeymoon couples, sightseers, and bird-watchers. The stream slowed in autumn and winter to a trickle—unless, that is, one of Miss Seeton's innocent exploits had been making off-season headlines. Even hard-bitten journalists had as great a need for their creature comforts as more sensitive souls, these comforts to include bed, board, booze, and access to the telephone.

While some of the post office shoppers still held to the theory that the girl with red hair had been lured (in some manner as yet unspecified) to Plummergen by Miss Seeton for the ultimate bloodthirsty benefit of Antony Scarlett, others were coming round to the notion that she could be a reporter on the trail of a Big Story before it broke: said story to be centred, inevitably, upon Miss Seeton (although again in a manner unspecified, even if some had their suspicions). While the two schools of thought differed in their basic approach, on one point they agreed. A meeting between the two women was inevitable and would be contrived before many hours had passed—and should not be missed. Curtains twitched at the southern end of The Street; enough flowers were carried to ancestral graves in the churchyard beside the pub to denude most of the front gardens to the north.

The advent of the middle-aged Mrs. Ogden two nights before had caused only a little less comment than that of the George's younger and more glamorous guest. She had seemed at first so ordinary: so lacking in speculative potential. The car parked on Charley's grey asphalt forecourt was a respectable family saloon. Its tax disc was up-to-date; its number-plate was rusted in position and thus not false. Its owner had paid her hotel deposit in cash and had taken a stroll up one side of The Street and down the other before ambling over the bridge to gaze into the quiet waters drawn into their canalised path by the design of Prime Minister Pitt against the threat of Napoleon. She had been observed studying the concrete pillbox built against a more recent and terrible threat . . .

The pillbox was visible from the back windows of Sweetbriars, which fact was all that was needed to overcome the initially poor potential. Speculation was now rife.

Mrs. Ogden's ordinariness was a blind. She and Miss Seeton were in cahoots. Young women were at risk (if unmarried) of perversion; if married, they were at risk of corruption into that same perversion as active, rather than passive, participants. To which group did the girl with red hair belong? Was she a virgin or not? Her signature on the hotel register gave (according to Maureen) no title, merely her name. Reporter or victim? Without further evidence it was impossible to tell. Doris and Charley were famously disinclined to gossip about the George's guests. Given time, Maureen might have found out much, but after polishing a few half-hearted saucepans she had been sent home and told to pull herself together before she returned to work. Maureen had imparted to Emmy Putts by telephone the paltry intelligence already gleaned, then had dragged herself to an early bed, complaining of headaches. If Plummergen wanted to know what was going on, it must find out for itself . . .

The girl with red hair had asked for tea and—as an afterthought—toast to be served in her room. Maureen had known this much, but no more. Doris could have told of muffled sobs heard through oak panels, of reddened eyes, and cheeks blotched with tears: but Doris, as ever, kept her own counsel. Left alone, the girl sipped tea, nibbled toast, and set the tray outside her door before casting herself in despair upon comfortable feather pillows in search of sleep.

The chink of crockery as Doris removed the tray woke the girl some hours later. She looked at herself in the mirror and shivered. She dragged a thick sweater from her bag and put it on. She washed her face in cold water; ran a brush through her tousled locks; pulled on coat, hat, and gloves; and with another shiver emerged cautiously from her room to descend the stairs to the main door.

Doris, on her knees beside the reception desk with a milk-soaked cloth in her hand, was busy bathing the leaves of Charley Mountfitchet's cherished cheese plant. She looked up at the sound of footfalls. "Popping out for a bit, are you, dear? You're wise not to leave it too long. Once the sun's gone down, there's a regular nip in the air."

The girl gazed at her from under still-swollen eyelids. "I . . . don't like the cold," she said. Doris hid a smile. From the look of the poor young thing, this admission came as no surprise.

"Your room's all right, isn't it?" she enquired hastily. "If you haven't got enough blankets, you just let me know. And the radiator's nice and warm—or it ought to be."

"It is . . . thank you." The girl managed a weak smile. "Everything's . . . very nice, really."

"Then a good brisk walk before supper," said Doris, "will give you an appetite as well as get your blood going, though you don't want to go too far. Why not pop down to the bridge to watch the sunset across the marsh? A lovely view, that is." She hesitated. There was something in the graceful way the girl moved, in the bones of her cheeks and the rich tumult of her hair, that made her add: "Artists come to paint it, you know."

"I . . . didn't know." The girl turned to look back up the stairs. "I've a small sketchbook in my bag, but . . ."

Doris remembered how little of the toast had been eaten. She had no wish for a second fainting fit on her hands so soon after Maureen's efforts in that direction. "Oh, you don't want to keep running up and down when you've only just come," she advised. "Time enough for all that tomorrow once you've had a good night's sleep after a good hot supper and a proper breakfast to set you up for the day."

"I could sketch the sunrise," suggested the girl, her smile a little stronger now. "If I . . . stood on the bridge and looked the other way . . ."

"So you could," agreed Doris cheerfully. If it had been meant as sarcasm, she'd save her breath for better targets.

Too many of these London types tried to get clever with folk and were slapped down as they deserved, but there was something about this poor young creature, looking half-starved—and so pale, despite the red eyes—that made her, well, feel sorry for her. "But that's for tomorrow," she said briskly. "You get along now and enjoy your walk, and when you come back, there's a nice fire in the lounge and the television, where folk often take their tea and biscuits, though you don't want to spoil your appetite so close to supper, do you?"

The girl agreed that she didn't. She would take Doris's advice and walk to the bridge: she would admire the sunset; she might visit the church. She would be back before dark.

She went out of the door into the first faint hint of twilight and turned left to walk past church and vicarage to the narrow lane leading to the canal bridge.

"Good evening," said Miss Emily Dorothea Seeton.

Brinton and Buckland were back in the former's office, with steaming mugs of tea in front of them on Brinton's desk and pensive expressions on their faces. To the simmering disapproval of Desk Sergeant Mutford, the uniformed constable had been temporarily signed off patrol duty by his plainclothes superior, who hadn't realised quite how much he would miss the presence of Detective Constable Foxon when he wanted to try out his wild hypotheses on the recent history of the half-dozen houses hitherto only tentatively linked in the Pauper Pensioner Puzzle.

Hitherto. But now . . .

"Maybe I'll let you off that tenner you owe me, lad." Brinton grinned across his blotter at the startled Buckland. "Just as well we went into Sussex after all, wasn't it?"

"If you say so, sir." Buckland's was not a nature that enjoyed the taking of unnecessary risks. He had the nasty suspicion that his head, being the most junior, would be the first to roll when the authoritarian axe was wielded. While Inspector "Fiery Furnace" Furneux might just about view with equanimity a passing visit from the car of a neighbouring force, Sergeant Mutford would simmer beyond boiling point were he to learn (as sooner or later he was bound to do) of the recent cross-border foray on official time when (until now) there wasn't really any justification for such a trip.

"Because now," said Brinton, echoing Buckland's unspoken thought, "we know what's been going on, don't we?"

"We can guess, sir," said the cautious Buckland.

Brinton snorted. "Seems a fair enough bet to me—and I don't mean ten quid's worth. There's something big behind all this, if my instincts are right. Think about it, lad."

Buckland did so.

Admittedly, he'd had his suspicions, but it had taken the sight of the last house on the super's list to convince him that there was, in the super's words, something big behind it all. Once more, this time across the county border, they had arrived outside a property of slightly run-down appearance, more than overdue for the renovations a spell of fine weather would no doubt initiate. Overdue for all renovations—except one.

"Always makes me want to grab a broom and start sweeping," growled Brinton with a jerk of his head towards the maroon asphalt drive artistically speckled with white. "It looks as if someone's emptied confetti all over the place and it needs tidying up."

"I couldn't agree with you more," came an unexpected voice. The two policemen jumped as a bright-faced little woman popped up on the other side of the dividing hedge and nodded to them. "Gravel is so much less demanding, don't you think? Whereas next door simply cries out to me, as it obviously does to you, *litter*." She shuddered and gestured towards the hedge. "Wild cherry," she said expressively. "Can you imagine how I feel when this is in bloom? Oh, it may be a clever method of softening the harsh effect of so much asphalt at once, but it's incredibly irritating to anyone with the least inclination to tidiness. And after what happened the first time around, I would have supposed they would have learned their lesson—but there, you can't tell people who don't want to listen, can you?"

"You certainly can't," said Brinton, thinking of some notable closed ears of his professional acquaintance.

His new acquaintance took this heartfelt agreement as an invitation to continue, which she did with a decided twinkle in her eye. "Mind you, if they *had* listened to me, I would have had to admit they'd have been wrong—in one respect, that is. You won't convince me it looks neat, but at least it . . . it's *lasted*, which I never thought it would, and I told them so. But it hasn't run, despite all the rain we've had this year, and if it hasn't by now, I suppose it never will. But oh, my goodness, you should have been here when it did before!"

"A bit of a sight, was it?" prompted Brinton, daring Buckland to breathe and interrupt the flow.

The bright-eyed neighbour of the asphalt drive threw up her hands with glee. "Sight? Smell, you mean! Peppermint from one end of the road to the other!"

Brinton's ears pricked at this. Buckland smothered a chuckle. "P-peppermint?" enquired the superintendent, his voice almost steady.

"That's what they'd used for the decoration or whatever you call it." Bright eyes twinkled all the more as another gesture indicated the property next door. "The contractors didn't use the chips of white stone they'd promised, but peppermints—the hard sort, not creams—broken into pieces and squashed in by hand with a roller. I was on holiday at the time, or of course I would have smelled a rat straight away.'' She giggled. ''Or a peppermint— though not until it rained, of course. Peppermint toffee, that's what it was once it did!''

''I believe you,'' said Brinton. ''I'll bet the flies and wasps around here had a field day.''

''Yes, indeed they did, much to everyone's relief.'' She gave her audience no time to register surprise. ''So many of the little beasts stuck fast in the stuff—they must have scented it a mile or more away—that for weeks afterwards you couldn't find a single creepy-crawly on the hoof, as it were, if you tried. It wasn't until the breeding cycle began again that they came back. It was like an enormous mint-flavoured flypaper for them, you see. Basically red, with huge smears of white—going grey, you know, as more and more insects landed and couldn't escape . . .''

''Ugh,'' said Brinton obligingly as she paused. Once more he was rewarded with a twinkle.

''It was absolutely revolting.'' Then, with a sigh and a shake of her head, she became serious. ''And simply the last straw for poor old Mrs. Grainger. She'd been finding it hard enough before this mess to keep the place going— she was a pensioner, you know—and if only I'd been here I could have warned her to have nothing to do with them, no matter how plausible they sounded, which I gather they did. But they wouldn't have fooled me!'' Brinton was prepared to believe this, too. ''*I've* watched men repairing roads,'' she went on with a decisive nod and a frown. ''Keep your wits about you, that's my motto. Always be *interested* in things, and you won't go to seed. Well now, nobody uses an ordinary garden roller to lay asphalt, do they? Or even to squash fancy patterns into it?''

''They don't,'' said Brinton. ''Full-blown bulldozers and steamrollers, that's what they use.''

''Mrs. Grainger was ninety-two and her eyesight wasn't

terribly good." Mrs. Grainger's former neighbour sighed. "The poor soul wouldn't have known one piece of machinery from another if it made enough noise to sound like the genuine article, as I gather it did. They were here and gone within the day—and nobody's seen them since, of course. Charged her the earth and vamoosed, the devils. Oh, if I could only get my hands on them I'd teach them to swindle half-blind old ladies out of their savings!"

Brinton had believed that, as well.

He looked now at PC Buckland. "There's something big behind all this," he said slowly. "Every single house we visited has had recent problems with a stretch of asphalt, and all the houses were owned at the time the asphalt was laid by an elderly person living alone. Some of 'em, like Miss Addison, are still there, and so's the asphalt, with grass growing through it and potholes from the frost." He paused invitingly.

"And some of them . . ." ventured Buckland.

Brinton nodded.

Buckland coughed. "Well, most of them . . . have either died or sold up. Either way, other people own the houses now and they've inherited the problems. Sir."

"And had a go at solving them," prompted Brinton. If the lad wanted to join his pal Foxon in CID, which he'd made a few noises from time to time he'd like to try, a spot of on-the-job training wouldn't hurt his chances.

"They've had the cheap, low-grade stuff ripped up, sir, and replaced with proper new. Or with gravel or stone—or they're in the process of doing it, anyway. Sir."

"Let's hope they have better luck second time around," said Brinton. His hand moved towards the telephone, then pulled back. "So what d'you reckon, lad?"

Buckland scratched his head. This was rather more than he'd been expecting. He blinked. Brinton glared at him. "I . . . I reckon," offered Buckland, "there's a—a pattern to all this, sir. Not just our area, I mean, or Sussex, but probably other places, too, if we knew. I mean, if the chummies have found something that works, they're not going to . . . stop doing it, are they? Until they're caught, I mean. It's—it's easy money, cheating old folk.''

''Damnably easy.'' Brinton, pleased with his pupil's deductive abilities, nodded and reached for the telephone again. ''Get me Scotland Yard . . .''

"Superintendent Brinton here, Ashford. I'd like a word with Chief Superintendent Delphick, if he's handy. Thanks." The wires clicked and hummed. There came a rattle as a receiver was picked up. "Sergeant Ranger? Your boss around?"

His voice, he knew, was unmistakable. So was the instant anxiety in the voice that answered him.

"Oh—hello, Mr. Brinton." Bob's guarded greeting was followed by a pause as Delphick (Brinton guessed) lifted the other extension. "Er," said Bob before hanging up. As he hadn't been specifically instructed to keep listening, he wouldn't; but he did, well, wonder. "Er—is everything . . . all right in your neck of the woods, sir?"

"As far as I know, she's fine," Brinton assured him. "This is something else—more or less," honesty compelled him to add. "But she's only on the fringe of it, and unless she's likely to be talked into having her front garden asphalted over by a firm of blasted cowboys, I can't see there's anything to worry about."

"Touch wood when you say that," warned Delphick in his most oracular tones. "Although," he went on cheerfully, ''with Stan Bloomer near at hand and notably jealous of his territory, your remark seems less, ah, fatally provocative than similar remarks have been on previous occasions, given what we know of the cowboys' usual procedure.'' Smoothly he ignored the startled exclamation that burst from Brinton's lips. ''Perhaps, however, as his adopted aunt is, albeit peripherally, concerned in your current predicament, the sergeant should continue to eavesdrop—with your permission, of course.''

''Okay by me,'' said Brinton, recovering himself. ''You mean you *do* know this crowd I was ringing about?''

The Oracle backtracked slightly. ''We have some knowledge of what may be the same crowd manifesting itself at different times in different parts of the country, yes. It would appear that there has been quite an epidemic over the past couple of years, although the fine detail escapes me, and for all I know there may be several independent copycat groups. Until now it has been more the province of Fraud rather than of Serious Crime, but . . .''

''Until now? Why, what's happened?''

''One of the victims, an old soldier, refused to pay up.'' Delphick's voice was grim. ''He was attacked in his own home and left permanently crippled. His wife, who was already in a wheelchair, witnessed the attack and was, the doctors tell us, literally terrified to death.''

Brinton drew in his breath with an angry hiss. ''Heart, I suppose. We've had a similar case like that here, if I'm reading it right. The poor old chap ended up in a home, completely doolally—so much so the medics say he'll never snap out of it. His mind's gone. No chance of getting a statement out of him—and the other suspected victims are either dead or gone some other way.''

Buckland, who had heard only one side of this exchange, here stirred on his chair. Brinton looked up. ''Oh! Yes, with one exception. A poor old biddy who's still on the spot was frightened half out of her wits when young Foxon appeared on her doorstep with a black eye and was a bit slow telling her who he was. I should think he struck her as just the sort of hooligan who'd amuse himself by beating up old ladies who didn't pay their debts—if that's how these blighters work?"

"It would seem so." The Oracle didn't waste time by asking the reason for Foxon's black eye. The boy, a mere six-footer, was seven inches shorter than Sergeant Ranger: and even Bob, over the years, had received his share of honourable wounds in the war against crime. "As in your case, witnesses are somewhat thin on the ground, but our old soldier was, let us say, forthright in his account of what happened." Delphick cleared his throat. "He . . . had nothing left to lose, he said."

Brinton found himself blinking. "Go on," he muttered. He coughed. "No, hang on. Buckland, hop across and listen in on the other phone—if that's all right by you, Oracle?"

"I deduce," Delphick observed after a reflective few seconds, "that the presence of PC Buckland in your office has something to do with DC Foxon's black eye. Buckland, my compliments for accepting the heroic role of understudy." Buckland mumbled something, and the tips of his ears turned pink. "I won't," went on the Oracle, "ask for details just yet—unless Foxon ran foul of the asphalters, that is."

"Some young totty kicked up a fuss when he tried to arrest her boyfriend," Brinton told him. "And then a chap whose hedge he was peering over got a bit—ah!"

"Oh!" said Sergeant Ranger, sounding guilty. "Er—sir, I'm sorry. The, uh, computer's still working on that one. As soon as we get anything . . ."

Brinton snorted. "Yes, well, so much for modern technology. Let's have some details of good old-fashioned fraud instead, shall we?"

Delphick once more assumed the lead. "Details as far as we know them," came the quick qualification. "However. The working method, if we may call it that, is fraudulent in the extreme, but so cleverly conceived that there must be many victims around the country who never realise how, or indeed that, they have been defrauded." The Oracle paused. "In fact, it was the growing unease within the legitimate building industry, rather than complaints from any of the fraud victims, that first alerted the authorities that something might be—in fact, was—wrong."

"Oh?"

"The gang make their initial approach in the guise of established contractors, though they neither make verbal claims to the identity nor put anything in writing."

"Clever," agreed Brinton with a sigh.

"They say," Delphick went on, "that they have been doing some work in the vicinity—usually carriageway repairs on a nearby main road—and just happen to have half a load of asphalt left over, which they would be prepared to . . ." He hesitated. "To install? To lay," he amended. "To offer to the householder at a favourable price," he concluded.

Brinton groaned. "And if that's not an argument to appeal to the old folk, I don't know what is."

"Exactly." Delphick sighed. "The gang members wear uniforms resembling those of recognised companies; their vehicles and plant are dressed in near-genuine colours, and with trade names and logos almost identical to the real thing. Who, when the overall appearance is one of such authenticity, is likely to notice a griffon for a dragon—a letter *m* for an *n*—orange rather than yellow paint?"

"Not too many," said Brinton. "Especially if they're getting on in years and don't spend as much time as younger folk charging up and down motorways with plenty of opportunity to see what's really what."

"Or," interposed Buckland before he could stop himself, "getting stuck in traffic jams."

There was a pause. "Quite so," said Delphick. "There speaks one who has served his time in Traffic Division. The comment came from the heart, Constable Buckland."

"Yes, sir. Sorry." And once more the tips of PC Buckland's ears turned pink.

"Go on," invited Brinton, directing no more than an upward roll of his eyes for the hapless young man at the other desk. When he started chucking peppermints, the lad could feel at home. Until then . . .

"The gang," said Delphick, "alter their appearance every few months—or, as we have already mentioned, there may be several gangs using the same trick. In either event, more than one well-known construction company with a deserved reputation for high standards of customer service has been called upon to repair the shoddy work supposedly carried out by some of its employees. In the interests of public relations, they have generally done so."

"Explains why you haven't heard too much about all this until now," said Brinton. "I take it the building types don't care to let on how they've been gulled, either."

"They don't. Once the trick became general knowledge, the risk of this sort of blackmail would be enormously increased. Reputation is all too easy to wink down," said Delphick, adapting Swift, "and all too hard to, ah, wink up again."

"Oh, they're clever devils," Brinton said.

"They are. Of course, word has gradually spread among those with what we might call a right to know. Chairmen of large companies rub shoulders with chief constables at a variety of public and private functions. Discreet chats take place. Concern is expressed; warnings are passed along the line to those who, being on the spot, are most likely to notice any deviation from routine procedures." Delphick's tone became one of moderate frustration. "Of course, by the time anyone has pointed out the risks that might be being run, it is too late. The fraudsters have come—and gone, vanishing without trace."

"To gloat a bit and slap a fresh coat of paint on the van," muttered Brinton, "and start up their tricks all over again somewhere else. So how exactly do they work it?"

"As I explained, they put nothing in writing. It seems they offer a verbal quotation for the cost of the complete job, and once it is completed they insist that the quoted price was per square foot, not per square yard as the householder believed." Delphick paused to allow assimilation of this nine-times-the-original-cost formula. "While," he went on after the pause, "their accounting methods may leave something to be desired, there is no doubting the efficiency of their intimidation techniques as practised on anyone who tries to argue with them."

Brinton whistled. "But even a footpath will be several square yards—a driveway can run into dozens!" He glanced across at the equally shocked Buckland. "And blokes who do manual work have to be tough specimens. The old folk aren't going to argue with 'em. Something big, I said—and big it is—in more ways than one."

"It is," said Delphick. "Big enough, perhaps, for other people to jump on the same bandwagon—or, as it still might be, for the same people to risk the same trick in more or less the same area after the passage of a few months. We don't know for sure, but there are indications that this is what's started to happen. Assuming it is, we have absolutely no idea how or why they decide to take that risk . . ."

"But it seems," said Brinton, "they've been taking it here. On my patch. And I don't like it, Oracle. I don't like it one little bit. I'd like to collar the blighters and throw the book at them, and you can't give me any idea where to start . . ."

"Keep an eye open for strangers," said Delphick.

"Good evening," said Miss Seeton as she emerged from the vicarage front garden. "I am so sorry." Afternoon tea with the Reverend Arthur Treeves and his sister had been a pleasant affair, although the dear vicar was still convalescent after his shocking cold and growing a little tired towards the end, when she had of course excused herself and taken her leave. Colds always seemed to go to his chest, poor man. One had from time to time wondered whether the deep breathing techniques practised in yoga might be beneficial for weak lungs, but to suggest it might be seen as interfering, which one tried never to do. Or (even worse), it might be seen as a slight on the care all Plummergen knew Molly Treeves took of her brother, such as the way she was at present trying to encourage his lost appetite by inviting a different friend to tea every day of the week, when the vicar would (according to Miss Treeves) be obliged, as host, to do rather more than peck at his food, which until now was all he had been doing (again according to his sister). Miss Seeton was flattered to be considered a friend of such standing that the true motive behind the invitation would not be suspected. The vicar was notoriously ill-at-ease with strangers. Some people, after an acquaintance of seven years, might consider shyness with regard to Miss Seeton an affectation on his part, but Miss Seeton (like Molly Treeves) knew that it was not, as well as knowing that a convalescent should, as far as possible, be humoured. Which she, the invited guest, had done her best to do.

Strangers. "I am so sorry . . ." Miss Seeton nodded and (unseen in the twilight) blushed her apology as she greeted the beautiful girl into whom she had, turning to latch the vicarage gate with her umbrella swinging from her free arm, almost bumped. It was only good manners to make a stranger feel welcome . . . although somehow one had the feeling that she was not. A stranger, that was to say. The way she held herself; those eyes, those bones were unmistakable, even if—Miss Seeton shook her head—one could not quite remember where . . . But there was surely something about the tilt and carriage of her head on that slender neck, the grace of her movements . . .

"H-hello," said the beautiful girl. "I'm . . . sorry to have—I mean, it was my fault, really. I . . . wasn't looking where I was going."

"Both of us," said Miss Seeton absently as she continued to gaze at what she could see of the girl's loveliness—of which, she was sure, she had seen more on a previous, better-lit occasion. "And in the dusk," she went on, trying to remember, "it is perhaps not so easy to judge—especially moving backwards, when I should have been looking over my shoulder—so careless—one's mind on other things—his chest, you know, and the breathing—and tempting his appetite, poor man—"

"What? Oh! How could you be so cruel?" And the lovely girl burst into tears.

Dismay descended upon Miss Seeton. It had been, or so she'd thought, only a slight bump—some loss of balance, a stumbled step . . . but (one had to admit) easy, in the gloaming, to misjudge the effect. But . . . cruel? The young, of course, were often given to exaggeration—and yet . . . And, to be fair, with the lovely stranger (if stranger indeed she was: there remained that tantalising hint of memory) not knowing, perhaps, where exactly she might be in relation to anywhere else; not appreciating the difference between a careless bump and—however unlikely, in Plummergen—a deliberate attack . . .

"Shock," decided Miss Seeton as the girl, with her face

buried in her pale, shapely hands, tried to stifle her sobs and could not. If anything, they were growing more wild. One recalled such incidents from school. Gentle firmness and, where possible, a glass of water should be administered.

Or . . .

"Sugar," murmured Miss Seeton, whose preference was for weak tea without rather than strong tea with. The girl uttered a bubbling little cry and sobbed even harder. Miss Seeton found herself clearing her throat in sympathy before delivering a breathless admonishment.

"Come now—this is hardly the time or the place, my dear—so many houses nearby, although fortunately there is no traffic just at present—and you don't wish to make an exhibition of yourself, do you?"

"An exhibition? Oh!" cried the girl, bubbling still more and showing no sign of stopping. Miss Seeton regarded her anxiously. Deaf to entreaty she might be, and creating what even in charity one would have to call a scene, but one couldn't leave the poor child to sob out her heart on the corner of The Street, where—yes, curtains were already twitching in one or two houses—everyone could see. So undignified; so embarrassing to look back on later when the paroxysm of grief had passed, as in time it would, although one accepted that the young could never understand this and tried not to be too impatient with them. Their feelings were always so . . . immediate. Intense. One might almost say, in some respects at least, unbalanced. Miss Seeton, who had never been anything other than serenely balanced on life's emotional scale throughout her entire six decades and a half, found herself sighing. Romeo and Juliet, of course, who were even younger; Carmen and Don José, whose behaviour—either of them—had been hardly discreet. But all of them foreign. And the climate warmer, which in January in England was really no excuse at all.

"You must try to stop," said Miss Seeton, audibly more stern than sympathetic. "All these tears can't be good for you—why, I don't suppose you have a proper handkerchief, have you? Paper ones are far from practical when they are wet as opposed to merely damp."

"What? Oh!" After a startled moment or two in which she digested this sage advice, the girl had muted her sobs to a bubble which, Miss Seeton realised with relief, held more of burgeoning mirth than of misery. "Handkerchief," said the girl in a quavering voice and lowered her hands from her face to thrust them into the pockets of her overcoat. "Oh . . ."

"Now that's quite enough," said Miss Seeton sharply. Too sharply? "What you need—my dear—is a nice cup of tea. And a biscuit or two, perhaps, or a slice of cake."

"Oh . . ." said the girl, quavering again, this time once more like tears than laughter. Her hands fluttered out of her pockets and described agitated shapes in the air.

Miss Seeton had no intention of allowing the situation to develop, as she suspected it might, into a full-blown scene. There had been far too much of that sort of nonsense in her life of late. She frowned. There was that elusive memory again . . . "If," she said quickly, "you would care to come home with me," she invited, flourishing her brolly towards Sweetbriars across the road, "you would be most welcome. It is the least I can do in recompense for having . . . disturbed you as I did."

"No," said the girl, "it wasn't you—your fault—you mustn't think that—it was . . ." She gulped. Her fluttering hands fell to her sides. Her shoulders drooped; in her pale face, her eyes were dark pools of raw, burning emotion. Miss Seeton, ducking her head, took an automatic step backwards. One was uncomfortably reminded of—

"Kristeena!" she cried, remembering. She looked up

into those burning pools in their unmistakable, wonderfully sculpted sockets. "Of course!"

And the eyes of Antony Scarlett's one-time model opened wide in her pale, beautiful face.

"Yes," whispered the girl as she warmed her chilled hands around one of Miss Seeton's best bone china cups. "I'm— I was—Kristeena." She took a deep breath. "Tina Holloway. But . . . how did you know? I thought—he said—I'd changed so much, and . . ."

Miss Seeton blinked. "If you will forgive the impertinence of a personal remark, I could explain, although really I would have thought it obvious."

Tina's answering smile was shaky, as if she had almost forgotten how to express any feeling except grief. "Not to me," she said sadly. "Besides, I've heard personal remarks for most of my working life . . ." She gulped. Miss Seeton, fearing another bout of hysteria, uttered a gently warning cough. Tina shivered; stifled a sob; tried to speak calmly. "More—personal—*personal* than ever—in . . . the past few months." She drew a deep breath, looked up to meet Miss Seeton's approving eye, and essayed another smile, which came more easily than the first. "But I . . . can't imagine you would say anything . . . unforgivable, Miss Seeton."

Miss Seeton chose to ignore the bitter note creeping into the young woman's voice and replied to her original question. "Well, my dear, you may be slimmer, if you will excuse me, in the face and body than when you were modelling for Mr. Scarlett, but the basic structure and shape of bones does not change. The skull, feet, and hands in particular—your eye sockets, the set of your ears and nose, your jaw—and most of all your hair. Quite unmistakable, even from seeing only reproductions in the art pages. And so much press coverage last summer . . ."

With a horrified blush, she realised what she had been

about to say, what unhappy memories she had been on the point of reviving. She saw tears well up, despite a clear effort to suppress them, in Tina's anguished eyes. "Have some more tea," she offered to cover her embarrassment. "Or a biscuit—some cake—"

"Oh!" The offer was too much for her guest. Tina's cup, which she had barely tasted, was pushed to one side so that she could once more bury her face in her hands.

"You mustn't start crying again," said Miss Seeton, more embarrassed than ever and amazed at her own severity. Of course, one had never been able to view self-indulgence with approval, even in children so young they could not reasonably be expected to understand the importance of willpower and, well, moderation. One simply hoped to teach by example, or hope that others would already have done so. Parents, for instance. And Kristeena Holloway was no child—in years, that was to say, although in her behaviour . . . Yet she was clearly very distressed, and to scold her for something over which she might indeed have no control might be . . .

"Now, don't cry," urged Miss Seeton, gently scolding. "It serves little purpose—on the whole," honesty made her add, whereupon practicality appended: "Besides, your tea will grow cold. Let me top it up for you before it does." She suited the action to the word, wisely ignoring the glint of Tina's tearful eyes peeping in astonishment from between her fingers. So great was the astonishment that she had, indeed, almost stopped crying.

Miss Seeton nodded as she replaced the tea-cosy on the pot, the pot on its stand. Then she sighed. Advice, no matter how well-intentioned, could so often be seen by the one to whom it was offered as interference that one did one's best not to volunteer it. There were, however, times . . . "Perhaps," she ventured, "you might feel better about whatever distresses you if you could only . . . think about it." Oh, dear. Did that sound too blunt? Discourteous? Opinionated? "I think." She coughed. "Calmly and quietly." She coughed again. "Face up to the problem, I mean, instead of . . ."

"Running away?" Tina Holloway's hands dropped from her face into her lap. That porcelain skin covering those finely moulded cheekbones was stained with tears, yet even tears could not detract from her beauty. "You're . . . right," said Tina with a sigh. "I'm a miserable coward, though you were kind enough not to spell it out." Miss Seeton attempted a shocked apology and was waved down. "I'm not—I haven't been—calm," Tina said, straightening her bowed shoulders and looking Miss Seeton squarely in the eye. "Or quiet." Her lips twisted in a grimace of wry self-knowledge. "I've been . . . making a fuss. Running all the time these past few months—only this time I was . . . trying to fool myself that I was running *to*. Not away," she enlarged as she saw Miss Seeton's puzzled frown. "I thought," she said, "that I was . . . making a choice. Being decisive in coming here—and now I see that I—that it—wasn't."

"But you are," said Miss Seeton, still puzzled, grasping at the one coherent thought in all this. "Here, I mean. In Plummergen." Rapidly she considered England's geography and place names. "Unless . . . did you make a mistake and wish to be somewhere else? Plumstead, perhaps, in Norfolk?" The girl's lovely grey eyes opened wide as she stared. Miss Seeton rebuked herself for so foolish a suggestion. The far side of London did seem unlikely. "Plumpton?" she offered. "In Sussex, you know—our neighbouring county. It's near Brighton, I believe. Or—"

She broke off. Tina had leaned forward to lift her despised cup from the table, and she now raised it high in a toast. "B-Brighton? Miss Seeton, you're wonderful!" Her voice barely quavered; her hands did not flutter as those lovely grey eyes glowed at her elderly hostess across the teacup, and she drank to the celebrated home of the naughty weekend. "Wonderful!" she repeated, setting down the cup and, arching her delicate brows to ask Miss Seeton's permission, reaching—with only a little hesitation—for a thick slice of rich fruitcake. "Thank you." She took a deep breath, then laughed. "Brighton . . . Oh, you've done me more good in just a few minutes than"—the quaver was slight and soon suppressed—"than anyone else in ages," she finished and took a mouthful of cake. Slowly she smiled as she began to eat.

Miss Seeton smiled, too. Such impassioned thanks—for what, she wasn't entirely sure; an invitation to tea had been the least, in the circumstances, she could do—seemed somewhat excessive. The young, of course. But it was a pleasure—she smiled again—to see how quickly the child had recovered from her little upset; gentle firmness and a dose of common sense had, thank goodness, worked as they usually did. And it was such a relief that she was now behaving like a sensible, rational adult that her hostess had no cause to believe that she, well, wasn't. Apart, that was to say, from such a fulsome tribute to oneself—due, no doubt, to the artistic temperament, which after the years of modelling was probably, well, inevitable. "Catching," murmured Miss Seeton as she helped herself to a chocolate biscuit and pushed the plate closer to her guest.

With a convulsive gulp, Tina swallowed her last bite of cake. She stared at the biscuit plate. Her voice was low, with no hint of laughter, as after a moment she responded to Miss Seeton's remark. "Yes . . . you're right. I'm afraid I—I did come to Plummergen hoping to . . . catch him." She looked up and met Miss Seeton's kindly, if perplexed, gaze. "I suppose you'd say it was . . . wrong to come chasing after him like that, but—I've—been—so . . . miserable . . ."

"Now, don't cry again," begged Miss Seeton, once more dreading the worst. Tina shuddered, swallowing with the effort of keeping back the tears that were never far away. She reached out blindly for her empty cup, which clattered on its saucer and almost fell off.

"Oh," cried Miss Seeton instinctively, "do be careful! Cousin Flora's very best bone china!"

Tina froze. She stared at Miss Seeton. "That's what he said," she exclaimed. "Nothing but—but skin and bone!" Within the anguished depths of the grey eyes a black fire smouldered as she suddenly unburdened herself to this sympathetic audience. "Skin and bone, he told me, and I was no—no use to him anymore if I couldn't get my appetite back and put on all the weight I lost, because whoever heard of Rubens painting anyone—anyone *thin*?"

Her voice broke on the final word. Miss Seeton, hoping to deflect the threatened bout of hysteria, began: "As I recall, Rubens—"

Tina ignored her. "Skin and bone, he said, as if it was all my fault—and it's not fair, Miss Seeton, because it wasn't! And I *never* blamed him, no matter what anyone else might have said—those wretched newspapers—it was the gallery; they should have maintained the air conditioning properly—but of course he wasn't going to start arguing with people who . . . mattered to his career, was he? People who could help him, people with influence—but I understood, I kept telling him I did—I knew he was angry, that he needed to let off steam, and I didn't blame him, truly, when he was so—so difficult to live with, but it was *cruel* of him to keep on and on at me about calories when he knew how—how ill I'd been, how I simply couldn't face the *idea* of food, never mind eating it . . ."

The chocolate biscuit she had picked up without noticing now dropped from her tortured fingers back to the plate. It landed with a rattle Miss Seeton thought it wiser, in the

face of so much raw emotion, to ignore. "I hate chocolate," whispered Tina. "I never did . . . before. I used to
eat it by the ton . . . He encouraged me, you see. He'd buy
those jumbo slabs, and the biggest boxes . . . Now he uses
chocolate all the time, twisting the knife in the wound . . ."

A queer little groan escaped her pale lips, almost as if a
macabre laugh were being stifled. Miss Seeton shot her a
quick, startled glance. She had recalled that sad saucer of
white melted manhood next to the moulding of Antony
Scarlett's nude body at the Galerie Genèvre. Surely—the
poor child was upset, anyone could see that, but surely she
could never have been so—so bitterly destructive?

Or could she? She was blushing now under Miss Seeton's shrewd gaze, her hands writhing together on her
lap . . .

"Twisting the knife," poor Tina said in a trembling
voice. She gulped. She licked her lips and took a deep
breath. Miss Seeton thought it best to say nothing.

So, it seemed, did Tina. "Reminding me," she at last
went on, "that I'm no use. No good. I can't bring myself
even to try working for anyone else—I still need him the
way I thought—thought he needed me, Miss Seeton—and
he doesn't! He . . . he's changed—and so have I—but he
. . . can live with himself now. And I . . . can't."

Miss Seeton regarded her gravely. Guilty conscience or
not—the damage (whoever had done it) had disturbed Antony Scarlett far less than this child's wretchedness evidently disturbed herself—was Tina threatening to do away
with herself if Scarlett refused to take her back? That booming, bullying presence: so unsuitable for a sensitive young
woman, one would have supposed, although there was no
accounting for taste. And she was . . . well, young. Older
than Juliet, of course, but obviously just as susceptible as
the Italian teenager to extravagant behaviour when her feel-

ings were involved. "I don't see why not," said Miss Seeton.

Tina, the risk of confession passed, preparing for further flight into the emotional stratosphere, felt the sudden reverse-thrusting slam of common sense. "Why . . . not?" was all she could say as Miss Seeton's grave regard was tinged with a hint of impatience.

"You are," Miss Seeton told her crisply, "a young woman of striking good looks in, as far as I can tell, the best of health. While there is nothing whatsoever wrong in being large if that is what nature intended," said Miss Seeton, seven-stone-nothing and five feet tall in her stockinged feet, "clearly, in your case, it did not. Your bones," she explained, as Tina could only stare. "Puppy-fat may be one thing, but for a grown woman to—to gorge herself on chocolate just because it would suit the convenience of someone else to have her weigh more than she sensibly should is, if you will excuse my saying so, ridiculous." She drew a deep, indignant breath. "As artists can . . . outgrow their models, my dear, and move on, so can a model move on to another artist more congenial, as it were, to herself. Her *true* self," stressed Miss Seeton, mistress of the truthful vision. "Not the self somebody else thinks she ought to be." She paused. Tina continued to stare. Miss Seeton blushed. Had she, yet again, been too . . . opinionated? "I think," she concluded. "If you don't mind my saying so."

There was a longer pause.

"No," said Tina slowly. The grey eyes gleamed for a moment longer with that bleak, black fire, then dulled into a sudden serenity. "No, I don't mind." She drew herself up, and when she spoke her voice hardly trembled. "I don't mind. I . . . think so, too, Miss Seeton."

She reached out a second time for the chocolate biscuit and took a large, defiant bite.

CHAPTER 12

Brinton, yawning, was studying a pile of reports on last night's break-in at the biscuit factory when his telephone rang. "Brettenden," he said into the receiver, stifling another yawn.

"Ah." The voice on the other end of the line hesitated. "Do I gather," came the well-known accents of Chief Superintendent Delphick, "that there has been nocturnal skulduggery in the wider regions of your empire?"

"Oracle." Brinton rubbed his eyes. "Sorry, I was half asleep. Yes, you're right—but I take it you aren't ringing to commiserate with me and my troubles. What's up?"

Delphick's voice became grave. "You, too, are right. I'm not—in fact, I may be adding to them. After we spoke about your pauper pensioners and the asphalt fraud, I passed the word around the various divisions to find out how many similar cases might have occurred without necessarily being correlated, as it were, by our basement computer."

"And now you've got some answers," said Brinton.

"Results rather than answers, perhaps, although there are inferences to be drawn from which answers might reasonably be deduced.'' The Oracle sighed. ''Inference or not, the facts are that there has been a noticeable increase around the southeast of England—including your area, of course—in the numbers of undernourished old people being admitted to nursing homes and to long-stay hospital care.''

''And nobody's saying why,'' suggested Brinton as Delphick paused. ''Or . . . are they?''

''No, they aren't, for the same reasons you yourself have found. The entrants, if we may so describe them, are all salt-of-the-earth noncomplainers: decaying gentry, retired professionals, solid artisans and craftsmen. All of them owner-occupiers with depleted savings, although their mortgages are more or less paid off, and their property is— or rather was—their own.''

''And not a council-house tenant on the list,'' offered Brinton at once.

''Not one.'' Delphick sounded pleased that Ashford had evidently reached the same conclusion as had Scotland Yard. ''I'm reluctant to call it conclusive, but we have a definite pattern, Chris. Town councils, of course, are responsible for structural repairs to property under their control: and responsible to the ratepayers for the cost of said repairs.''

''Speaking as a ratepayer,'' returned Brinton on cue, ''I wouldn't be too happy if I thought the local mandarins were wasting my hard-earned cash paying a load of cowboys to do shoddy work that needed more repairs five minutes after the blighters had disappeared with a sizeable cheque in their hot little hands.''

''Councils,'' agreed Delphick, ''have more clout than the private individual. They can demand greater safeguards and pursue more vigorous enquiries than the man or woman in the street. It must be more trouble than the fraudsters would think worth the effort to achieve collusion on an unimaginable scale with numerous Clerks of the Works and similar public officials.''

Brinton grunted. ''Makes sense. They're cunning devils, as I think I've mentioned before. They'll go for the easy money every time—and they've got to be stopped, Oracle. Easy come, easy go—and they start to feel that way about other things, too.''

''Such as the sanctity of human life,'' said Delphick as his friend fell silent, brooding.

''I don't want another Philippa Byng on my patch,'' Brinton said. ''On anybody's patch, come to that. I don't want any more Addie Addisons terrified out of their wits when a bloke with muscles knocks at the front door. What I *do* want is this asphalt gang, Oracle, though I'm damned if I can see how to find 'em—and,'' he continued as Delphick coughed, ''don't say a word! I know just what you're thinking, and I won't say I haven't thought it, too, on and off. But in a funny kind of way I'm fond of the old girl. I wouldn't want her on my conscience if anything . . . went wrong. I had to get shirty with young Foxon for trying to drag her in even on the edge of all this. They're a nasty bunch, and she's not getting any younger.''

''Miss Seeton bears a charmed life,'' Delphick reminded him. ''I'm sure she would, in a good cause, be prepared to take the risk—''

''But I'm not. Having her . . . fall into adventures the way she does is one thing, but deliberately setting her up as bait for a crowd like this is something else. Her front garden's about six inches long. The most desperate crook couldn't hope to convince her she ought to have asphalt on that path—and if you think I'm borrowing a house and popping her in it for an indefinite period, think again. They all know one another's business in Plummergen, especially Miss Seeton's. Put her in a strange place—even if she'd go, which I doubt if she'd be happy about for long, and she's no actress so she'd probably give the game away the minute the gang arrived—but if she went, how could we possibly keep an eye on her? Potter covers half a dozen villages besides Plummergen, remember. You can bet it'd be when he's somewhere else they'd turn up, and she's had too many close shaves in the past for me not to know there's got to be a time when her luck runs out. We've got to think of some other way. Can't you talk to the computer again?''

To which plea the Oracle responded with a promise to do what he could when the basement monster would permit.

Lady Colveden sat brushing her hair before the bedroom looking glass, relishing the slow luxury of pure bristle on her scalp. It was the first time for several days that she had done more than run a quick comb through her thick, wavy brown locks: the Reverend Arthur Treeves was not the sole inhabitant of Plummergen to have succumbed to a nasty cold. Her ladyship had been confined to barracks by her husband and son while she took aspirin and afternoon naps until she thought herself on the mend. One hundred strokes before bedtime had been the nursery routine that only this evening she had felt able to resume.

After she had settled into the familiar rhythm she allowed her gaze to focus beyond her own palely convalescent image to that of her husband, propped against a mound of pillows with his nose buried deep in *Under Drake's Flag*. It seemed a shame, in a way, to disturb him, but . . .

She coughed and said, ''George.''

Major-General Sir George Colveden (baronet, Knight Commander of the Bath, holder of the Distinguished Service Order, Justice of the Peace) turned a page. He and his friend Admiral Leighton shared a devotion, nurtured in boyhood, to the works of G. A. Henty. Secondhand shops and jumble sales occasionally provided Meg Colveden with another volume for her husband's still-growing collection: the complete set he would have loved as a child had failed to materialise in those far-off days. When a chance remark advised the Buzzard that the general had acquired *In Freedom's Cause* for Christmas, the naval proposed to the military man a short-term exchange for their mutual edification and delight. No doubt the ginger beard was at this moment bristling with just such excitement as did the toothbrush moustache.

But . . . "George, do listen." Her ladyship, having reached one hundred strokes, tripped in her slippered feet lightly across the floor and climbed into bed beside one who barely noticed her presence, so thrilling were the adventures of Sir Francis and his crew.

"George," said Lady Colveden, this third time waiting until the end of a chapter. Sir George, with a grunt, looked at her vaguely from a distance of four centuries. "George, have you noticed anything about Nigel over the past few days?"

"Nigel?" The baronet blinked at the wardrobe, as if expecting to see the form of his son and heir materialising from behind its mahogany bulk. "What about him?"

"I think he's met a girl." Sir George blinked again. "You know what he's like when he has," enlarged her ladyship. After a moment, Sir George nodded. Nigel in love—a state into which young Galahad Colveden was all too prone to tumble upon the slightest provocation—exuded an air of suppressed distraction by which nobody who knew him well was fooled for long.

"Can't say I've noticed," said Sir George as his wife, cuddled under the eiderdown, waited. "Mind's been on other things," he said, as if she hadn't known. "Blasted weather, for one. If the ground doesn't dry out soon—"

"George, please. I have enough ploughing at mealtimes,

and if I hear the word 'hedging' once more I shall scream.''
Ten dainty aristocratic toes kicked at the eiderdown and let
in a blast of cold, emphatic air. ''You and Nigel do nothing
but moan about the weather—or rather, *you* do.'' Her ladyship smiled. ''That's what first made me wonder, because
Nigel hasn't moaned half as much as you since the night
of the darts match.''

''Darts?'' The baronet frowned, then grinned. ''Cupid,
you mean. Well, high time the boy settled down. Make him
a full-blown partner. Save buying spoons.''

Lady Colveden sighed and ignored this ingenious suggestion. ''No, not Cupid. The match at the George, when
Murreystone were such bad losers and Constable Potter had
to phone for reinforcements. I think he met her there.''

''Potter?'' Sir George, whose preferred pub game was
dominoes, had drifted most of the way back to Drake. ''Respectable married man. Can't see Ned Potter, of all people,
carrying on with a Murreystone girl. Nobody else from
Plummergen either, come to that.''

Lady Colveden let out an exasperated little cry. It was
true that PC Potter (husband to Mabel, father of Amelia)
was as unlikely a target for illicit passion as Nigel was
likely for the licit; it was likewise true that no Plummergen
male who valued village tradition would ever court a Murreystone maid. The legendary feud had been in full docu-
mented swing by the time of the Civil War, was believed
to have flourished during the Wars of the Roses, and was
thought to date from the ninth-century invasion of Romney
Marsh by marauding Danes, when Murreystone (claimed
Plummergen) had refused to go to the aid of Plummergen
five miles away—or, as Murreystone still insisted, when
Plummergen had made such refusal.

It was true: but it hadn't been what she'd meant. She
thought. ''George,'' exclaimed Lady Colveden, popping up

from under the quilt, "you don't think *that's* why he hasn't told us about her?"

"Who?" enquired Sir George absently as he turned another page. "What?"

"Nigel!" cried his wife, then winced in case her cry had reached beyond the bedroom wall to the ears of her sleeping son. "Nigel," she repeated quietly, wrapping the eiderdown around her shoulders. "No, somebody would have told us if he had. Besides, I'm sure he never would," she reasoned, nestling into the pillows for reassurance. "He'd know it wouldn't work ... unless both of them moved away from here." She stifled a yawn. Sir George took no notice. "Post Restante for letters," she went on dreamily. "An ex-directory telephone number ... an assumed name ..."

"Name?" As his wife fell asleep, Sir George woke up. "Tina ... Something." He continued to take no notice as her ladyship's eyes flew open. "Pretty girl. Red hair. Staying at the George: hasn't been too good recently."

Lady Colveden experienced the conflicting emotions of irritation that her spouse had apparently known all along and hadn't told her and concern for the welfare of her only son. "She's been ill?"

"Run down, they tell me." Sir George huffed through his moustache. "No surprise, living in London. Do her good to have some fresh air and honest rations." He turned to twinkle at the startled face on the pillow beside him. "Bit too thin for my taste, of course."

The implied compliment was ignored. "Do you mean you've actually met her? And never told me? Honestly, George."

"Not our business, m'dear. If Nigel wants us to meet, he'll arrange it. Friend of Miss Seeton's," he added as her ladyship shook her head for this masculine obtuseness. "Bumped into them on the canal bridge, sketching. Girl's a model.'' He strained to recall exactly what aesthetic composition Miss Seeton had been attempting to describe. ''Wrong time of year, she said. No flowers.'' He frowned. ''Tina . . . Miller? Doesn't sound right—though she did say the hair was perfect.''

''Oh, George, I wish you'd paid more attention. Flowers? And what has her name to do with her hair? But never mind,'' said her ladyship happily, sinking back under the bedclothes with a smug look on her expressive countenance. ''I really ought to call on Miss Seeton to thank her for sending such kind messages while my cold was so bad and for letting Martha change her day to help in the house. I'm not infectious any longer, and think how rude she'd think me if she saw me drive past tomorrow without stopping . . .''

Five minutes later, Sir George finished another chapter. ''Never do to be rude,'' he agreed with another twinkle; but Lady Colveden was fast asleep, her lips curved in a smile.

''An attempt—and I fear a poor one—at something in the spirit of Millais,'' explained Miss Seeton, blushing for her artistic presumption as she modestly displayed (the hostess will always follow her guest's conversational lead) the most recent pages of her sketchbook. ''Ophelia, you know, except that I thought *before* she drowned—reaching out to hang her flower garlands on the overhanging branch, except of course that there is no tree. But far safer to balance on the bridge than on the bank, with the grass so very slippery after all the rain. And her hair is quite beautiful—as, indeed, is she.''

''So George says,'' said Lady Colveden, adding ingenuously: ''And I gather Nigel thinks so, too, though he's hardly said a word to us, of course. She sounds a nice girl. Do you think she would be offended if I invited her to tea one afternoon before she goes back to Town?''

''I think,'' said Miss Seeton after a moment, ''she would be delighted.'' How much could she say without being thought interfering; without betraying a confidence? ''But perhaps, plain rather than chocolate biscuits and fruitcake,'' she said, ''if I may make the suggestion. She has no plans to return to London just yet, as far as I know—though there is, of course, no reason why she should inform me of such plans—but chocolate is not one of her favourites, I do know that.''

Tina had come on wonderfully since her first encounter with Miss Seeton's crisp common sense, though the cure was not yet complete. She no longer drooped, but held herself erect as she walked and risked the occasional smile when hailed by passing Plummergenites as she waited at the bus stop. The Murreystone darts match had been a turning point. Charley Mountfitchet, fearing disturbance to his guests, had warned both Miss Holloway and Mrs. Ogden that if they wished to dine off trays in private, he would be happy to arrange room service to suit their convenience, provided they didn't leave it until too late to tell him. Mrs. Ogden, thanking him with a laugh, had soon settled for sandwiches at the bar. Speaking, she said, for herself, she found things a little on the quiet side, even for somebody close to retirement age. She had always been one to enjoy a bit of liveliness once in a while.

Tina, faced with the same choice, had hesitated. A meal in her room, away from watchful eyes guessing how much, or how little, she ate, was very tempting . . .

''You'd be putting us to no trouble,'' Charley assured her, thinking her hesitation due to courtesy. ''It's what we're here for—and we grudge no extras for any friend of Miss Seeton's, o' course.''

Miss Seeton's new friend blushed and remembered the gentle scolding of her mentor. ''I'll . . . eat downstairs, thank you,'' she said, and felt that she had overcome another obstacle on the road to recovery.

It was inevitable that Tina's path should cross that of Nigel Colveden, she being a beautiful young woman and he an always susceptible young man. Tina was leaving the dining room to take a final stroll before retiring upstairs to contemplate the events of the day: Nigel was huddled with a few cronies by the reception desk, discussing where no Murreystone ears could eavesdrop Plummergen's last-minute tactics and strategy. Tina's glorious hair gleamed richly gold in the light of the chandelier; Nigel caught his breath. Their eyes met . . .

It was inevitable that Nigel, driving to Brettenden the next day and seeing one of the George's guests at the bus stop, should offer her a lift. The guest to whom he was so quick to make this offer was not—although they had met and chatted in the public bar the previous night—Mrs. Ogden . . .

''I believe he took her out to dinner the day before yesterday,'' Lady Colveden told Miss Seeton over the teacups. ''He tried to give us the impression it was an ordinary Young Farmers' night, but you know what Nigel's like when there's a girl involved.'' Miss Seeton, smiling, nodded without speaking. Could there be anyone in Plummergen ignorant of Nigel's lovelorn likeness? ''With my cold,'' said her ladyship, ''I suppose I haven't been paying as much attention as I ought, although as George says, Nigel is old enough to know his own business.'' She sighed. ''And I'm a nagging, nosy mother to want to know—oh, it's kind of you to disagree,'' she added as Miss Seeton uttered a muted protest, ''but I am, really.'' She giggled, then sighed. ''I can't help wondering if it's more serious than usual. You know how George always teases the poor boy whenever a new girlfriend appears on the scene.'' Miss Seeton achieved another silent, smiling nod. ''Well, unless

it's been out of deference to my convalescent nerves and I
haven't heard him, I don't believe he's said a word. Don't
you think that must mean something?''

Miss Seeton, who had little personal experience of matters of the heart, ventured the opinion that it might: or,
again, it might not. Sir George, she understood, had been
much preoccupied of late with the weather. (Lady Colveden
emitted a groan and told Miss Seeton that she could say
that again.) The normal family pleasantries (continued Miss
Seeton with a reciprocating twinkle) could well seem out
of place at such a . . . such an anxious time.

''You mean he won't start teasing until the sun shines?
I'd never thought of that, but of course you could well be
right.'' Lady Colveden reached out to help herself to a slice
of Battenburg, then quickly drew back. ''Oh, dear—my
waistline. George will be furious if I have to buy any more
clothes . . .'' Her lovely eyes, mischievously glowing, met
those of Miss Seeton. ''Except for special occasions, that
is. Do you suppose it would be tempting fate if I started
planning my wardrobe?''

Miss Seeton poured them both another cup of tea while
she considered the matter. ''A new hat,'' she suggested
after a moment, ''might perhaps be an acceptable compro-
mise . . .''

Whereupon the tea party chatter became a paean of
praise to the millinery skills of Miss Monica Mary Brown
(of the celebrated Brettenden hat shop) and moved on to a
discussion of the relative merits of May (silage-making),
June (ditto hay) or July (harvesting of various vegetables)
for the wedding of a farmer's son.

CHAPTER 13

Tina Holloway admired with the eye of an aesthete the display in Monica Mary's window. However strongly tempted, she did not fall. She had come to Brettenden to buy not a hat but sketching gear to add to the little she had summoned up enough energy to bring with her from London. Miss Seeton's benign influence still held: the girl's spirits were improving by the day, her confidence growing. A few days spent sightseeing—one morning in the company of a delighted Nigel Colveden, the rest of the time bus-hopping by herself—had proved the final (and best) spur Tina could have wished to start work, for once entirely on her own account rather than being, as she'd been for most of her working life, dependent on the patronage of others. She had always suspected that she might be able to draw, if not paint, as well as any of the artists she had met. She'd had plenty of time to think, as she posed hour after tedious, poorly paid hour, about . . . all sorts of things. About likely subjects for her own masterpieces—those masterpieces she could now see only her chronic lack of self-esteem had prevented her from trying to achieve . . .

Tina shook her head dismissively at a frivolous confection of vibrant pillar-box feathers curled about a mocha velvet base. Scarlet and chocolate. She felt it was . . . symbolic: and she would have none of it. Who, of those she had met, had done most to impress that lack of self-esteem upon her—had done so for what she now saw had been to suit his own egotistical purpose, with no thought at all for how it might suit Tina Holloway? Antony Scarlett . . . who had oh-so-persuasively smothered Tina (dainty butterfly Tina, barely escaped from the miserable chrysalis of adolescent puppy-fat) in layers of chocolate blubber and called her Christina—no, even her identity had been smothered out of existence. Kristeena, he'd told her it was better spelled, and she'd believed him, blinded by his glamour, by the aura of success he exuded, by the envy she saw in the eyes of other girls as he made his grand entrances with her on his arm—weighing him down. She saw that now, too. On how many of those envious girls had his roving eye lighted? How many silent messages had passed between the glamorous figure in the swirling black cloak and the slim young females with all the energy, vim, pep the once-more-overweight Tina—Kristeena—lacked?

But those days were gone—as was Tina's urgent desire to confront her Scarlett Svengali and either beg him to take her back, skinny—in his cruel phrase—as she now was, or attack him for destroying her creative soul. She was free for the first time in years. She could be . . . herself: the self she wanted to be. Slim, attractive Tina Holloway, an artist—as was Miss Emily Seeton—in her own right, with her own individual style.

Miss Seeton had given Tina more than encouragement and the first stirrings of confidence: she had also given her the address of the Brettenden art shop from which she bought much of her equipment. Coloured crayons, lead pencils, pastel and charcoal sticks, cartridge paper by the block or the individual sheet: Tina in her new, buoyant mood resolved to have nothing but the best—and (symbolism again) more of it than she needed. The money she had inadvertently saved over the past months by not eating more than she needed (despite Antony's frequent demands) had caused feelings of guilt whenever she saw a bank statement: but she would feel guilty no longer. She would spend her money now on what she, not another, wanted. She would start again. A new life was ahead of her. She was restless, eager to begin as she turned to walk away from the milliner's. Brettenden High Street, without knowing it, had just witnessed the ultimate rebirth of Tina Holloway begun in a Plummergen cottage . . .

Miss Molly Treeves and Miss Emily Seeton bumped into each other in the post office. As one bought stamps, her friend bought groceries; the first to complete her purchases waited for the second to join her in a companionable stroll back down The Street towards their separate homes.

"Definitely on the mend," said a beaming Miss Treeves, as—having listened with some sympathy to Molly's pungent opinion of the telephone engineers who were being so slow to correct a fault that had plagued south Plummergen for the better part of twenty-four hours—Miss Seeton made polite and tactful enquiry after the health of the Reverend Arthur, who had suffered a slight relapse. "He even asked for another egg this morning." Miss Treeves tapped the basket on her arm. "With Marmite soldiers instead of plain bread and butter, which he never feels like doing when he's really under the weather."

"That is excellent news," said Miss Seeton, fully appreciating the effort involved in dipping dainty fingers of bread into runny yolk rather than spooning it mouthful by tentative mouthful. Feeling a little guilty that the relapse might in part have been caused by her accepting of Molly's invitation to tea the other day, she added: "You must allow me to give the dear vicar some of mine, with my compliments. Brown eggs seem so much more cheerful than white, don't they?''

Molly chuckled. ''Don't tell Arthur, but the last time we ran out, I boiled white ones in weak tea. It works very well, provided the shells don't crack. Some people might not think so, but *I* think they taste almost as good—and then, if they don't, with a cold in his head he won't notice the difference—all in a good cause, you know.''

Miss Seeton wondered privately about the integrity of such a scheme, while admitting there was something to be said for subterfuge where serious loss of appetite was concerned. Loss of appetite? ''Why,'' she exclaimed, relieved at this coincidental chance to change the subject yet again, ''there she is!''

''Who?'' Molly, preparing to launch into a discussion of the relative merits of Hamburgh hens (white eggs), Anconas (cream) and Rhode Island Reds (brown), was confused by the unexpected interruption. ''Where? Oh,'' she said, following Miss Seeton's gaze and pointing umbrella to the blacksmith's forge diagonally across The Street. In the deep shadows cast by the double doors, a slim female form could just be seen. ''Your young artist friend, of course. She seems to be enjoying her stay in these parts, though I would have thought it on the quiet side for someone her age. She does a lot of sightseeing, I gather.''

''I believe so,'' agreed Miss Seeton. ''I know little of her plans—a chance acquaintance more than a close friend—but I know she has been taking the bus a good deal.''

''Seen her at the stop myself,'' said Miss Treeves, then coughed as the bus-taker turned from where, bent over her sketchpad, she leaned against the massive doorpost to wave her pencilled hand towards the approaching pair of amiable gossips.

Miss Seeton, discreetly pink, waved back. Miss Treeves, who had not been formally introduced, bowed and smiled in her character of The Vicar's Sister. Tina Holloway waved again, brandishing her sketchpad with evident pride. Miss Seeton, with swift understanding, made gestures of approval and congratulation with her free hand, then excused herself to Miss Treeves on the grounds that she believed her opinion might be being sought. Miss Treeves, knowing her friend's former occupation as a teacher of art, bowed again, nodded amiably to Tina, and continued to wend her way homewards as Miss Seeton crossed The Street.

"I haven't seen you for ages, Miss Seeton!" Miss Seeton stifled a gasp. This bright and lively girl was a far cry from the pale, sad, self-doubting guest of just a few days ago. "I've been having a marvellous time," Tina babbled as her elderly acquaintance drew near. "I did as you suggested and bought myself a fresh sketching kit"—Miss Seeton looked startled at the idea her casual words had been considered firm advice, but said nothing—"and I've been hopping on buses all over the place. I went to Rye—look . . ."

She leafed through her sketchbook until she reached the pages dedicated to half-timbered buildings in black and white, cobbled streets, and lobster pots. "What do you think of him?" she asked of a gnarled old man in a peaked cap, repairing nets by the quayside.

"The minimum of strokes," said Miss Seeton after a moment, "to the maximum effect. There is . . . life in this drawing, my dear. It's good."

"I'm glad you think so." A few days ago, Miss Seeton's slightest disapproval would have cast the young artist into the depths of despair: now her decided approval produced no more than a pleased smile from someone clearly confident of her own abilities. Tina was sharing her work with Miss Seeton as one artist to another, not as a nervous pupil begging for reassurance. She flipped to another page.

"Recognise him?"

"Naturally," said Miss Seeton with a twinkle. "Though I must confess my ignorance of exactly what he is doing."

"But you've known Nigel since you first came to live in Plummergen!" Tina was amazed that someone who had spent more than seven years in the country should be so ignorant of country pursuits: then she realised that her amazement might sound, well, insulting to the older woman who had been so kind to her. "He's, um, laying a hedge," she explained quickly. "Hawthorn." Miss Seeton, not in the least insulted, was all polite interest. Relieved, Tina went on: "You cut almost through the stems just above the ground, then bend them over and weave them in place with stakes and pegs. Nigel told me a properly laid hedge can last for years and only need trimming each winter to keep it tidy."

"With ditching," said Miss Seeton with a nod, remembering. "Yes, of course. They hold competitions sometimes."

Tina giggled. "Nigel told me about the last time a team from Murreystone entered." Miss Seeton recalled the report in the local paper and sighed. "I had no idea," said Tina with another giggle, "that life outside London could be so interesting. I really must visit Murreystone before much longer. Nigel says I need to widen my horizons."

"This," said Miss Seeton, one of nature's literalists, "is certainly the place for that. The marsh . . ."

"Oh, yes. I remember how you showed me from the bridge that you can practically see all the way to Dungeness and the coast, and it's—how far? Ten miles? Nigel's going to take me to the bird sanctuary there, he says."

It was news to Miss Seeton that Mr. Colveden had developed a taste for ornithology, but when there was a pretty girl in the case, his actions were seldom without purpose.

"Which will be very interesting," agreed Miss Seeton, herself no mean wielder of binoculars.

"And the power station, if he can spare the time." The lovely eyes gleamed. "They say you can go on guided tours, and it would fit in wonderfully with my plan—the British Workman, Miss Seeton. Honest toil, and so on." Tina opened her sketchbook to show the first swift lines depicting smith Daniel Eggleden hammering an iron bar. "And Nigel's friend from the garage . . ." She turned back a few pages. "What's his name? Jack something . . ."

Miss Seeton had no time to murmur "Crabbe" before another sketch was presented for inspection. "Nigel asked him," Tina said, "if he'd mind my watching him fix a car, and he said he didn't. What do you think?"

"Again, good." Miss Seeton smiled at the sight of Jack Crabbe with a spanner in one hand and some anonymous piece of motor vehicle engine in the other; and at an enormous pair of boots on the next page, shown protruding from underneath the chassis of a car. Boots and no more: but they clearly belonged to the invisible Jack. There was more than everyday talent there. "A series?" guessed Miss Seeton. "Your own exhibition, perhaps?"

Tina nodded. "When I'm ready—but I'm not going to rush it. I wondered at first, you know, whether I mightn't try for the Stuttaford Prize. Victorians were great ones for encouraging honest toil, weren't they? So it would be quite in the spirit of the founder, and if I could put something together before the end of the year . . . But then . . ." She became grave. "I saw that it would be . . . vindictive. I'm not saying I'd stand a chance of winning, any more than I think"—only the briefest hesitation—"Antony does, but I wouldn't normally enter anything like that because—well, I'm not sure art ought really to be competitive. You can't judge—oh, sculpture and painting on equal terms, can you?

It would be like asking someone to choose between lobster and ice cream.'' She did not hesitate to use this culinary simile; neither did she blush or look uneasy. It seemed that Tina's cure was complete.

''The terms and conditions, as I read them in the paper, did seem somewhat . . . imprecise,'' agreed Miss Seeton. ''No doubt those wishing to enter will be given more detailed information when they send for the entry form.''

''No doubt Antony has already done so.'' Tina's voice was not so much grave now as scornful. ''I knew there had to be some reason he kept rushing down here every five minutes, as all my so-called friends have been only too eager to tell me—but I don't know what it is, and I don't care.'' Miss Seeton, who both knew and cared, sighed, but said nothing. ''No more grudges,'' said Tina with resolution. ''I won't exactly forgive and forget, but I'm not . . . out for his blood any longer. If I met him in the street tomorrow, I would nod and smile and walk away. I've . . . outgrown all that, Miss Seeton.''

Miss Seeton regarded her thoughtfully. In the end, she smiled. ''Yes, my dear,'' she said slowly. ''I believe you have. Well done.''

And Tina, once more glowing, began to show her mentor the sketch she had made of a Brettenden road-sweeper leaning on his broom while his partner poured tea from a flask.

Gallery owner Genefer Watson, masterminding the publicity campaign of her latest protégé, had decreed that Antony Scarlett must give The People Who Mattered the best possible chance to acquaint themselves with his doings. The Neurotic Hermit had been last year's success: this year's was to be the Genius Extrovert. Antony's flamboyant garb and distinctive mannerisms of swirling cape and booming voice would be wasted if he went everywhere by car. She had toyed with the idea of making him ride a penny farthing, but decided that in London's traffic there was too great a risk of his cape catching in the spokes and tipping him into the path of a motor vehicle with faulty brakes: besides, Antony had little liking for physical exertion. It had not been for aesthetic reasons alone that he had required his model to resemble one who lived her life entirely between bed, board, and sofa rather than one who rose early, visited the swimming baths after breaking her fast on crispbread, and jogged the rest of the day away before dining on lettuce and spring water.

It had been with a delightful sense of creative inspiration that Genefer had instructed Antony in how to be Visible from one end of his journey to the other. He must walk to a bus stop two stages from his home and take none but a red double-decker to the nearest Tube station. Should the rush of air up the down escalator, or through the tunnels, cause his cloak to billow artistically in the face of a passer-by, so much the better: he must apologise at full volume and at length. Could he bring himself to kiss the hand of the victim (if female), better still. A nonsmoker, he must object forcefully should anyone light up in his presence. Should he decide to take even a small bag with him, he must ensure that he (a) found a porter to carry it and (b) tipped said porter with a bar of chocolate (what else?) as well as with coin of the realm. He must spurn any offer of a taxi at the other end and take the bus (regrettably green, but you couldn't have everything) from Brettenden to Plummergen . . .

It was the afternoon of market day when Antony arrived for what felt like the umpteenth time at Brettenden railway station. Truth to tell, he was growing weary of these trips down to Kent to talk Miss Seeton into changing her mind. Despite the repeated assurances of Miss Watson, he had a nasty feeling Miss Seeton wasn't going to change her mind. The more he saw of the woman (on those occasions when he caught her unawares), the more she reminded him—in character, if not in physique—of his Aunt Hilda, deceased this past decade but still a family byword for obstinacy (his female cousins) and sheer awful bloody-mindedness (male ditto). Miss Seeton made him feel uncomfortably as if he were a schoolboy again, not Antony Scarlett the rising young—though not so young as that—conceptual artist. While she had been surprised by his first visit, surprise (he suspected) had soon given way to polite irritation. There hovered about her still the distant air of chalk and sharp knuckle-rapping rulers by which he had been made so wretched at school. The nearest he'd got to making her pay him any serious attention had been when that brolly of hers had clumped him on the chin and almost laid him out; and she hadn't let him in the house since . . .

The house. Sweetbriars: the perfect site for "Briars Sweet," his sure-to-be prize-winning tribute to the eminence of Sir Andrew Stuttaford. But—perhaps, just perhaps—perfection was beyond his reach? And, if so, *could* he settle for second best? Antony hadn't admitted as much to Genefer, but there had been a recent damp and cloudy night when, doffing his distinctive cape, he had sneaked (by taxi) across suburban borders to a library where, unrecognised, he'd consulted a few files of large-scale Ordinance Survey maps for a similar-to-Sweetbriars configuration of canal, road, and dwelling. He had grown bored before long and sneaked home again, but there was at the back of his mind the feeling that he might possibly do as well to cut his losses and try somewhere—someone—else for his Ideal Location. Genefer might say that for True Art No Sacrifice Was Too Great, and it was certainly a good PR line, but Antony had his doubts that Miss Seeton would ever willingly play the PR game. There was always the risk she might make it look as if he'd been bullying her, which would do him no good at all with the signally philanthropic Stuttafords . . .

A gust of wind caught the folds of Antony's cape as he climbed into the waiting bus. For an instant, he froze with one foot on the step, one off. All heads—and, this being market day, there were many—turned to look, then turned hastily away. Plummergen feet shuffled as people prepared to leave their seats. That mad artist bloke as kept visiting Miss Seeton was back and pulling faces like a regular lunatic. Best keep out of range, just in case . . .

"Damn this wind," muttered Antony, sitting down to scowl at his reflection in the window opposite as the conductor rang the bell and the bus juddered into life. "Damn this miserable journey! If only the wretched woman would agree . . ." If she did, his success was assured once his master work was complete. He would never need to visit Plummergen again—except for photo calls arranged, of course, by the Galerie Genèvre, for which he would arrive by taxi. Fame and fortune and creature comforts would be his, along with the Stuttaford Prize . . .

"Thank *you*," said the bus conductor, in a third-time-of-asking voice. Antony surfaced with a blink from his blissful visions of a future financially secured on the strength of his artistic genius and (inevitably) the efforts of the Watson publicity machine. "Plummergen?" guessed the conductor, jingling his money pouch. He remembered (who could forget?) Antony Scarlett from previous visits. "Return?"

"Naturally." Antony, radiating delight at this evidence of his growing fame, fished through a flap in his cape for the coins in his trouser pocket. His volatile mood was now so buoyant that he was tempted to tell the man to keep the change, holding back only because an accusation of bribery of a transport official was the sort of publicity he (and by association Genefer) could do without. Handing over instead a bar of chocolate as per instructions, he nodded graciously as he accepted his ticket, then settled with impatience to observe the passing scenery as the outskirts of Plummergen rattled slowly into view.

The market shoppers, still wary of what he might do—he'd been groaning and pulling faces something awful—waited until the artist had left the bus before hurrying to the doors in a huddle and clustering together beside the bus stop as Antony disappeared southwards down The Street in a black, red-satin-lined flurry.

"Well!" was the general opinion, offered in muted tones in case the madman should overhear and, enraged, turn back. With one accord everybody moved to the door of the post office, ready to dash inside if danger threatened, but until that time watching eagerly to see what might happen next.

The Street is long, wide, and almost straight: almost. The gentle curve of its length meant that what happened next was better seen by those Plummergenites who were at home, peeping through the windows of their front rooms, than by those who weren't. Antony Scarlett, his cape flapping, strode south in the direction of Sweetbriars. Tina Holloway, her sketchbook in her hand, emerged from the door of The George and Dragon heading north towards Crabbe's Garage, where Jack had promised to do something else, rather more mechanical, for her to admire. Both Antony, leaving the bus, and Tina, making for the garage, walked on the same side of The Street . . .

Where in due course they met.

CHAPTER 14

Miss Seeton, poised to pour boiling water from the kettle to the pot, stayed her hand as the doorbell rang. A visitor: perhaps more than one: perhaps the telephone engineer. She would leave making tea until she knew how strong it needed to be. Her preference for weak (one spoon for each person and none for the pot) was shared, she knew, by few. One could always water strong tea to an acceptable weakness, but it wasn't easy to strengthen, as it were, what others might call weak tea to make its taste acceptable to a true-blue English palate.

As she set down the kettle and prepared to welcome her guest, personal or professional, the doorbell rang again, impatiently. Not, then, a visitor with whom she was well acquainted. The telephone man, then, eager to finish work for the day. Miss Seeton, with a faint sigh, walked—briskly, as a hospitable concession to impatience—down the hall. Unless, of course, it was some kind of emergency, which she hadn't thought being without a working telephone for twenty-four hours had been, when one could always go to Mr. Stillman at the other end of The Street, where the phones were still working. But an emergency . . .

Miss Seeton walked a little faster and opened the door with something approaching a jerk.

She stared in surprise at the figure drooping before her with a sketchbook in its hand.

"Oh, Miss Seeton!" The tearful face of Tina Holloway gazed at her from the step. "Oh, thank goodness you're in—it's dreadful!"

Rightly surmising that it was not her presence at home, but some other circumstance that so exercised her young acquaintance, Miss Seeton clicked her tongue gently, reached out a firm hand, and drew the girl inside. Tear stains and incoherent speech did not mean, thank goodness, too serious an emergency: the young were always so intense. "Suppose," she suggested, "we have a cup of tea. You will feel so much better, and you can tell me all about it—if, that is, you wish to," she added. One did not care to pry, even if Tina had seemed more than happy to tell her all about it last time and indeed had asked for her opinion. Depending, of course, on what "it" was this time. And it was somewhat embarrassing to be thought, as the poor child had implied that she did, an oracle. Miss Seeton tried to hide her involuntary smile. Dear Mr. Delphick—tall, distinguished, quick of wits and polished of manner—how very different from her own retiring self . . .

"Oh!" Tina had seen the smile and misinterpreted it. "Oh, Miss Seeton, please don't laugh—it's so cruel . . ."

Miss Seeton's heart sank. Where was the child's hard-won self-confidence in which she had revelled for the past few days? She was as distressed—as deflated—now as she had been a week ago. The hands that clasped the sketchbook were knotted and white with tension, the voice thick with further unshed tears. "My dear Tina," said Miss Seeton, after a moment leading her visitor past the sitting room to the kitchen, "this isn't like you. What could have happened to upset you so? And don't start crying again," she warned as Tina's lovely eyes began to brim. "Sit at the table—that is, no." She remembered how it never did any harm to take a fretful child's mind off its woes. "If you could fetch the cups and plates from that cupboard, while I make the tea? Thank you," she added with a smile and a nod of approval, as Tina, surreptitiously wiping her eyes, hurried to obey.

The table was laid, the tea was stirred, the leaves were left to settle: a strainer, while undoubtedly practical, still becomes clogged if used too early in the proceedings. Tina tried not to wince as Miss Seeton produced a tin of her favourite chocolate biscuits and arranged some on one of the larger plates. The girl's shudder did not go unnoticed by Miss Seeton, quickly though it was suppressed. As she poured tea, Miss Seeton's brain made swift calculation. It was several days—no, blessedly more than a week—since Antony Scarlett had been seen in Plummergen. She had begun to hope he might have abandoned his ridiculous notions; that his last visit had been, well, his last. She had, however, a strong suspicion that her hopes were about to be blighted by the intelligence Tina, once a cup of tea had soothed her nerves, would impart.

"I see you have been sketching again," said Miss Seeton, searching for a neutral topic and smiling towards the block her guest had released from that frenzied grip only once her duty as a crockery-fetching guest had been made clear.

Tina burst into tears.

Miss Seeton was shocked. "Have some tea," she said and held out the cup. Automatically Tina took it. Her eyes met those of Miss Seeton. Something in their calm regard made her gulp twice, sniff, and force a grin. "Before it gets cold," urged Miss Seeton, and obediently Tina drank.

"I'm sorry," she mumbled into her cup. Miss Seeton said nothing. Tina drew a deep breath. "I'm sorry," she

said again, sitting upright. "I'm better now, thanks. It was
. . . shock, I suppose. Partly. I mean, I know that I came
here on purpose to see him, so you'd think I wouldn't be
surprised when I did, but honestly, Miss Seeton, I meant
what I said before—about not caring one way or the other
any longer—and if only he hadn't been so—so sneering—
so rude—so full of himself . . ."

Miss Seeton sighed. Her suspicion had been all too correct. "Mr. Scarlett?" she asked, just to make sure.

Tina gulped and nodded. "I was on my way up to the
garage and stopped to look across at the forge—the sparks
from the fire were bouncing off the flagstones in the most
beautiful arcs—and when I turned round, there he was!"
It was obvious that she did not mean Dan Eggleden. "He'd
had plenty of time to notice me, of course, before I noticed
him. Time to . . . to work out something . . . clever to say."
Having said which, Tina closed her lips and said no more.

Miss Seeton gave her an encouraging smile. She knew
the girl did not care to repeat Antony's words, no matter
how clever—or (which was more probable, from what she
herself knew of the young man) not. "I'm sure you behaved with great dignity, my dear," she said.

Tina smiled back, a little shakily. "I tried, honestly I did.
I said hello, and what a coincidence, and I gathered he was
working on something special and—and so . . . and so was
I, and he . . . laughed at me, Miss Seeton. But it was the
way he laughed that made it worse! He was so horribly
pleased with himself, as if . . . as if I didn't count for anything—and I couldn't bear to have him sneering at me, and
I told him so." She blushed. "I wouldn't like to tell you
what I called him. Before he was so rude, I'd even been
prepared to . . . apologise for having made such an exhibition of myself earlier in the year, but afterwards . . ." Her
expressive hands writhed together on her lap. "It was all
so . . . undignified," she said sadly. "Humiliating. I thought

I could cope, and I . . . couldn't. I've let myself down, Miss Seeton—and you, too, when you'd been so kind . . .''

"Nonsense," said Miss Seeton. "I wouldn't say you have let anyone down, my dear, least of all yourself. All you've had to do is . . . readjust your ideas a little, perhaps, but then your first encounter with Mr. Scarlett was always likely to be somewhat awkward, wasn't it? And with the particular circumstance of his seeing you before you noticed him, your feeling of shock is quite understandable. But now that it's all over, I'm sure you won't need to worry any longer.''

She sounded so very sure that Tina's eyes, after a few uncertain moments, began to glow at her across the table, and she smiled. "Oh, Miss Seeton, thank you! Listening to you puts it all into perspective somehow.''

To avoid further embarrassing gratitude, Miss Seeton was quick to twinkle at her young friend. "Years of practice, my dear," she said with a wise look. "As a teacher of art, that is to say. Will you have some more tea?''

Tina smiled. "And a chocolate biscuit, if I may," she began, but was interrupted by the doorbell. Miss Seeton, in the act of passing the plate, stayed her hand. "What a busy afternoon I am having," she remarked, rising to her feet. "I expect this time it *is* the telephone man. Do, please, help yourself while I'm gone.''

She was not gone long; and when, smiling, she came back she was not alone, for Nigel Colveden followed her into the kitchen. At first he was almost incoherent with delight at recognising Miss Seeton's other guest. "Tina! Oh, gosh—I say, what luck to find you here. It's seemed ages—and it just goes to show how virtue is its own reward, because if I hadn't been doing my mother a good turn I wouldn't have seen you at all.'' Tina blushed again, this time less from embarrassment than from pleasure.

Miss Seeton nodded amiably as she offered tea and biscuits, which the future baronet did not scorn. "I hadn't forgotten," she said, "but it was kind of you to take the trouble to remind me, Nigel. I'm having supper tonight at the Hall," she explained as Tina looked puzzled. "And with the telephones still out of order—I tried twice this afternoon, but with no success . . ."

"Ah," said Nigel, looking wise. "Well, as I was coming down The Street I did happen to spot a couple of chaps up a ladder, doing things to the overhead wires with spanners and so on." Tina brightened. Nigel grinned. "Yes, another of your British Workman possibilities—if only the sun wasn't on its way down, fast. By the time you got there . . . well, would blobs of torchlight have the same effect?"

Tina thought they probably wouldn't. Miss Seeton felt that pale hands in darkness might have as striking an effect as heavy boots protruding from beneath a car, but accepted that everyone saw things in a different, as it were, light. Tina giggled. Nigel guffawed politely. Miss Seeton beamed. She had rather more romance in her soul on behalf of others than others sometimes realised, and her mind was working as she looked from Nigel, munching cake and describing the antics of the telephone repairmen, to Tina, modestly glowing at him across the table. Miss Seeton's general rule was not to interfere, but there were times . . .

Such as now. Miss Seeton addressed her words with care to the baronet's son. "I have had a great deal to occupy me in and around the house for most of the day. I know you were kind enough to agree to collect me tonight, Nigel, but the weather is so much better than it has been of late that a stroll on a frosty night has its appealing side, if one is wrapped up warm, which of course I would be. Should you think me very ungracious if I were to refuse your kind offer and, well, to walk?"

Nigel's academic record might not be impressive, but he was a far from slow-witted young man. He swallowed a

gleeful mouthful, grinned, and said that he wouldn't think
her in the least ungracious: but would she think *him* ungracious if he said he might not, as he'd first thought, be
dining with her at the Hall? He smiled at the beautiful girl
sitting opposite. "Remember you promised to have dinner
with me again one night soon: well, why not tonight? You
aren't too full, are you?"

"Of course she isn't," said Miss Seeton, as Tina, still a
little shaken from her confrontation with the Rubens of Refreshment, hesitated at the idea of a three-course meal in
public, no matter how agreeable the escort. "I'm sure,"
said Miss Seeton, sounding even more certain than on previous occasions, "you'll have a lovely time."

Tina's sudden laughter was a rippling cascade of golden
notes. "Oh, dear—oh, no, it's not you," she told Nigel,
"it's me. Do you know what I was just thinking? *What on
earth shall I wear?*" She glanced at Miss Seeton, rippling
again. "Oh, dear . . . I'd say I was over it, wouldn't you?"

As Nigel, puzzled, stared from one woman to another, a
smiling Miss Seeton agreed that she would.

Nigel arranged to collect Tina from the George at seven
o'clock sharp, gulped his tea, excused himself, and rushed
home in so rapturous a daydream that he forgot to switch on
his car headlights. Tina, her eyes brighter than the early stars
by whose rays her swain was navigating the length of Marsh
Road, once more thanked Miss Seeton for her support, and,
quite as rapturous as Nigel, hugged her elderly friend before
pecking her on the cheek and floating out of the door back to
the hotel. "I'll come and tell you all about it tomorrow," she
promised, waving her hands eloquently in the air. "What I
wore and where we went and what we ate . . ."

It was a promise she was not, sadly, destined to keep.

Antony Scarlett had been quite as startled to see Tina in
Plummergen as she, concentrating on blacksmith Daniel

Eggleden, had been to see him. He'd had several yards'
warning before the necessity to address her had arisen: he
had, he thought, acquitted himself well in the verbal
stakes—but she hadn't responded in the way he'd expected
to his crushing repartee. It was galling to remember how
she had . . . defied him as she did. Antony had grown accustomed to the adoring doormat Kristeena, sinking into
oblivion once her time was over. Liberated Tina, oblivious
of her oblivion, was . . . an unnerving experience.

But what was worse, far worse than the girl's newfound
independence, was the way she and that irritating old
woman were evidently in league against him. No wonder
Miss Seeton had been so firm in refusing him the rights to
her cottage when Tina—Kristeena—had filled her mind
with poison! He had watched his former model turn and
run from him down The Street and up the short front path
of the cottage into which he himself had been welcomed
only twice—and Miss Seeton had invited her in without a
qualm! How many times had she been there before? What
plot were the two of them now hatching? Was his prize-
winning design—his "Briars Sweet"—doomed beyond all
hope because of a vengeful young woman his Art, and his
alone, had raised from obscurity? Was he to be blamed—
was he to suffer—simply because he had outgrown her—
because she had been unable to accept the fact that Genius
Must Be Served?

Tina's presence in the house he had come to think of as
his was a difficulty he had not foreseen. Until she was no
longer inside, he would be unable to approach Miss Seeton
with his renewed request that she reconsider her refusal:
the idea that his artistic fate might be decided on the opinions of one whose sympathy with his creative spirit had
long since faded was anathema to him. Any sign that Miss
Seeton might be weakening would be noticed not only by
himself, but by Tina, who would all too quickly encourage

the old woman not to yield to his entreaties, no matter how well presented. Kristeena—Christina—Holloway was, in short, a damned nuisance, and the sooner she was gone, the better.

As for being gone, he himself could not yet be so until he had justified his journey to the wilderness of Kent by speaking again with Miss Seeton. The woman must be brought to realise that only under the greatest artistic provocation would the cosmopolitan Antony Scarlett deign to visit her hayseed village more than once. She should be flattered that he thought her—or rather her house—worth his consideration; she must understand just how necessary that house was in his great design: she must bow to his demands; she must, in short, agree to sell him Sweetbriars—and the sooner, the better.

Antony strode up and down, brooding, and benefiting not at all from the fresh country air as he did so. On the contrary, his head began to ache as his jaw and neck muscles went into slow spasm with repeated grindings of his teeth. The door of Miss Seeton's cottage remained resolutely shut. As the sun drew near to the western horizon, lengthening shadows darkened and chilled The Street. Antony consulted his watch, scowled, and sighed. The last bus had gone: he would have to take a taxi, at this rate. So much for his public appearance.

A red sports car rattled merrily past to pull up outside Miss Seeton's front door. Antony, whose head had shot up on observing the car's colour, then recognised its make as an MG and its driver as the one who had refused him a lift on an earlier visit to Plummergen. Antony scowled as Nigel Colveden jumped with easy grace from the MG and marched up Miss Seeton's path to join the party, then ground his teeth again. This young man had the bearing of an athlete, or at least of someone not unused to the . . . physical side of life. It would be . . . undignified for an artist to risk tangling with such a man, especially a man from such a village as Plummergen. Why, he probably chewed straws in his spare time! Only once this miserable place had been put on the map by the Scarlett masterpiece would any dignity or honour pertain to the Plummergen name . . .

Antony shivered as a sunset breeze shook the folds of his cape. He cursed, swung on his heel, and headed for the public bar of the George and Dragon. He had come to a decision. If it was going to prove as impossible as now seemed likely to speak to Miss Seeton this evening, then he would make the supreme sacrifice. He would not return to London, to civilisation: he would stay here overnight and catch her first thing tomorrow morning. There was nothing else, after all, to be done.

"Mr. Mountfitchet likes us to take the full deposit for folks who arrive without luggage," reiterated Doris, whose stint behind the reception desk had seldom been so exasperating.

"I assure you," proclaimed Antony Scarlett in ringing tones, "I have every intention of paying my way tomorrow morning like any honest citizen." *Even if*, he added in thought, *I am far from being as they. I am no bourgeois, hidebound by convention: I am a free thinker! I am Antony Scarlett!* "My good woman," he went on as Doris opened her mouth to repeat her instructions for the fourth time, "have you no idea who I am?"

"I know who you are," said Doris.

Antony preened himself. This was more like it.

"You," said Doris, "are the bloke who's going to pay a deposit—in cash—before I let him have a room."

"Ignorant provincial!" boomed Antony, flinging out his arms in a studied gesture of frustration. His cape, billowing behind him, enveloped and tipped over the enormous cheese plant standing in its heavy earthenware pot beside the desk. Doris uttered a horrified cry. If Charley, who doted on that plant, saw what had happened . . .

"Well, go on," she snapped as Antony recoiled and prepared to condemn the management for its policy of over-intrusive greenery. "Pick it up!"

Antony caught her eye, remembered that he really did want that room, and bent to make a few vague sweeping movements with his hands. Housework was not something in which the True Artist often indulged: why else did so many men of genius insist on live-in models?

Doris, in whom the flame of women's liberation burned faint but willing, overheard a few of the things he muttered as he swept. She was not pleased: but her efficient nature could not bear to watch his clumsy attempts at tidiness. "Never mind, I'll fetch a dustpan and brush," she said at last. "After we've settled the room," she added as Antony stood up and dusted his palms with another studied gesture, this time of satisfaction. Doris, however, had no intention of letting him think he'd pulled the wool over her ignorant provincial eyes. "Cash," she reminded him and glared at him again.

Ten minutes later Antony was in the bar, ensconced in a seat near the window overlooking the southern end of The Street and, by extension, the front gate of Sweetbriars on the corner. Deflated by Doris, he had tried to boost his self-esteem by asking Charley Mountfitchet for a Brandy Alexander, which (to his irritation) the landlord knew exactly how to mix. Charley, like most of the village, had learned a few tricks since Miss Seeton took up residence in Plummergen. Far too many smart-alec reporters appeared from London when she was engaged in one of her little exploits for the locals not to have developed a fine sense of self-preservation: and on this particular occasion Charley had heard from Doris while Antony was upstairs washing earth off his hands. With no more than a nod he had shaken together brandy, fresh cream, and (Antony's automatic choice) chocolate flavoured crème de cacao with ice and, after straining them into a glass, had sprinkled them with nutmeg. "Put it on your bill, shall I?" he enquired: and Antony had ground his teeth again.

"Strong stuff, this." Charley, who didn't care to have people drink too much on an empty stomach, was shaking and straining for the third time of asking. "Rich." He pushed the glass across the counter. "Will you be eating here?"

Antony gazed about him. He had no way of knowing, but food at the George was generally considered good, if plain: Plummergen did not approve of fancy foreign cuisine. Alexander and his twin, however, had given the artist some Dutch courage. "Eating here?" He frowned into the cream-smeared depths of his glass. "Is it recommended?"

"It won't kill you," said Charley in tones that suggested some other cause just might, if Antony kept on the way he was going.

"Oh, I'll have a packet of crisps," said Antony, doing this yokel barman a favour. "While I'm making up my mind."

"Crisps," echoed Charley, his mouth set. "Right. And what size would you like 'em?"

Antony blinked over the rim of his glass. "What size?"

Charley shot out a hand to one of the tall pint glasses favoured by some of the younger set for lager or shandy. His fingers closed on the slender cylinder—and kept on closing. Antony gulped as the glass shattered into a thousand pieces in Charley's powerful grip. "Crisps," said Mr. Mountfitchet, as glittering splinters fell from his open palm to the wooden surface of the bar. "Large ones, those are." He reached for another glass. "Or we can do you the small size, if you'd prefer . . ."

"I'll be eating here," said Antony with a gasp, and Charley Mountfitchet smiled.

• • •

Mrs. Ogden, newly returned from a house-hunting expedition, was commiserating with Doris on the aftermath of the cheese plant's accidental de-potting as Tina Holloway danced in through the George's main door.

"Someone looks happy," observed Doris with a cheerful wave of the duster with which she had been polishing the final traces of calamity from the leathery leaves.

Tina radiated happiness. "Isn't it a lovely evening? Hello, Mrs. Ogden. Doris, I'd better let you know now that I won't be eating here tonight." She pointedly ignored the snort of muted fury that burst from over by the entrance to the bar. "Nigel Colveden is taking me out to dinner."

"Somewhere nice, I'm sure," said Doris, in turn ignoring what sounded like a second furious snort. "Young Nigel, he knows his stuff when it comes to a fancy dinner."

Mrs. Ogden, taking her cue from the others, also chose to ignore the snorting figure on the far side of the foyer. "I've seen a number of classy restaurants while I've been driving around and about." She chuckled. "Not that somewhere posh to eat is the best way of choosing a place to retire, is it? Still, once in a while you do like to splash out, so I've popped into one or two for lunch—and their looks don't lie. You're an honest crowd in this part of the world, you know."

"So we are," said Doris, pitching her voice a little louder. "There's been nobody try any tricks about payment at the George for quite a spell, believe you me."

"I believe you," said Mrs. Ogden with a wry smile.

Much of the by-play was lost on Tina, whose main concern was to prepare for her night on such town as Nigel decided to show her. "I don't know when I'll be back," she said to Doris. "What time do you lock up?"

Mrs. Ogden's titter was drowned out by the most furious snort so far, although Antony was still so cowed by recent experiences that he did not dare to speak. "Oh, Miss Holloway," she said with a light laugh, "you make this lovely old pub sound like a prison!"

Doris smiled, then pursed her lips. "Well, dear, that depends on how busy we are, except being winter like it is we won't be open all hours as we would in summer. Did you want someone to stay up for you?"

That she hoped Tina wanted no such thing was so obvious the girl's response was immediate. "Goodness, no thanks, if you can let me have a night key instead." The distant sound of grinding teeth was music to her ears. "And I suppose it would be a bit silly if I handed in my room key when I left, wouldn't it? If there'll be nobody at the desk to give it back to me later, I mean."

"Because you don't how much later," Doris agreed brightly. "You could always ring, I suppose, if you don't leave it too late," she said with a nod for Mrs. Ogden, whose sleep might be disturbed by midnight callers. "And *if* they get the phones fixed like they promised, which I doubt."

"Nigel said he saw some repairmen up a ladder," Tina told her. "He said they said it shouldn't be long—but it would be a shame to wake anyone up just to let me in," she added sweetly. "Yes, I'll take a night key, if I may."

Doris grinned as she handed it over. Mrs. Ogden smiled, and Tina floated blissfully up the stairs, quite failing to notice the large male figure, clad in black, looming with folded arms beside the newel post.

Doris and Mrs. Ogden exchanged amused glances. Antony, intercepting them, emitted one final snort and stamped back to the bar. Charley Mountfitchet, without a word, mixed a fourth cocktail . . . and handed him the menu for dinner.

Antony took the hint and was in the dining room waiting for his soup by the time Tina climbed into Nigel's MG and was whisked off into the starry night. Morosely the artist wondered where the man was taking her, how long they would be gone, and what plots they might contrive to hatch while they—both friends of Miss Seeton—were some-where he, the victimised Scarlett, could not hear them . . . and yet if the pair were indeed elsewhere, they couldn't be here, could they? *There.* Over the road in Sweetbriars, pro-tecting Miss Seeton . . .

Antony ordered a bottle of red wine in celebration.

Vegetable soup, steak and potatoes, and chocolate (of course) sponge pudding leave a man with a comfortable feeling inside. Antony demanded a second cup of coffee while he brooded some more, then wrapped himself in his cape and went out of the George to do battle again with Miss Emily Seeton. A crisp breeze whistled south down The Street to ruffle the black gaberdine folds and send a draught down the Londoner's neck. He shivered. The coun-try: you could keep it. Thank heaven he had only a matter of yards to walk before he was at her door . . .

There were no lights on at the front of the house. There were—Antony squinted down the narrow passage between the house and the high brick wall—no lights in any of the side rooms, either. Even he did not have the nerve to check the back: and in any case, if he had, he could have guessed at the outcome. Miss Seeton was not at home.

"She was here earlier," he reminded himself as, to make absolutely sure, he rang the doorbell. "I should have kept a closer watch, but . . ." But he did not remind himself of his rout at the hands of Doris, the cheese plant, and Charley Mountfitchet. "To be out on a night like this . . ."

Another northerly blast ruffled his cape and made him shiver. He pulled the black folds more closely about him as he extended a frozen finger to press the bell again.

Miss Seeton did not answer. She was definitely not at home. "Out," groaned Antony Scarlett. "And who knows

when she will return? That means tomorrow to speak to
her . . .''

He so far forgot himself as to fling his arms sideways in
the familiar Artistic Gesture. ''Gone!'' he cried as the
breeze billowed his cape into an icy balloon. ''Gone with
the wind . . .'' He gathered the black folds about him.
''When tomorrow is another day . . .''

He paused. He spoke the line again. He nodded, pleased
with himself; then he turned on his heel and stalked ma-
jestically down Miss Seeton's path, out of her gate, and
back across the road to the George and Dragon.

CHAPTER 15

As the sun went down and the darkling world became stark and cold and cheerless, in a lonely house in a quiet village somewhere in Kent an old man stood at bay.

He was not yet afraid: he was angry. On age-bowed legs he squared up to the burly workman looming over him, ignoring the even burlier companion in the shadows. He shook his withered fist as the large, unwelcome visitor repeated his extortionate demands and he defied him in a voice that sixty years ago had barked orders across a parade ground.

"What d'you mean you want three hundred pounds? Thirty, you said, and thirty's all you're getting—and lucky to get that, the shoddy job you've made of it!"

"Thirty pounds a square yard, squire. You weren't listening properly—but at your age that's no surprise." The old man uttered an outraged cry, but the burly man talked over him. "Ten square yards in your driveway—that makes it three hundred quid in anyone's book. And we're not leaving here till we get it."

"Then you'll have a long wait, because you won't get it from me! I didn't spend the best years of my life being

gassed in the trenches to feather the nests of rotten, cheating
scum like you. That stuff you've laid out there's so thin
you can almost see through it in places, and if it lasts more
than a week once the snow and frost arrive, I'll be very
surprised. Three hundred quid for a job like that? Even
thirty's too much!''

The burly man loomed over him. ''Depends on your
sense of values, squire. Thirty quid's dead cheap, I
reckon.'' In the shadows, the burlier companion sniggered.
''Dead cheap,'' repeated the burly man, looming closer,
breathing hard into the old man's face. ''For three hundred,
now—that's still a bargain. Like insurance, if you know
what I mean. You never realize what it's worth until you
use it.'' Now it was his turn to snigger. ''Or lose it, as you
might say. Don't want to lose—anything—do you,
squire?''

The old soldier's heart beat faster, but he took only one
step backwards before saying: ''Don't you dare threaten
me! Get out of my house before I call the police!''

''Not without what's owed,'' said the burly man. ''One
way or another,'' he added as his companion took a silent
step forward. ''You say we owe you—well, *we* say you
owe us. Three hundred pounds, or . . .''

The old man was more than half a century too late to be
able to withstand what happened next.

The roar of the motorbike faded swiftly northwards as
Wayne tried to catch up the time he had lost waiting for
Maureen to finish her face before accepting his escort to
work. As the devoted youth disappeared in the direction of
Brettenden, Maureen, smothering a yawn, ambled into the
George for the ritual morning scold from Doris.

''There's Mrs. Ogden already up and gone for the day,''
Doris told her as she teetered on her platform shoes, ''and
breakfast to start clearing for lunch while I check the gro-

cery order—except you'd best leave the two corner tables a bit longer, on account of how Miss Holloway and Mr. Scarlett have both put 'Do Not Disturb' on their doors, and there's no telling when they'll be down.''

Maureen stared. After a moment she sniggered and put her hand in front of her mouth. "Have they?"

"They have," said Doris. "And there's no call to think such idiotic thoughts, my girl. Miss Holloway was out with Nigel Colveden till past midnight, and Mr. Scarlett was in the bar most of the evening, saving a short walk for some fresh air after dinner. Don't stand there gawping like that, Maureen. Get along with you to work—do go on!''

She chivvied Maureen into the dining room and warned her not to use the vacuum cleaner until at least one of the two guests roomed above should wake. Maureen, feeling hard-done-by, clumped wearily from table to kitchen and back with her hands full of plates and dishes, while Doris retreated to the larder armed with a notepad and pencil. Of Charley Mountfitchet there was no sign.

The whites (and rims) of Antony Scarlett's eyes matched his name as he at last put in an appearance. His face was pale, in his temples beat a pulse visible even to unobservant Maureen, and he kept taking long, shuddering breaths. "Coffee," he croaked, collapsing on a chair and closing his eyes against the sight of Maureen in the full morning glory of her make-up. "Black," he added. "Strong."

Maureen sighed. "Instant okay?" It would be too much effort to drag out the grinder for one miserable cup, which was all he looked as if he'd be able to get down him before, well, the worst happened. If it hadn't already, of course. And if it had, she wasn't going to be the one to do his room once he signed out, not blooming likely she wasn't.

Antony sighed, too. "Instant." Anything more witty and cosmopolitan was beyond him, and he could not have nodded—or boomed—to save his life. "Okay," he said and closed his eyes in dismissal. His head fell back, and the artistic lock of hair across his brow slipped to one side, disclosing a darkening bruise. Maureen vaguely assumed he must have taken a tumble getting into bed last night. It wasn't likely anyone had thumped him. Was it?

The thump of the service door was a torment to Antony, and when a second thump was followed by the clatter of cup on saucer as Maureen dropped them on the table, his torment was even greater. He opened his eyes again. "Ugh," he said as he saw what it was. Maureen chose to take this remark as a personal affront and clumped off in the direction of the service door, behind which she vanished, never to return.

"The cheek of him," she moaned to Doris, who had temporarily abandoned her shopping list to check the balance of the loaded dishwasher before switching it on. "Rolled his eyes at me real horrible, too, he did."

"Did he?" Doris darted back to her list, scribbled "lge" after "salt," dashed back to the machine, and switched it on. Maureen blinked at the energy of her example and yawned in heartfelt sympathy as Doris said: "He made a night of it last night, by all accounts. When you come to do the rooms, best leave his for last in case he wants to go back and sleep it off. Save changing the sheets twice." She dashed back to her pad and made another note to charge him for a second day if he did.

"Well then, there's only Mrs. Ogden," said Maureen, "with Miss Holloway still not down." She yawned massively and sat down on the nearest chair. "So I might as well leave the whole blooming lot to do together later. Save disturbing anyone with the vacuum, and that."

Doris, underlining "lge," wondered whether Maureen's instinct for survival was rather more than the George could be expected to cope with. Lazy Maureen, obedient to instruction because she couldn't be bothered to be anything else, was one thing. Maureen thinking for herself might result in mutiny. "Now, you just get along," snapped Doris, "and don't argue, all right?"

"Oh . . . all right," said Maureen. Doris had sounded unaccountably fierce. Maybe it had been her who'd thumped Mr. Scarlett, though why she should Maureen couldn't imagine, Doris not being the sort men got fresh with even if they'd drunk the barrel dry. It was too early in the morning, however, for the spark of rebellion to stay alight for long. "Just get along," she'd been told.

She got. Yawning again, she drifted out of the kitchen through the green baize door into the hall, pausing en route to pick up a feather duster from the broom cupboard. Feathers didn't make a noise. She could do the stairs, the corners of the corridor ceiling, and . . .

And answer the telephone, which was shrilling rhythmically on its rubber mat in one corner of the reception desk. Maureen glanced over her shoulder before approaching it. No sign of Doris; of Mr. Mountfitchet. She wasn't paid to do it, but she supposed she'd better.

She picked up the receiver. "Hello," she said, with no elaboration beyond a weary sigh.

"Is that the George and Dragon?" enquired a young man's voice, sounding hurried and a little puzzled.

"Yes," said Maureen, sighing again.

"Oh." Despite the hurry, there was a pause. "Is that Maureen?" came the next enquiry as the puzzle was solved.

"Yes," said Maureen: of this fact she was sure. Gears began to mesh slowly in her mind. "Who's that?"

"Nigel Colveden. Look, I'm calling from a box in Ashford and I'm short of change, but I just wanted a quick word with Miss Holloway. Can you fetch her?"

"She's not down yet." In sympathy, Maureen yawned for the umpteenth time. "She had a late night, Doris says."

"Yes, I know." Nigel's smugness was twofold: Tina's

late night had been spent with him, and he, a working farmer, had managed to rise at six the next day. "I suppose she's posted 'Do Not Disturb,' so I won't ask you to put me through to her room, but could you take a message?"

"A message. Hang on." Maureen looked about her for something on, and something else with, which to write. The frantic cries of Nigel, abandoned with a clunk on the rubber mat, called her back.

"Maureen, wait! There's no time—I told you I was running out of change—just tell her, please, that she's not to worry, I found her earring in my car and I'll drop it in around lunchtime when I've finished here. Could you—?"

"Could I what?" Maureen regarded the telephone doubtfully as it beeped in her hand. There was no knowing what Nigel Colveden might not ask a girl to do . . . if she was lucky. If what folk said was true. As if the likes of her would ever find out! The disconnection beeps turned to the dialling tone, and she sighed. She replaced the receiver, sighed again, and picked up her feather duster. Some girls had all the luck. That Miss Holloway—looked good, lovely clothes, lived in London . . . Some girls didn't know they were born, unlike others stuck in Plummergen from one year's end to the next. It wasn't fair.

Maureen's nature was too idle to bear a grudge, except against her worst best friend Emmy Putts, but her feeling of wistful envy turned to dull resentment against the more fortunate Tina Holloway. The feather duster was exchanged for the vacuum cleaner, and Maureen bumped it step by step up the stairs to start rolling it at full throttle back and forth along the corridor in which lay Tina's room. Lazy cow. If Nigel Colveden could wake up, so could she. Everyone else was out of bed, even Mr. Scarlett . . .

Antony was still downstairs, recovering over his coffee; Mrs. Ogden was (Maureen supposed) out on her regular retirement cottage hunt. Maureen herself was left to trundle the cleaner up and down and to bump it against the skirting board and the base of Tina's door for a quarter of an hour before Doris wondered where she was and came looking for her. The cleaner was an old and noisy one: Doris wasted no time in shouting. She bent to switch off the plug at the socket, and as Maureen turned to find out where the power had suddenly gone, Doris let rip.

"You stupid girl, what are you playing at? Can't you read? Didn't I tell you there was 'Do Not Disturb' up and you weren't to do along here until everyone was down?" And more in similar vein.

"Sorry," mumbled Maureen when Doris finally ran out of steam and realised that her shrill harangue must have been the final straw for the weary, trying-to-sleep-late Miss Holloway. "Didn't think."

"You never do." Doris stifled a groan. As Maureen's superior, she must shoulder the ultimate blame for Maureen's faults and make such reparation as seemed suitable. A bit knocked off the bill, perhaps? Apology alone wouldn't be enough. Breakfast in bed today at no extra charge? She couldn't have slept through that little lot. Room service would be a start . . .

Doris tapped on Tina's door. "Miss Holloway!" There was no reply. She tapped again with the tip of her pass key, a distinct, unmissable sound. Still no reply.

"She'll be in the bath, I dare say," said Doris. She tapped once more, announced herself, and cautiously opened the door, calling Tina's name as she did so.

"Miss Holloway, it's reception, just asking if you'd like anything brought up." There was no response to this well-meant offer. "Miss Holloway?"

"Miss Holloway!"

The fourth time Doris called Tina's name, it was not as a simple question.

It was as a shrill exclamation of horror.

CHAPTER 16

Nigel Colveden emerged from the jeweller's feeling pleased with himself. Why he'd noticed it in the first place, he couldn't have said: it hadn't been one of the pieces he'd looked at when choosing Christmas presents for his sister, Julia, and young niece, Janie: but somehow or other the necklace now nestling in a box in his pocket had impinged itself on his memory and proved (as he'd thought the moment he saw them) an almost perfect match for the earrings Tina had worn last night.

Christmas was past, and he had no idea when her birthday might be. It hadn't been one of the things they'd talked about while they were together: truth to tell, he couldn't remember *what* they had talked about before, during, and after dinner—except that they'd talked, and he'd enjoyed it, and as far as he knew Tina had enjoyed it, too. Tina Holloway. Christina. Christina Colveden . . . No harm in an un-birthday present, surely . . .

"Is that the George and Dragon? It's Nigel Colveden. Look, I'm calling from a box in Ashford and I'm short of change, but I just wanted a quick word with Miss Holloway. Can you fetch her?"

• • •

Police cars with grim-faced drivers and flashing blue lights sped quietly through the Ashford streets en route for Plummergen. Superintendent Brinton had issued stern warnings against the use of the two-tone sirens unless, in traffic terms, absolutely necessary. The press and other snoops would find out soon enough that there had been murder committed in Miss Seeton's village.

No doubt, from Potter's preliminary report, that it was murder. While it might just about be possible to throttle yourself if you were really determined, you couldn't do so without a ligature of some sort—tights (did any female under the age of thirty wear stockings anymore?) or a belt or (in winter, which of course January was) a scarf. Potter was a good man. He'd made it clear that, closely as he had examined the bruised and swollen neck of Miss Tina Holloway, there had been no trace of anything other than pressure-marks from strong, probably masculine, fingers . . .

"And if Potter says so, I believe him." Brinton settled his bulk more comfortably in the passenger seat. "Forensics and the scenes-of-crime lot will go through the motions and tell us the same in the end, but . . . Potter's a good man."

"Yes, sir." Foxon, summoned from his sickbed to assist in the emergency, changed gear for a sharp bend ahead. "But what I find hard to credit is that she could have been killed by Charley Mountfitchet. My money's on the artist bloke from London, if he was the only other man staying at the George last night."

"Mountfitchet's been a good friend to the police over the years," Brinton conceded. "You would expect him of all people to know he'd never get away with it . . . but this is England, laddie. Even if he *is* the raving nutter everyone seems to think, we can't accuse this artist without evidence—and then, the most surprising folk can suddenly go wonky for reasons nobody normal can understand. You've been in the force long enough to know about hidden depths.''

''Well—yes, sir. But Scarlett's been way past wonky since the first time he came to Plummergen—everyone knows that. And Charley's a good sort. Always cooperates with the police—law-abiding—friendly—useful cricketer—''

''And the odd after-hours drink with no questions asked.'' Brinton shifted again on his seat. ''A cynic might argue he'd been notching up Brownie points as camouflage for when he decided he was ready to go right off the rails.''

Foxon, despite his long experience of those who were not so much off the mental rails as way beyond the lawful pale, was shocked by this suggestion. Did Superintendent Brinton seriously think the landlord of the George and Dragon had such a devious mind?

The superintendent retorted that the minds of villains were as twisted as corkscrews, and then some. Everyone knew appearances could be damned deceptive. Just look at how old Miss Addison had been convinced her doorstep visitor was a villain of the deepest dye because of the way he looked—and as for Abinger . . .

''Point taken, sir.'' Foxon, too busy driving to rub either of his black eyes, could only sigh: which he did with energy. ''But the way this artist looks is pretty villainous, by all accounts. Even MissEss called him theatrical, and you know how she usually falls over backwards to be nice about everyone—''

Brinton sat bolt upright. The seat belt jerked across his chest and made him gasp. ''Foxon, shuttup! Do you *have* to bring that woman's name into this business so blasted early in the proceedings? Time enough for the Battling Brolly once we get to Plummergen. She's bound to be mixed up in all this somehow. She always is.''

"She has," agreed Foxon, "had her dealings with Dracula, sir. I mean," he hastily amended as an oath blistered from Brinton's lips, "with Scarlett. Buying Sweetbriars to fill it with chocolate and knock it down—I told you he keeps pestering her about it—that's why half of 'em think she's procuring young women for him, because he's always dropping in to see her, prancing about the place in that daft black cape—"

Brinton snorted tremendously.

"Yes, sir, I know, but sometimes there can be a—a grain of truth in the most ridiculous stories. Suppose he does have a—a taste for girls? And a gorgeous specimen, as they say, is staying in the same hotel. She asks him back to her room innocent-like for coffee, and he gets the wrong message and takes it out on her when she objects . . ."

"Funny to start drinking coffee way past midnight," said Brinton. "One of the best ways I know to ruin your chances of a decent kip until the caffeine's worn off."

"Well, sir, it was just an idea. But suppose—"

"Suppose the girl's not as innocent as she seems and changes her mind after leading him on? Suppose she's on the game and changes her mind about the price when he's already agreed to pay? Suppose she's been blackmailing him and he's had enough? There are dozens of *ideas* we could try, Foxon." Brinton glanced sideways at him and cleared his throat. "One of which I think you'll like even less than the idea of Charley Mountfitchet doing away with one of his guests—and I know you've been trying to keep me off this, and I know he's a pal of yours—and his father's a magistrate, dammit—but coppers don't play favourites, laddie."

"No, sir."

Brinton waited for more. It did not come. He nodded.

"Look, I don't like it any more than you—but facts are facts. Forensic'll tell us if she was killed somewhere else and moved after death—but who in their right mind would go in for the exercise? So—it happened right there, in her bedroom at the George. And it must have happened after midnight, when everyone goes to bed, because the girl went out for the evening and let herself back in with a late key, according to Potter, according to Doris. So—suppose the bloke she was out with let himself in with her?'' Brinton shook his head. ''He's about the most unlikely person, I know, but our mutual friend Nigel Colveden is definitely in the frame for this one . . .''

It was inevitable that by the time Brinton and his cohorts had driven the fifteen miles from Ashford, Plummergen would know not only that they were on their way, but why. In few parts of England does the grapevine function with greater efficiency. The superintendent accepted that there would be no advantage in attempting any secret approach via the back roads through Hamstreet and Brenzett: he might as well use the fast Brettenden route and brazen it out by driving down The Street in full view of people who already knew that he was expected.

''We know damned well,'' he growled to Foxon, ''most of the beggars will be gawping outside the place long before we get there. With—ugh, telescopes, most likely.'' He only just bit back a reckless mention of binoculars. Miss Emily Seeton must stay out of his case for as long as he could manage it: which, knowing her, wouldn't be long, but he'd do his damnedest to last a few hours, at least, without her and her blasted umbrella getting in the way.

As for getting in his way, the gawpers were, as predicted, there, although none had a telescope; and (had he ever known) it might have cheered Brinton to learn that the nearest anyone had come to using binoculars was old Miss Wicks in her cottage next-but-one to the smithy. Cecelia Wicks had wondered what rare specimen of bird life must be perched on the roof of the hostelry opposite and took out her dear mother's opera glasses for a better look. Seeing nothing of particular avian interest, she replaced the glasses in their worn leather box and went back to mending the torn lace ruffle on her nightdress without giving another thought to what her neighbours were doing outside in such numbers on so chilly a morning.

The gawping crowd parted to let the police cars pull off the road to the parking space in front of the George, then surged back again, elbows at the ready, to its prime viewing position on the pavement (publicly owned) rather than on the private forecourt. Landlord Charley Mountfitchet, once he was over the initial shock, had been quick to issue stern warnings about Trespass to which PC Potter had given the full support of the law, although Charley made extra sure by standing sentinel on the step with his arms folded and a threatening light in his eye.

Brinton might have suspected a double bluff on Charley's part, but he was grateful not to have to fight his way to the door through ranks of clustering gossips. Even from the distance of several yards, however, he couldn't miss the muttered mention of a certain name . . .

"Knowed her, didn't she?"

"Afternoon tea, they *called* it—as if that'd fool even a copper . . ."

"Stands to reason she'll be involved, no more'n a cough 'n' a spit from the very door . . ."

Brinton tore at his hair as he fled from the pursuit of those insistent voices. Was there to be no escape from the woman? Even when she wasn't there, she still haunted him. "Miss Seeton," he groaned, exploding with relief into the safe haven of the foyer of the George.

"Good morning, Superintendent."

Brinton rocked back on his heels, almost knocking Foxon flat. He stared. He could not say a word.

Miss Seeton rose quietly from the chair on which she had been waiting. She smiled a tentative greeting to Foxon, now busy repeating Charley's up-the-stairs-and-third-on-the-left instructions to the forensic hangers-on from the second car, and as Brinton remained speechless with shock, she hurried to explain her presence at what might be called intrusively close to the scene of the crime.

"I hope, Mr. Brinton, that I do not intrude—but when Martha told me what had happened to poor Miss Holloway . . ." Miss Seeton cleared her throat, blinking rapidly once or twice. "It is one of her days, you see, and when she saw so many people . . ." Mrs. Bloomer had been unable to resist the lure of the crowd. A Londoner born and bred, Martha had grown more Plummergen than Plummergen in the years since her marriage to native Stan, though she exercised more caution than most of the village over what she said about—and to—whom and when she chose to say it. Martha did not forget that Tina Holloway had been a guest at Sweetbriars: could not forget it, given the many voices all too eager to remind her of this inconvenient fact.

"Of course," said Miss Seeton, "I recognise that you will need to enquire into every aspect of poor Tina's life for the purposes of investigation, and so because she left it at my house yesterday . . ." She hesitated and blushed. "I had, naturally, every intention of apologising when she came to collect it this morning . . ." Brinton didn't even try interrupting her to ask why Miss Seeton should apologise to a guest for that guest's absent-mindedness.

Miss Seeton plunged on with her explanation. "And then—because after a late night I wasn't in the least surprised that she should be breakfasting late, too—when Martha told me the shocking news and I realised I still had it . . . It was by accident, I feel sure, as I had already given my opinion, and she was so much looking forward to her

evening out that it is a pardonable error—which is why I
knew at once that I must bring it back. In case,'' she concluded in her most earnest tones, ''anyone should make a
detailed list of her belongings and find it gone. One would
not wish there to be any misunderstanding.'' Miss Seeton
again turned pink. ''Not, of course, that I would presume
to interfere in your work, Superintendent, but were anyone
to suggest that it had been stolen . . .''

''You didn't steal it,'' Brinton finished for her. He'd not
made too much sense of the rest of the rigmarole, but this
much he was pretty sure he'd got.

He'd got it wrong. Miss Seeton looked startled: dismayed
''Oh, no—oh, dear, I'm sorry, Mr. Brinton—but it never
occurred that anyone might suppose that I . . .'' Her cheeks
turned from pink to pinker as she fumbled with the catch
of the capacious handbag hanging over one arm. ''It was
Doris, you see—and Maureen. I should not wish anyone to
think . . . Doris is so very honest and reliable, and Maureen . . .'' Miss Seeton boggled slightly over a suitable ad-
jective for the slowest worker in Plummergen. ''I believe
she is a very respectable young woman, Superintendent.''
This could be said almost without a qualm: did Maureen
not still live at home, despite the attractions (as Miss Seeton
assumed there must be) of leather-clad Wayne and his motorbike? ''And, of course, Mr. Mountfitchet. Not that anyone of sound mind could consider it a justifiable excuse
for . . .'' She sighed. ''For murder.'' One had seen such
things on television and heard plays on the wireless, but in
real life—if that was not an unfortunate phrase . . .

''Of course,'' she went on while Brinton still tried to
catch his breath, ''I have little experience in such matters . . .'' This startling claim drove what breath he might
have finally caught right out of Brinton's gasping lungs.
For someone who over the past seven years had been in-
strumental in apprehending a score of murderers, not to

mention lesser crooks without number, how MissEss managed to keep up the pretence that it was nothing to do with her never ceased to amaze him.

"But," she went on, having paused politely to let him finish choking, "it is my impression that the mind of anyone willing to commit murder is thought to be—well, far from sound. In most cases," she added, trying to be fair. "As indeed it must be to commit any sort of crime, for one's sense of right and wrong must be, at the very least, considerably distorted. Which I think you will agree, once you have spoken to them, could be said of none of them. I felt, you see, that if I didn't bring it back, even though it is too late for me to apologise, you might wonder, which would have wasted valuable time when there is, sadly, a genuine criminal to pursue. To her, not to you, Superintendent, though of course I am sorry if I have caused any confusion."

Was she? Brinton gritted his teeth. *Had she? Damned right, she had! And what the hell was she doing now?*

Miss Seeton, having explained everything to her own satisfaction if not the superintendent's, now opened her handbag and produced a brown-paper package oblong in shape, about half an inch thick, and tied neatly with string. "I remembered about fingerprints, you see," she said with a touch of pride, handing the package to Brinton, who received it in silence: he couldn't think what else to do. "I hope," she said, "they haven't smudged. I know that the proper procedures must be followed, even if both Miss Treeves and I have seen her using it, and would be willing to vouch for it should that become necessary." She stifled a sigh, recalling a previous occasion. "Except that a public appearance in court . . . a most uncomfortable feeling, to be the centre of attention . . . but, as dear Mr. Delphick explained at the time, it is the penalty one sometimes has to pay for doing what one believes to be right. Which I do:

as, I feel sure, does Miss Treeves. It's only that . . .''

As she ran out of steam, Brinton took a deep breath. ''This parcel was the property of the young lady calling herself Christina Holloway, was it?''

''It was,'' said Miss Seeton, ''her name.''

''And she left it with you . . . by accident? Not for what you might call safekeeping?''

Miss Seeton blushed. ''She had every reason to suppose it would be safe in my house, Mr. Brinton, and no reason to suppose it would not.'' That blush, Brinton suddenly realised, was tinged with guilt. ''Which is why,'' she went on, ''I had intended to apologise to her this morning, or whenever she came, as she had promised, to tell me about . . .''

She stopped. She sighed. ''Poor Nigel,'' she said. ''He will be most distressed to learn what has happened. She was so young—her whole life ahead of her . . .''

''Not anymore,'' said Brinton.

''Sorry, Miss Seeton.''

Brinton's head jerked back at the unexpected sound of Foxon's voice. If there were any more apologies without a decent reason, he'd throw something. Or worse. ''Ready upstairs whenever you are, sir,'' Foxon told the superintendent carefully. ''When you've, uh, finished here.''

Brinton decided he was finished—for the moment. True, he hadn't made too much sense of what MissEss'd been telling him, but when the old girl was in full flight that was about par for the course: besides, he'd got the gist of it. He excused himself as he sent Miss Seeton on her way with thanks for her help and the warning they'd be over later in the day for another chat, just to confirm a few details. No, he wouldn't need to ask her to identify the body: Mount-fitchet and PC Potter between them had been able to save anyone else the trouble, poor girl. Miss Seeton, with a sigh of thankfulness that she had been spared an unpleasant duty, picked up her umbrella from where she had rested it against the arm of the chair and went more than willingly home.

"Sorry, sir." Foxon's voice was low as they trudged side by side up the main stairs. "Did you want me to interrupt you or not? You looked a bit—well, you looked . . ."

"I can imagine how I looked. You know how that woman affects me at the best of times, which the start of a murder investigation isn't. Miss Seeton's a pal of the victim, of course. Seems the girl dropped in yesterday for elevenses or afternoon tea or whatever, and left this behind." He brandished the brown-paper package in his free hand. "Miss Seeton meant to give it back to her today and didn't want us to think anyone had pinched it . . . whatever it is." On the top step, he paused. Squeezed. Frowned. "Feels a bit like an enormous paperback book," he said at last, trying not to think what else it might resemble.

"A sketchbook," suggested Foxon, not quite bold enough to suggest that Brinton should open it and find out for himself, and sympathetic to his unspoken reasons for not doing so. "This Tina was some sort of artist, sir, Ned Potter says. She's been sketching people like Jack Crabbe and Dan Eggleden while they work."

Brinton, who'd instinctively winced on hearing Tina's calling, relaxed a little and nodded. "Makes what MissEss was saying a bit clearer, then: it's logical artistic types will pal up with one another when their paths cross. Unless the girl came to Plummergen on purpose to meet her—or was a former pupil or something. We'll find out later when we start talking to people—but first things first, laddie. If they're ready for us, we'd better go."

CHAPTER 17

They reached the third doorway on the left of the main corridor and halted on the threshold to survey the scene within. Those blocking their line of sight—the photographer, a man with a tape measure, another with an assortment of labelled plastic bags—moved hurriedly out of the way and received their official congé from Brinton, who dismissed them about their business with the warning that he expected full reports to be on his desk by the time he was back in the office.

"Potter, you stay," he added as the rest of the team disappeared in the direction of the stairs. "First things first. Who certified the death?"

"Dr. Knight, sir. Charley—Mr. Mountfitchet," amended Potter quickly, recollecting that his friend must be legally as much of a suspect as the scarlet stranger, "he thought she was dead the minute he saw her, but with young Maureen having hysterics and even Doris in a state, not to mention that artist bloke"—once more Brinton winced—"with a hangover, he phoned up to the nursing home even before he phoned me. Sir."

Potter had observed the wince and stood sharply to at-

tention as he pressed on with his apologia. "With him being on the spot anyway, so to speak, I didn't think it was
worth troubling Doc Wyddial all the way from Brettenden.
Sir."

Brinton grunted. Potter shuffled his boots but said nothing further. Brinton nodded. "Dr. Knight still around?"

"Yes, sir, downstairs in the restaurant. I got Charley—
that is, Mr. Mountfitchet—sorry, sir," he apologised as a
curse burst from the superintendent, who then looked about
him for some suitable missile to relieve his complex emotions. His grasp tightened on the brown-paper package, but
with a visible effort he held himself in check. "I asked
Charley," said Potter, giving up, "to keep an eye at the
front—stop folk peering through the windows as they'd
otherwise be sure to do."

Again Brinton grunted and nodded. Slowly Potter's
shoulders relaxed. "And seeing as I had to secure the scene
of the crime, sir, and couldn't be in two places at once, and
with Scarlett—Mr. Scarlett—under the weather and no
knowing how he might react, I asked the doctor if he
wouldn't mind sort of keeping an eye on him until you got
here, sir, and had a word with him. If that's all right, sir."

"All right, Potter. I doubt if I could've arranged it any
better. Well done." Potter allowed himself a grin of relief.
Brinton decided to make him earn it. "Talking of keeping
an eye, you go on down now and ask the doctor to join us,
if he will." He handed him the brown-paper package. "I'll
take a look later, but you keep an eye on this at the same
time you keep the other on this Scarlett who seems to be
Suspect Number One in most people's book—but who's
innocent until proved guilty," Brinton added grimly. He
had no need to add the name of an even more promising
Number One. Nigel Colveden, as he had said earlier to
Foxon, was definitely in the frame for this one . . .

"Right," reiterated Brinton as Potter clumped off in the

direction of the dining room. "Can't put off the evil hour any longer, Foxon."

"Er—no, sir."

"Come on, then." The superintendent took his first cautious step over the threshold of the bedroom of the late Miss Tina Holloway.

The two detectives stood for a few moments in respectful silence beside the young woman's body before Foxon ventured to speak. "She must have been a real looker, sir. That figure—that hair . . ."

"She *might* have been," Brinton corrected him gloomily. "Unless there are any Before photographs of the poor kid, we've only got the After to go on, and with her face in such a state we can't tell, can we?"

"No, sir." Foxon sighed for the tragic waste of a human life, especially a human no older (as far as he could judge) than himself. "Well, blue's never been one of my favourite colours." Cracking a joke—it didn't matter how feeble— was often the only way a police officer could keep his sanity when the circumstances were warranted to send those unused to horrors screaming from the room, as had happened with Maureen and, more discreetly, to Doris.

Brinton averted his gaze from that bruised, bloated face with its undignified scarlet petechial dots. Thank goodness her eyes were closed. With that hair (if it was natural, which they'd know soon enough) her eyes would most likely be green—or grey. He shuddered. Grey was horribly close to blue; to black. Bruised black and blue . . .

Time to get to work. "Attacked from the front," he began. "No sign of a ligature, so it's not the old catch-her-by-surprise over-the-head-and-pull trick. She'll have seen him coming—could have been chatting to him friendly as you please and been so startled by the change there was nothing she could do about it." He did not mention Nigel Colveden as the most likely male to have been chatting in friendly fashion to Tina alone in her room at midnight.

Foxon knew the way his chief's mind was working. "He could have pushed inside when she opened the door and caught her off guard that way, sir. Just because there are no obvious signs of a struggle doesn't necessarily mean she knew him well enough to have, uh, asked him in."

Brinton grunted. "He was right-handed," he observed after a pause. "Look at the bruises on her neck."

Foxon looked; nodded. With this, at least, he was happy to agree at once. "Fingers on the left, thumb on the right, fainter marks the other side: yes, sir. And he moved her afterwards," he went on, though he hardly needed to. Tina lay with her arms across her chest and her legs together, discreetly covered by the folds of the long skirt she had worn for her night out with Nigel—was there no avoiding that young man's name? Victims of violent death never fall so neatly. "Tidied her up, if you like."

"Odd how some of 'em do that." Brinton scowled at the silent figure on the floor by his feet without seeing her. "They don't want to think they've really done anything so very bad, after all. Reduces the impact for 'em if they don't leave her lying in a heap the way she fell, but nice and tidy as if she'd just dropped off to sleep. The trick cyclists have a fancier explanation for it, I dare say." He glanced at Foxon. "What do *you* say, laddie?"

Foxon sighed. One of them had to say it: and he was the junior officer. "She was a tall girl: no featherweight, even if she was slim. Not easy to drag her around without leaving traces unless . . ."

"Unless he was a weightlifter. Of sorts," Brinton finished for him. "Mountfitchet spends half his time humping barrels of beer and crates of wine up and down the cellar steps. Young Colveden's a farmer—and show me a single farmer who's a nine-stone weakling. It's no good, Foxon. Artists just don't need that much muscle, do they?"

"Depends what sort they are, sir. I mean, dabbing paint from a brush is one thing—but a sculptor . . ."

"Ah. Yes. You did say something about that, I remember." He brightened. "Yes, a sculptor. Before he got on to chocolate he'll have used chunks of stone, lumps of metal, bits of concrete. Good. Maybe we won't go rushing off to Rytham Hall the minute we're done here." He brightened further. "Maybe we'll have more than a preliminary chat with Antony Scarlett, after all."

Dr. Knight confirmed their theories, adding that Tina had died between midnight and dawn: the post mortem (which he, as an unofficial party, would not be conducting) ought to give them a better idea. She had put up only a little fight: her killer had indeed taken her by surprise. She would have lapsed very quickly into unconsciousness. The scratches and marks on her hands were probably the result of instinctive rather than deliberate movement.

"You mean she won't have marked chummie's face for him?" Brinton sounded disappointed to have his (unspoken) guess confirmed.

Dr. Knight hesitated.

"Interesting you should say that. As you know, I was summoned here by the admirable Charley to minister to Doris and Maureen. The silly young wench is enjoying all this, I'm afraid. Likes to score over her friend Emmy about being where the action is." Dr. Knight rolled his eyes. Brinton snorted. Foxon grimaced. "I gave her a good whiff of smelling salts and a lecture," said the doctor with relish. "Told her to make a pot of strong tea—yours is downstairs; hope you don't mind it stewed—but poor old Doris is in deep shock. I'd prefer it if you didn't talk to her until tomorrow, if you can wait—not that I think a woman did this, from my limited experience of these matters."

"Neither do we," Brinton told him.

Dr. Knight nodded.

"Once I'd seen to the ladies, Ned Potter asked if I'd take a look at the artist chap who's been staying here." The doctor smiled. "Stand guard, he meant. Well, I looked. He's in the late stages of a hangover, so he's not saying much, but if you'd like an off-the-cuff view of his mental state, I'd say he appears to be genuinely shocked by what's happened. Appears to be," he repeated. "Appearances can be deceptive, as you know. I'm a nerve man rather than a shrink, so I'm not going to swear it either is or isn't a nice convenient bout of hysterical amnesia . . . he's got a lovely bruise on his temple, you see. And he can't—or won't—say where or how he got it."

"Then maybe we should ask him," Brinton said. "As soon as we can. Thank you, Doctor." They would've spotted it for themselves, of course, but going in already knowing about the bruise would give them a head start. Especially if the bloke was also recovering from a heavy night. Unnoticed, the doctor departed as Brinton wondered whether Scarlett had taken to drink before or after Tina's death. And (if the latter) why so late at night. They'd have a word with Charley Mountfitchet first, to ask how much the man had drunk at the bar before closing time . . .

"He might've brought a bottle from outside, sir." Foxon adopted his customary Devil's Advocate role as Brinton tested his tentative hypothesis. "Perhaps the very first thing to do would be to search his room for empties."

"Leave him to sweat for a while?" Brinton approved this Fabian approach. Even an unimaginative bloke would start to feel a bit uneasy if left alone with a uniformed police constable watching over him, and artists were supposed to have more than their fair share of imagination, weren't they? He tried not to think of Miss Seeton. Not yet. Not just yet. "Hop along and get the master key, Foxon."

Foxon hopped and got. He was soon back, reporting that

he had looked in on the dining room, caught Potter's eye and exchanged a few words out of Scarlett's earshot, and had the pleasure of seeing the grey-faced man turn green. "He's sweating, sir," he concluded. "Nicely. If there are beans to spill, by the time we talk to him, they'll be rolling."

The personal contents of Antony's bedroom seemed to be few. "Slept in the altogether," suggested Brinton, directing Foxon to shake the covers while he opened various doors and drawers. "Or his underpants—it's the sort of thing you can do when you're young and don't have any luggage, especially the Bohemian types. Wonder what the beggar used to clean his teeth?"

"Charley keeps an emergency supply, sir. Travellers' samples of toothpaste, throwaway razors—bingo!" Foxon had shaken to good effect.

Brinton gaped. "Good lord. A nightshirt. Haven't seen one of those for years. Where the devil did he get it?"

"I told you, sir. Charley keeps an emergency supply." Foxon's grin was infectious: Brinton found himself chuckling. "He says if the George burns down in the middle of the night, he doesn't want his guests embarrassing the firemen or catching double pneumonia. Nightshirts are unisex, too. He only has to keep a few in stock, and they'll do for anyone—and who's going to pinch a nightshirt? They're all enormous. Pyjamas fold up small and are far more likely to go for a walk in somebody's coat pocket or handbag."

"Queer guests they get here," observed Brinton, pouncing on the last word with glee as he brandished the folds of the black gaberdine cape. "As you might say."

"Yes, sir." Foxon's voice was muffled; having searched the bed, he was now peering under it. "No bottles," he told Brinton, who was closing the door of the wardrobe. "Unless he's hidden 'em on top of there. Those old-fashioned types have a sort of parapet round the edge to hide hat-boxes and things—my gran's got a couple," he explained, seeing the question in Brinton's eyes. "If I climb on the chair and balance one foot on the bedside table, I can—"

"You could finish the day back in hospital, you young idiot. Twice in one week is going it a bit. Why not just buy a season ticket and have done with it? I need you in one piece, laddie, not crippled from tying yourself in knots doing—ugh—acrobatics." He was *not* going to think about yoga. Or Miss Seeton. "We'll assume Scarlett isn't the acrobatic type either. You can't turn handstands if you're forever wrapped in yards of cloth." His glare dared Foxon to comment on the flaw in this reasoning. The disappointed acrobat did not speak. Brinton grunted. "No extra booze, then. Whatever he got, he got from Charley: and you know what they say about drink loosening the tongue. We'll leave Scarlett to sweat a little longer, Foxon. I want to know what Mountfitchet might have heard from him last night on the subject of Tina Holloway . . ."

Charley Mountfitchet had grown accustomed over the years to the descent of members of Her Majesty's Constabulary upon his formerly quiet little country hotel. With an enthusiasm to gladden the heart of any modern Antisthenes, the landlord would serve drinks after hours; cut piles of sandwiches; and volunteer statements, opinions, and advice even when nobody had asked him.

Helping the police with their enquiries took on a new aspect when, for the first time, Mr. Mountfitchet found himself being addressed in formal terms by one officer he knew well, while another officer he knew even better wrote down in his regulation notebook everything he said. Charley was not exactly nervous, but he was relieved that his conscience was clear. Now it was simply a matter of convincing Brinton and Foxon that he had nothing to hide.

The preliminaries were done. The serious questioning began. Brinton, watching the other's face for the slightest giveaway, asked his opinion of Tina.

"Oh, a nice girl," said Charley at once and apparently with no reservation. "Not one of your flighty pieces, if you were thinking she might've been on the game. You get to know the type in this business, and I'll stake my oath she wasn't, for all she was so good-looking. A sad, shy little thing she was at first, mind you, so it didn't show, but once she'd been here a few days—Miss Seeton had her to tea, and that seemed to cheer her up, and o' course she'd met Nigel Colveden . . ."

There was an uncomfortable pause. Each man in the room could hazard a guess at what the other two were thinking.

"Anyway, she was a different girl," said Charley. "Had a smile for everyone, passed the time of day, stopped hiding in her room and got out and about on buses sightseeing like Mrs. Ogden—except *she's* looking for somewhere to retire, and young Tina, she was drawing all over the place, all sorts of people." He grinned. "Even drew me the other night, pulling pints behind the bar. Right handsome she made me, too. Something about an exhibition, she said. Poor kid," he added as memory returned. "Who'd want to do a thing like that to a nice girl like her?"

"Who, indeed." Brinton cocked his head to one side as he fixed the landlord with a penetrating gaze. "Someone a bit the worse for drink, maybe?"

"You mean Scarlett." It was not a question. "Well, she and him were giving each other funny looks in reception, so Doris said, like as if he was chasing after her and she didn't want to know—but I'll say this, Mr. Brinton, *if* he did it—and I'm not saying he did—then I doubt you can blame the drink. While I'll allow he was merry by the end of the evening . . . well, more than merry, to tell the truth—

but it was nothing . . . nasty. He never got going about Miss Holloway, if that's what you're asking. Never said anything unpleasant at all—not that he was over-friendly, the way they sometimes are. None of this draping himself about the place telling you you're his best pal. He's not the type to be friendly, even in his cups. The whole time he was full of himself, bumptious little squirt, bragging and chattering how wonderful he was—but it was all brag and bluster, and it wasn't as if he'd be driving home. You know I never let my customers get themselves in too much of a state. It's bad business, that is.''

Brinton nodded. There were never any complaints from the Watch Committee when the licence of the George came up for renewal. ''Chattering, you say. About anything in particular, if it wasn't about Miss Holloway?''

Charley shrugged. ''I'm not one for old films, but when a bloke wants to talk, then you try to keep up your end of the conversation if he asks, so I kept an ear open, but he didn't ask. Quite happy by himself most of the time, he was.''

''Old films?'' Probably wanted to mix reels of celluloid with the chocolate and the briar pipes. ''Is that all?''

''*Gone With the Wind*, he kept muttering about.'' Charley shrugged again. ''Laughing to himself. Quite a change from the way he'd been before dinner, grumbling and scowling with a face like thunder, but then he popped out for a breath of air and was chirpy as a cricket afterwards. That's when the bragging and boasting started. Waving his arms about all excited, he was. Tumbled off his stool once and bumped his head''—the two detectives exchanged glances—''but it didn't make no difference. I helped him upstairs in the end. Had to keep shushing him for singing his way to bed, with Mrs. Ogden asleep even if young Tina was still out . . .''

He hesitated. ''She wasn't . . . interfered with, was she?

When the hullabaloo started and I went to see, I didn't care to look too close, just got the womenfolk out o' there and rang for the doctor. But she was a decent girl, Mr. Brinton, and spoke everyone fair and caused no bother. I wouldn't like to think as—anyone—had done her wrong on wrong . . .''

It was a good point. The post mortem would confirm it, but Brinton's view was that sexual assault had not been the reason for Tina's death. The "tidying" of her body into a less disturbing pose might well have involved some readjustment of her clothing, but instinct honed over decades of detection cried that this murder had been a hurried affair, and its aftermath likewise.

Charley Mountfitchet was a steady, reliable, intelligent man. Granted, nobody could ever be sure of how anyone would react given the right (or wrong) provocation: it was his pub, and the girl had arguably been in his power. He might have lost his head: he might. But a sordid, spur-of-the-moment killing like this . . .

And if instinct was right and sex wasn't why she'd been killed, then didn't that rule out Nigel Colveden, too?

Brinton made up his mind. "Don't you go wandering off, because we'll want to talk to you again later," he told Charley. "But I think the person we ought to talk to next is this Antony Scarlett bloke . . ."

CHAPTER 18

"It's not that I'm prejudiced against the chap because he's a stranger." Brinton watched Foxon turn in silence to a fresh page in his notebook. "Oh, well, I suppose in a way I am." He shrugged. "But there's the artistic connection we mustn't forget, and I don't mean Miss Seeton." Now that the superintendent was at last in full cry, he was able to speak her name without wincing. "Tina's an artist— well, she was talking about an exhibition—and if you ask me she can certainly draw." He jerked a thumb towards the sketchpad where it lay in the middle of its brown-paper wrapping. For the past ten minutes it had been the centre of their attention. "Mind you, I'm no expert. Neither are you—but we've both looked through the book, and we like what we've seen."

"Yes, sir. That one of Jack Crabbe's boots . . ." Foxon smothered a gurgle of mirth. Things were too serious for laughter. "But she got him pat, sir, even though you can't see his face. And the others, too. You'd know them any-where, even if some of them're just a few lines in pencil, and there's others with every last little dot in ink."

"Experimenting, I suppose. We'll ask MissEss what she

thinks of the girl's stuff when we see her—and Scarlett might be a lunatic, but he's a sculptor. Of sorts. We'll ask her about him, too. If he's any good, she'll know the blighter—and not just because he wants to demolish her house. But to have two artistic types wandering about a place the size of Plummergen when it isn't the tourist season's too much of a coincidence for me, even before Charley started talking about Doris and funny looks in reception. I reckon Tina and Scarlett know—knew—each other—and not simply through a mutual acquaintance with Miss Seeton.''

"I reckon so, too, sir." Foxon rose from his chair. "Shall I fetch him out of the restaurant now? He's had a fair amount of pickling, and we don't want the civil liberties people after us."

"Fetch him out, laddie—and I'll wrap this up again while you do the fetching." Brinton fingered the sketchpad thoughtfully. "I don't know if it's anything to do with what's happened, but if it is, it might come better as a surprise than if the blighter sees it and has time to invent something."

There are cures for a hangover more ferocious than the hangover itself. There is the well-known Prairie Oyster: there is the George's lesser known, but locally infamous variation on that theme to which, in an ideal world, digestive resistance has been built up over several generations. Dr. Knight had been swift to dispense something fizzy and sinister from his little black bag once he realised to what extreme lengths the George's landlord had gone to sober his guest for what was to come. It had taken some minutes to work, but Antony Scarlett was no longer green. He might be pale, and still somewhat shaky on his legs, but he followed Foxon into what had become the interview room with his head held high.

"Morning, Mr. Scarlett." Brinton nodded to a chair. "I

won't call it good," he went on as Antony sat. "Not when there's been murder done."

"I should think not," muttered Antony. Despite the dual efficacy of the Plummergen Oyster and the sinister fizz, he didn't yet feel quite able to boom in the usual way.

"A very proper observation, sir. So what can you tell us about this shocking affair?" Never mind the preliminaries: catch him off balance and, with luck, keep him there.

Once the fizzing had settled, Antony's less-befuddled brain had started to work. "I didn't do it," he now said, letting his voice rise in pitch. "I am innocent!"

"I never said you weren't, sir."

"You do not think I am." Antony contrived, even while seated, to strike an attitude. "After all, I am the obvious suspect, am I not?"

"Are you, sir? Now what makes you say a thing like that?" Brinton had long since decided the man must be a lunatic: was he an exhibitionist lunatic? The superintendent's glance gauged the distance from the suspect's chair to his own; and he wondered if Foxon would, after all, end the day in hospital.

"Kristeena and I are—were—old acquaintances," said Antony. Brinton's eyes narrowed. He'd guessed as much, but he would've expected a bit more hedging than this. It was as if the bloke was enjoying himself. Well, he'd thought all along that he was crazy . . .

"Very old," said Antony. "No . . . more than that. Why should I beat about the bush, Inspector?" He was so intent on his confession that he missed Brinton's intake of demoted breath. "I," announced Antony Scarlett, "am a sculptor. For three years Kristeena was my model: I shared my life with her, in every possible sense." His tone implied that by this sharing he had conferred upon Miss Holloway the greatest of favours. "Last year," said Antony, allowing his voice to throb with tormented regret, "after an artistic disagreement of no concern to any but ourselves, we parted company.'' He sat up and fixed Brinton with an accusing eye. ''Whereupon the wretched girl chose to pursue what I can only call a vendetta against me. She slandered me to colleagues—damaged my most promising work—behaved in a totally irrational manner, Inspector.''

Antony flung out his arms to express the totality of Tina's irrational behaviour, but he had forgotten that his cape was still on a hanger in his bedroom. The gesture lost much of its customary force, although he did knock one of Foxon's spare pencils from the table to the floor.

''Totally irrational,'' reiterated Antony, barely losing a beat. The pencil lay where it had fallen. ''I resented that behaviour, Inspector. What artist—what red-blooded man—would not?''

''I wouldn't know. Sir.''

Antony, warming to his theme, ignored the careful interpolation. ''Then came the chance for which I had waited: the chance to bring my name before a wider audience: the chance to enter—to win—the Stuttaford Competition!'' His eyes were bright, his colour returned, and now he began to boom. ''I sought high and low, Inspector, for the ideal setting for the most ambitious undertaking of my career. I found it, I thought, in Plummergen—in the cottage owned by Miss Seeton on the corner where three roads meet near a bridge over the canal. It was . . . symbolic. I had to have it. I pressed my claim: Miss Seeton rejected it.'' Antony's gesture was suggestive of the folly of elderly, philistine spinsters. ''She,'' he went on, ''remained firm in her rejection, I in my purpose. I visited Plummergen repeatedly. The more Miss Seeton refused me, the greater became my desire to possess—I was a soul in torment, Inspector, unable to rest . . .''

''Are you pleading 'while the balance of the mind was disturbed'?'' snapped Brinton, wondering how much more of this he would have to suffer before the man got to the point. He seemed to be enjoying himself, blast him. Still, the more he talked, the more he might say that was worth hearing, buried in all the rigmarole.

He might.

"I was," replied Antony with dignity, "under considerable mental stress, Superintendent." Foxon hid a grin: so the bloke *had* been listening when he fetched him, after all. Pretty smart of Old Brimstone to let him rabbit on without stopping the flow: something would come out of it, sooner or later. He hoped, though, that it would be sooner. Too much of this barmy talk, and he'd start wondering whether it was him or—he grinned again—him. He hoped it wasn't.

"Imagine my feelings," Antony cried, "when I saw Nemesis stalking the Plummergen streets in the person of Kristeena!" He leaped to his feet. Foxon dropped a pencil of his own accord; Brinton involuntarily ducked his head. "Not only," boomed Antony, flinging out his arms, "had the wretched girl attempted to poison the minds of my colleagues against me—it was clear that her next aim was to sabotage my grand design! She insinuated herself into the confidence of Miss Seeton—the woman would never let me have her cottage now—she flaunted her affections for another man to arouse my jealousy . . . Can you wonder, Superintendent, that now I hear the chink of handcuffs in your every word?"

It was a stirring speech and a majestic final line. Antony collapsed on his chair, mopping his brow. Brinton shot a sideways look at Foxon. Foxon looked back at his superior. Their eyes telegraphed the same signal.

"I suppose," said Brinton heavily, "you'd like us to call your solicitor, wouldn't you?"

Antony waved his hand. "Miss Genefer Watson, of the Galerie Genèvre in London, will deal with all that," he said smugly. "I understand that I am permitted one telephone call. If you will allow me—"

"No," said Brinton. Antony blinked. There had been a note in the superintendent's voice he hadn't heard before.

"No telephone calls," said Brinton. "You haven't been arrested; you're just helping us with our enquiries, and it won't help if you take time out just to warn this Watson female that you've landed in the middle of a murder case that'll puff your blasted exhibition in every paper in the land. Do you take me for a fool? I know damned well why it's not your solicitor you want to call! You're trying to milk this for everything you can get—and I'm not going to let you. Maybe you killed that poor girl—though my gut feeling is you didn't, because I don't think you're bright enough to work a double-bluff—but she deserves more than having a—a posturing little twerp like you cashing in on her death! Oh, yes, you're a suspect—and I'm going to have every last inch of you investigated until you'll wish you'd never set eyes on Sweetbriars—*and* so you'll learn not to play games with the police when there's murder been done! And if you let one word of this out to the papers . . . Well then, be damned to your nonsense, because I don't care! Nobody likes a hypocrite—and they're not too keen on opportunists, either. Foxon, have you got all that?"

Foxon, who had been gaping open-mouthed at his chief, gulped. Did Brimmers want him to say yes or no?

Brinton hadn't really meant him to answer what had been a rhetorical question. "You can go, Mr. Scarlett, but don't try leaving the hotel. One of my men will be on the door, and not just to stop the crowd outside from coming in. I'm sure we'll talk again later."

When a crestfallen Antony had crept out of the room, Foxon drew a deep, shuddering breath. "I can't believe it, sir. Are you feeling okay? I've never heard you sound off like that at a suspect before—and he's the best we've got, if we don't want to finger Charley or Nigel. Why don't you think he did it?''

''As a matter of fact,'' said Brinton mildly, ''I think he did.'' Foxon stared at him. ''I think,'' said the superintendent, ''he waited up for Tina to come back from her date with Nigel, tried to reason with her, and lost his rag when she made it clear she'd well and truly scuppered his chances of getting Miss Seeton's cottage, never mind that she'd enjoyed herself with another man and wouldn't give tuppence anymore for him. I think once we hear from Forensics, we'll find the marks on her neck match his hands exactly. I know I said I didn't, but I do think he's quite smart enough to work out a double-bluff of protesting his innocence and kidding the dumb country coppers he means it when it's far too obvious he doesn't.'' Brinton moved restlessly on his chair. ''The man's an exhibitionist, Foxon, and mad with it—and I don't like dealing with loonies. I'm letting him pickle until I've got the expert evidence I need, which is going to take time—and *then* I'll throw the book at him, hard, when he isn't expecting it. It won't do him any harm to wait a bit.'' He pushed back his chair and stood up. ''Come on.''

''Come on where, sir?''

''Where do you think? Out of this hotel, so that Master Scarlett can relax again—so that I don't risk bumping into him every five minutes—*and* so I can get a second opinion from you-know-who.'' He jerked a thumb in the direction of Sweetbriars. ''I said I needed expert evidence, didn't I? I've never said she's a loony, but you can't deny Miss Seeton's not on the same wavelength as everyone else. It takes one to know one, Foxon: and she's an artist as well.'' He snatched up the brown-paper parcel of Tina's sketchbook. ''There may be something in here that would give us a firmer line to work on when we come to press charges. There could well be more to it than the cottage business or sheer jealousy of Nigel: the blighter's too willing to admit to them as motives, though I suppose that could be another blasted double-bluff. If,'' he added thoughtfully, ''that's the game he's playing. Monkeying about with my name, blast him! I don't play games, Foxon.''

''No, sir.'' It seemed the wisest reply.

''No.'' Brinton was striding towards the main door—nodding to Potter—ignoring the goggle-eyed crowd as he crossed the road with Foxon close behind him. ''Or maybe,'' said Brinton, almost to himself, ''I do. I could've arrested the blighter then and there—but . . .''

He flung open Miss Seeton's gate, marched up the path, and rapped on the knocker with a resolute hand.

In deference to the gravity of the situation, Miss Seeton's welcome to her visitors was muted. She instinctively offered them cups of tea, but when the tea arrived, it was served in the unpatterned cups, without cake, and with the very plainest of Marie biscuits. It would, she feared, be some while before she could readily contemplate eating chocolate biscuits again.

''A foolish fancy, of course.'' Miss Seeton sighed for her folly, then smiled faintly. ''When I recall that it was I who chided the poor girl for—well, for overreacting—and naturally I meant it for the best . . . but memory can be a most awkward taskmaster for one's conscience, can it not, Mr. Brinton?''

Brinton sat up. There had been something in the way she said that . . . ''I'd be interested in your memories, Miss Seeton. From a professional point of view, that is,'' he added and looked a little embarrassed as she sighed again. ''But nothing too . . . personal,'' he said quickly. ''I'd never want you to go against your conscience—but anything you feel that you *can* tell us about Miss Holloway—you seem to have got to know her pretty well during her stay here—

and if we don't ask you,'' he concluded, to clinch his argument, ''we'll have to ask young Nigel Colveden. And from what I've heard of his relationship with the dead girl I imagine he's a bit upset about what's happened to her—or he will be when he finds out.''

For a third time, Miss Seeton sighed. ''I had thought them rather well-suited,'' she said sadly. ''The attraction of opposites, you know. Dear Nigel—such an open-air young man—while poor Tina seemed at first so—so cosmopolitan, yet proved so willing to adapt herself—and with such success. And then . . .'' She shook her head and blinked once or twice. ''Oh, dear . . . He promised to take her bird-watching—and she enjoyed herself so much taking the bus to some of the nearby villages and towns to go sightseeing and to—to sketch . . .''

The delicate pink now mantling her cheeks did not pass unnoticed by Superintendent Brinton. Hadn't MissEss been blushing when she returned the dead girl's sketchbook? Just what was there about those drawings to make the Oracle's favourite sensitive so uneasy? Only one way to find out.

''Miss Seeton, you say Tina went out sketching. She showed you her sketches, of course. One artist to another, that sort of thing.'' Brinton's voice was urgent now. ''Was there anything about her sketches you weren't happy with? Anything . . . special?''

He snatched the brown-paper parcel from Foxon and handed it to their hostess. ''Show me,'' he begged as she accepted the offering with considerable reluctance, her blush deepening. ''Whatever it is in here that you think's not quite right—it'll help, I'm sure it will.'' He knew the old girl wasn't usually so . . . fanciful in her behaviour unless . . . She saved all that sort of thing for her Drawings, when her confounded instinct took over. And whenever it did, there was always *something* . . . even if just *thinking* about the way she did—whatever she did—made him feel uneasy . . . And maybe she'd done it this time by remote control, as you might say, through Tina Holloway . . .

A faint memory tugged at his brain, but he had no time to capture it before Miss Seeton sighed. "She drew so many sketches in the last few days, and all of them of the highest quality." She paused, as if not entirely sure of what she said. "It is," she went on firmly, "most gratifying to see a young person find something unexpected at which she might excel." Now she spoke without hesitation. "It was such a pleasure to her—rebuilding her confidence, you know, after the personal difficulties she had overcome, and she was so pleased and proud when she came to show me her work." Again that faint hesitation. "As I, naturally, was pleased for her. Tina showed more than ordinary promise, Mr. Brinton. Her death . . ." She coughed. "It is a tragic waste of more than just a life."

Brinton flicked through the book, sharing Miss Seeton's feeling for the lively talent that had formed the pictures in front of him and pausing as something he had spotted on his first study again caught his eye.

And tugged again at that elusive memory . . .

"Yes, she was especially pleased with that one." Miss Seeton moved awkwardly on her chair. "I teased her a little about it, you know, though of course in the nicest possible way, for she sketched it yesterday afternoon in Murreystone, of all places, before she came here. I told her she must on no account let Nigel or anyone else know where she had been for her little adventure . . ."

She blinked once or twice before continuing. "Raised voices, I understand, and some argument, although she had no idea why, and as soon as they noticed her, she moved away, as anyone would." Brinton thought privately that most people would stand with their ears flapping to find out what the fuss was about: Tina, it seemed, had been another like Miss Seeton. Or had let the old lady think she was, at any rate. A nice girl, as Charley Mountfitchet had said.

Miss Seeton smiled. "She'd forgotten, I think, about the feud, and indeed when I ventured to tease her, she expressed some surprise that the men in question, who were presumably Murreystone men, appeared to have forgotten it likewise, for she was sure she saw them again in Plummergen. Or at least driving through in their lorry, for if she hadn't been quick on her feet, she said, there might have been an accident as she crossed from the George to my house. It can be a tricky corner if taken at speed, which if they did was no doubt because they realised that they were, as one might say, on enemy territory." Miss Seeton shook her head for the folly of local rivalries. "Tina found it amusing, rather than a trifle absurd, after so many years. I am glad that her last hours were so much happier than . . ."

Miss Seeton, with a discreet sniff, fell silent. Brinton was frowning. What had she just said? An argument? An accident? MissEss had just chattered on without thinking them important—but why had that sketch in particular made such an impression? Not just on the art teacher, but on himself and on Foxon, too?

There was no doubt that it was a good sketch. The man leaning on the garden roller couldn't have been more clearly portrayed, and his colleague in the background pushing the decorated wheelbarrow was a model of muscular strength, with his sinews taut and his arms bulging, his forehead spangled with sweat.

Wait. Miss Seeton had mentioned a lorry. Gardeners didn't need lorries in the normal run of things. Leaves weren't heavy enough to demand the obvious effort required of the barrow man; and who rolls their lawn in January?

And what about that design on the side of the barrow— where had he seen that before? A sort of letter *H* made up from little squares, just like cobble stones or paving . . .

Memory returned with a blinding flash of mental light. Miss Seeton's sketch after her visit to Adelaide Addison— no wonder she'd been wriggling as her subconscious realised the girl had produced something not a million miles from what she'd drawn herself . . .

"Asphalt!" roared Brinton, making Foxon leap from his chair and Miss Seeton, sitting on the other side of the table, squeak with alarm. He turned Tina's sketchbook round to show the others, muttering as he did so. "I should've spotted it at once!" He flattened the book with a satisfied hand. "Garden roller, right?"

"Right, sir," said Foxon. Miss Seeton acquiesced with a silent nod. Brinton shook his head. "Wrong," he said triumphantly. "Well—right, technically," he conceded. "But wrong in the practical sense, because the blighters weren't using it to roll a lawn nice and level—they were laying an asphalt drive for some poor mug without using proper equipment, and Tina caught 'em at it and sketched them so's you'd know them again if you saw them—and they found out where the poor kid was staying—"

"Oh, no," whispered Miss Seeton. "Oh, Superintendent—then it was all my fault!"

CHAPTER 19

"Don't worry, I told her it wasn't," said Superintendent Brinton the following day to his friend Chief Superintendent Delphick as the two discussed the latest of Miss Seeton's triumphs. The Oracle sat enthralled in his office at Scotland Yard, while Brinton sat in Ashford with the telephone in his hand and Tina Holloway's sketchbook on his desk, with Miss Seeton's original sketch beside it. "Well, in a way I suppose you could argue it was, though you'd have to be pretty desperate. She felt guilty as hell, of course, until I pointed out that if the girl hadn't been going out with Nigel and expecting to come back after midnight, she would never have asked for a late key—or taken her own with her. If she'd joined the supper party at Rytham Hall she would've expected to be back at a reasonable hour and left the key in the usual way. Then they would have grabbed it from reception, sneaked into her room to pinch the sketchbook, and vamoosed without anyone being any the wiser."

"Theoretically possible," agreed Delphick, "if only the sketchbook had been in the room in the first place. Which we know it wasn't."

"Which is why MissEss blamed herself. Said if she hadn't wasted so much time getting ready for her date with the Colvedens she could've popped across to the pub with the sketchbook. Doris could've slipped it into the girl's room using the master key, and Tina would've been safe. Then I pointed out that unless they'd managed to pinch the master key, which knowing Doris I doubt if they could, they would still've had the problem of getting into Tina's room. That sort of crook can't pick a decent lock, and they wouldn't want to leave traces. They would still have had to lurk about the place waiting for her to return from seeing Nigel—and take her by surprise—and try to scare her into letting them take the book away . . ."

"And not succeeding," the Oracle finished for him as he fell silent. "Miss Seeton's encouragement, as we'll call it, had doubtless made the girl far less likely to give in to intimidation as she might have done in what we could call her Scarlett period—for which encouragement the poor woman presumably also holds herself to blame."

"She started to say something of the sort," said Brinton, "but I shut her up sharpish by reminding her that if it hadn't been for the fact she'd hung on to the book in the first place, we'd never have caught the one who killed Tina, because they would most likely have killed her anyway."

"Which," remarked Delphick, "given their track record, is not far from the truth. They're a vicious bunch."

"They are, and I told her so. Not that I mentioned poor old Sergeant Major Scott, because for one thing we didn't know about him then, but there were the others . . . So I said we were grateful to her in more ways than one—and it worked, I think. She seemed a lot happier when she realised she'd helped us lay the asphalt crooks by the heels. She'd felt pretty sorry for Miss Addison and the others."

"Whose confrères, at least, may rest easy in their beds, their savings and pensions intact. An argument to appeal to

Miss Seeton, of course." Delphick's voice held a smile.
"Not everyone over retirement age has an additional income in the manner of the force's favourite Art Consultant."

"No." Brinton coughed. "It was true, what I told her.
If she and Tina hadn't doodled the way they did—well, her
doodling made us pay attention to Tina's sketch—Buckland
would've driven past that lorry in Ashford without giving
it a second look. But as soon as he saw the logo on the
door, he recognised it from her sketch—I made damn sure
everyone had a photocopy as soon as we got back to the
station—and he was smart enough to make the connection.
There's money in paving paths—that's what the pair of 'em
were telling us in their different ways. Once we understood
them, we'd got the blighters on toast. The whole blasted
bunch of them are cooling their heels in the cells this minute, and the local briefs are licking their lips with all the
fees they're going to get once the case reaches court."

Both men sighed for the vagaries of the English legal
system. It could be a year or more before the Asphalt Gang
received the penalties due them.

"They had luck on their side," Delphick observed with
another sigh. "The George has no dragon on the desk.
Once they were sure it was where she was staying, it must
have been enough for Chummie to have a casual drink or
two in the bar, then make his way upstairs when the coast
was clear. With business so quiet, there was only a small
risk that anyone would spot him."

"Probably just think he was a pal of Scarlett's," Brinton
said. "A bloke like him—he's totally bonkers, Oracle—
must know some pretty weird people." He signed. "It's a
great shame he didn't do it: I can't stand the chap. I'd love
to have been able to throw the book at him, the play-acting
little creep. Talk about any publicity's good so long as they
spell your name right! I booted him back to London with

a king-sized flea in his ear, but I know it won't be long before it hops away—the Watson female who owns the blasted gallery will see to that.''

Delphick made sympathetic noises for a while, then began to muse aloud. ''I know we dislike coincidence in our business, Chris, but we can't deny it exists. The coincidence that it should be Miss Seeton's village to which Antony Scarlett persisted in coming—to which Tina Holloway likewise came, to be cured by Miss Seeton of her obsession with Scarlett and inspired by her to draw a series of sketches that included the very criminals Miss Seeton's own sketch had failed to identify, though they were working in the same area . . . How I look forward to reading your full report, Superintendent Brinton.''

Brinton was heard to snort on the other end of the wire. Delphick laughed. ''Copy to the computer, of course. The Yard's Unsolved files will enjoy a substantial reduction in number, I fancy. Oh, yes,'' he added as Brinton snorted once more. ''The query you raised the other day about Patrick Abinger. Did you say his wife's name was Lucy?''

''Foxon would know. I can't lay my hands on the right piece of paper at the moment. I think it is, though. Why?''

''Abinger is a fairly unusual surname, and coupled with the banking connection it wasn't too hard to trace in the end, though not through our own computer: he's clean from that point of view, Chris.''

''But?'' From the sound of it, this was going to be good.

''But,'' said the Oracle, ''an off-the-record conversation with a financial bigwig or two, passed along the unofficial grapevine, produces the intelligence that the only known Patrick Abinger is married to one Joanna. I should like to be a fly on the wall, Chris, when you tell young Foxon that the reason for his brush with friend Patrick was that the man thought him a private detective set upon him either by Lucy's husband, who wants a divorce, or by his estranged

wife, who doesn't. She doesn't even want a legal separa-
tion. She wants him back and is willing to go to almost
any lengths to get him.''

''He'll be the one with the money, of course,'' observed
Brinton once he'd finished chuckling at the thought of his
subordinate's face when he heard the anticlimactic nature
of the revelation. ''Paying out on two mortgages, though.
No wonder he bought the Pontefract place: with the work
that needed doing there, he'll've got it cheaper than most
other houses that size. Buckland tells me Lucy's looking
for a job in Brettenden. Well, that's no great surprise.''

Delphick volunteered the remark that it was not. Brinton,
after a pause, chuckled again. ''A private detective! His
idea of plainclothes isn't mine, but I've yet to see Foxon
in a trench coat and trilby hat . . .''

''You could always ask Miss Seeton to oblige,'' Delphick said. ''With her artistic ability—''

''I'll live in ignorance, thanks. Ask that woman to draw,
and the next thing you know she's Drawing.'' Brinton in-
vested the final word with an ominous significance not lost
on Delphick. ''And then,'' lamented Brinton, ''we'll be in
it up to our eyeballs again—which is more than flesh and
blood can bear when we haven't sorted out this last lot
yet—which, more thanks to Tina than to MissEss this time,
has been a nice neat job without any of her usual antics to
make a man tear his hair out by the handful or send his
blood pressure rising . . .''

Miss Seeton's yoga ensured that her own blood pressure
level remained excellent. She thought herself fortunate in
enjoying good health and good spirits: the artistic temperament, she was thankful to say, was not hers.

How—alas—unlike others. She uttered a sigh as the
black-clad figure swirled into sudden view at the end of her

front path. "Miss Seeton!" boomed Antony Scarlett, temperament personified. "Good day!"

"Mr. Scarlett." Miss Seeton, interrupted on her way to
the shops, drew herself up to her full height and prepared
to utter her umpteenth refusal to sell.

Before she could speak: "Miss Seeton, I salute you!"
With a final swirl he was upon her, seizing her hand in his
and raising it to his lips. The umbrella slid down her arm:
he pushed it back and boomed: "You have saved me from
false accusation, from incarceration—you have my deepest
gratitude—I am yours to command, Miss Seeton!"

"Thank you," said Miss Seeton, considerably startled:
so startled, indeed, that she had no thought of taking advantage of this assurance to petition for a return to her
former privacy, with the claims on her house retracted.

"Miss Seeton, you inspire me." Antony dropped her
hand (she had to snatch at the umbrella) and flung out his
own, palms upwards, as he gazed, Inspired, at the heavens.
"I called upon you the other evening—the same night as
the dreadful tragedy—and, absent in body though you
were, your influence remained about this cottage of yours
after which my soul has yearned."

Miss Seeton tried to say something here, but he ignored
her.

"You have never wished to sell, Miss Seeton. I have
always known, but I have always hoped."

She tried to say something else and was again ignored
as Antony again flung out his arms.

"There came to me that night, Miss Seeton, under your
benign influence, an Inspiration the like of which the world
has not seen for thirty-five years!" Miss Seeton blinked.
"*Gone With the Wind!*" She blinked again. "Greater than
the Selznick search for the ideal Scarlett—the Search for
the Scarlett Ideal! I told myself: Miss Seeton does not wish
to sell. She recommends that I find another such house—

but where is such a perfect house to be found? I asked myself: why should I, the genius of the nation, search through maps in secret? Let the nation search on my behalf! Let a *truly willing* Sacrifice be found—after weeks of dedicated struggle and disappointment—let it be laid upon the Altar of My Art—but only after everyone in the country has heard about it! Television—radio—the newspapers— the possibilities are endless, Miss Seeton . . .'' He seized her hand again. "And all thanks to you!"

"Oh," said Miss Seeton faintly. "I am . . . glad to have been of assistance."

"Assistance invaluable!" boomed Antony Scarlett as she took a backward step and tried to withdraw her hand from his grasp just as he let it go to fling out his arms once more in the familiar Artistic Gesture. Miss Seeton, losing her balance, stumbled a little but did not fall. Antony, his arms outstretched, staggered in sympathy and turned his ankle on the edge of the paved path. With a curse, he went down. Miss Seeton went down after him, dropping basket and umbrella as she bent to pick him up.

Awful visions flashed before her eyes as she helped the tall caped figure to his feet. She would have to ask him inside, and once inside he would change his mind about his Scarlett Search and renew his appeals to buy her house; she would refuse, of course, and he would go away—but he would be back again. And again. And again.

As she automatically brushed the dust from his cape with her free hand, she found herself wondering how long it would take to search the Ordnance Survey maps (which she knew were kept in Brettenden library) for a likely configuration of canal, roads and house. She had the feeling that however long it took her it would be time well spent. When Antony returned, as he was sure to do, she could give him a list of places, preferably at the other end of the country, and he could go away and bother her no more . . .

"And now," said Antony, "I must go." At this welcome echo of her thoughts, Miss Seeton looked up. Had she heard only what she wished to hear?

Evidently not. "I came but to thank you, Miss Seeton, and to say that I will never forget you—or your cottage—but now I must leave. The bus departs from outside the post office in"—he looked across at the church clock—"ten minutes, and I have a return ticket. Farewell!"

With a wave of his hand, he swung on his heel.

He stumbled. He stopped in his tracks. Miss Seeton saw the black folds shudder as he winced: his ricked ankle, of course. Must she accompany him to the bus stop half a mile away? They could never manage the distance in time. If she thrust out her umbrella, would the driver make an unauthorised stop outside her cottage? If he didn't, did that mean she must after all invite Mr. Scarlett inside while he waited for the next bus—and risk his changing his mind? If—

"If," said Antony, "you would be so kind, Miss Seeton, as to ring for a taxi, I should be exceedingly grateful." The bus stop—Brettenden Station—London—Miss Genefer Watson were all a long way away. Let others make willing sacrifice: genius would not!

Miss Seeton sighed with relief, smiled, and hurried back up the path in the direction of the telephone.

ABOUT THE AUTHOR

Hamilton Crane is the pseudonym of Sarah Jill Mason, who was born in England (Bishop's Stortford), went to university in Scotland (St. Andrews), and lived for a year in New Zealand (Rotorua) before returning to settle only twelve miles from where she started. She now lives about twenty miles outside London with a tame welding engineer and two (reasonably) tame Schipperke dogs.

Sweet Miss Seeton is Hamilton Crane's twelfth book in the series created by the late Heron Carvic. Under her real name, Sarah J. Mason has so far written five mysteries starring Detective Superintendent Trewley and Detective Sergeant Stone of the Allingham police force.